Channel Surfing in the Sea of Happiness

Channel Surfing in the Sea of Happiness

stories by

Guy Babineau

Cormorant Books

We acknowledge financial support for our publishing activities: the Government of Canada, through the Canada Book Fund and The Canada Council for the Arts; the Government of Ontario, through the Ontario Arts Council, Ontario Creates, and the Ontario Book Publishing Tax Credit.

LIBRARY AND ARCHIVES CANADA CATALOGUING IN PUBLICATION

Title: Channel surfing in the sea of happiness / stories by Guy Babineau.
Names: Babineau, Guy, author.
Description: Previously published: Toronto: Gutter Press, 1998.
Identifiers: Canadiana (print) 20240327535 | Canadiana (ebook) 20240327551 | ISBN 9781770867499 (softcover) | ISBN 9781770867505 (EPUB)
Subjects: LCGFT: Short stories.
Classification: LCC PS8553.A2437 C42 2024 | DDC C813/.54—dc23

United States Library of Congress Control Number: 2024930501

Cover and interior text design: Marijke Friesen
Manufactured by Friesens in Altona, Manitoba in March, 2024.

MIX
Paper | Supporting responsible forestry
FSC® C016245

Printed using paper from a responsible and sustainable resource, including a mix of virgin fibres and recycled materials.

Printed and bound in Canada.

CORMORANT BOOKS INC.
260 ISHPADINAA (SPADINA) AVENUE, SUITE 502,
TKARONTO (TORONTO), ON M5T 2E4

SUITE 110, 7068 PORTAL WAY, FERNDALE, WA 98248, USA

www.cormorantbooks.com

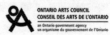

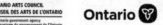

CONTENTS

Chairman Mao and the Spiders from Mars

"WHAT DID YOUR parents say?" Rose whispered.

I kept my voice low. "They laughed. They told me I'd outdone myself."

"Really? Mine would've killed me."

"Yeah, well my parents don't live on this planet. Tell me honestly, do you think it kind of looks like him? Even a little bit?"

I removed my father's old felt fedora. I'd swiped it from on top of a box in the attic. I thought it would cover up the catastrophe. Rose peered at me for what seemed like forever, then took off her wireframe glasses.

"Sort of," she said. "When you're blurry there's a faint resemblance."

"I got it cut at that place on West Georgia, Crimpers. I told them to copy the cover of David Bowie's *Pin Ups*. They wanted to dye it too, but it cost too much so I did it myself at home. Big mistake. It's pretty hopeless, isn't it?"

"It's pretty orange," Rose said, putting her glasses back on.

"It's pretty homo if you ask me," snarked Harlan, craning his neck around.

He'd beelined for the desk right in front of mine when he came into class. He was saving the two desks on either side of the aisle from him. Mike and Sammy. Nightmare City.

"I didn't ask you, did I?"

"I didn't *athk* you, did I?"

"I don't have a lisp."

"Fuck man, like you need one."

"I don't do that with my wrists either."

It was Monday morning, the first week of October, three weeks into the first semester of grade eleven. Second period was Twentieth-Century World History, where Indian Summer sunshine shimmered in bright amber pools on the classroom floor. A light breeze through the open windows had a fresh tang of salt from the beach a few blocks away. Though warm for the time of year, and still several weeks away from frost, there was a slight undercurrent of seasonal nip. Outside, the maples, chestnuts, oaks, and elms lining our school parking lot were just starting to turn, random leaves sparking to a radiant glow of tangerine, blood red, and gold. Beyond the parking lot, above the changing leaves, towered a dense stand of teal Douglas firs. They thrust upward like daggers into a vivid, periwinkle, rock 'n' roll sky.

Blushing, Rose began to search for something in her huge, tapestried handbag. When she opened it, she released a bouquet of trail mix, apple, and a hint of old lady's perfume. Rose was introverted. I didn't know her very well. In elementary school we hadn't shared homeroom and in high school our periods didn't coincide, until now. In the hallways she blended into the background. I couldn't tell you where her locker was. But I did know what everyone else knew. Rose's family was loaded. They'd been in the seed business since forever. Esterhazy Seed Company packages with bright watercolours of the potential growth inside were on hardware, supermarket, and garden centre racks across the country. I only sat beside Rose this morning because she was at the back of the classroom where I'd hoped against hope to hide my new, spiky, Day-Glo Ziggy Stardust hairdo. She pulled out a paperback of *The Female Eunuch*, opened it to a bookmarked page, and started to read.

The room was filling up. People turned around to get a good look at me. Mike and Sammy stopped at the door for a moment to gape, then took their places on either side of Harlan. Sammy's glass eye stared at me like a dead fish while he sat down, the other one spazzing all over the place. Mike had the sneer he'd been perfecting all summer as an accessory to his new military haircut. He used to be too stoned to sneer.

"You're so antediluvian," I said to Harlan, loudly enough for everyone to hear.

Harlan raised his eyebrows and smirked, slid down in his seat, stretched his legs across the aisle, and crossed them. He scratched an armpit. I had spent grades nine and ten with a crush on Harlan, before I met Phillipe. Harlan was cute in a collegiate, all-American, apple pie kind of way, and the captain of the soccer team. We used to get along. Now he had a chip on his shoulder. It probably had to do with a party I went to near the end of grade ten. I drank almost a whole bottle of Baby Duck and told Harlan I loved him. Talk about hangovers that don't go away.

Mike whispered something into Harlan's ear. They both laughed and glanced at me. Mike wore a faded tight Emerson, Lake & Palmer *Brain Salad Surgery* T-shirt that used to hang like curtains off his skinny frame, back when his hair was almost down to his waist. In June, just before summer holidays started, his mother found twenty hits of purple microdot in his jeans. So, his parents sent Mike to a summer boot camp somewhere up the coast near Sechelt. It was supposed to have built character. If anything, it'd built muscles and eradicated his slouch. Now he looked like a member of Hitler Youth, in acid rock camouflage. It was kind of sexy.

Harlan leaned over to Sammy and whispered, obviously repeating what Mike had said. They laughed. Sammy had his yarmulke on. He was going through a see-I'm-Jewish phase even though his mother wasn't Jewish and the only religion his father, a doctor, practiced was mixing martinis. I'd overheard my parents say so when I eavesdropped on one of their conversations. Sammy's true heritage was anyone's guess. He was adopted. The yarmulke looked out of place with his shag haircut and puka shell necklace, not to mention his glass eye.

Mike and Sammy didn't exactly tilt the IQ meter. When they were together, they were of one mind, thanks to sharing. Harlan ruled them. We'd studied all about the emotional ravages of adolescent testosterone in Sex Ed and I kept waiting for the onslaught to turn me into a lurching moron too, but so far, no dice.

"You don't know what antediluvian means, do you?" I said, even more loudly.

Harlan fiddled around with the squeaky top of an inkwell. Even though the school was housed in a modern building, a school board shuffle had dumped a pile of ancient desks on us. A corny heart with an arrow through it was carved on the top of my desk, but the names had been rubbed out by time. I wondered where the owners of the smudged initials were now, if they were still in love, if they still knew each other. And if not knew, remembered. I didn't want to end up a memory on a desktop. Or worse, old.

"Big deal," said Harlan. "So what if you've read the dictionary? What's that supposed to prove?"

"Why don't you tell us what it means, Trevor."

Mr. Cuthbert, our history teacher, smiled at me. I melted. He stood by his desk in front of a large poster of Mao Zedong pinned up over the blackboard beneath a roll-up map of the world. The electric eggshell-blue background on Mr. Cuthbert's poster was even more shocking than the sky outside. The leader of the Chinese revolution was airbrushed and retouched with colour. His skin had an orange glow, his cheeks were too pink, and his lips were a luscious red, as though the Long March of the Communists had straggled into a bad makeup school instead of the Shaanxi province.

Two weeks earlier when he found out that hardly anyone — except, it turned out, me and Rose — knew who Chairman Mao was, Mr. Cuthbert handed out a one-thousand-word assignment on communism in China, any aspect we wanted. I got hooked on the Cultural Revolution because it sounded cool. When I found out that Mao and a pile of teenagers called the Red Guards imprisoned and brainwashed millions of artists, teachers, and intellectuals, I didn't get Mr. Cuthbert or his poster. I'd spent the whole weekend writing a screwy essay about the Cultural Revolution, partly to get my mind off Phillipe, partly to set Mr. Cuthbert straight on a few important issues. It was due today, but I was having second thoughts about handing it in. I needed to get a grip.

I could have lived without Mr. Cuthbert's moustache but despite that he made me weak in the knees. I stared into his dreamy eyes, unable to speak or think.

"We're waiting, Trevor," said Mr. Cuthbert.

I became aware of everyone staring at me and fumbled with my father's ridiculous hat as I put it back on my head. The brim fell to just above my eyebrows. I was mortified.

"It means outdated, a throwback," I mumbled, wanting to kill myself.

"I'm sorry Trevor, I don't think everybody heard you."

"It means old-fashioned," Harlan said loudly.

"It means ignorant," announced Rose, staring at Harlan through her mass of frizzy hair.

"Thank you, Harlan," said Mr. Cuthbert. "And thank you, Ms. Esterhazy, but I think yours is a matter of interpretation."

Rose smiled. "No Mr. Cuthbert, it's a matter of poetic licence. Harlan can probably tell us what homo means though. He's apparently an expert."

Everyone laughed, even Mike and Sammy, until Harlan gave them a look. Surprised, I looked at Rose. The bell-bottom jeans with hand-sewn tie-dye inserts had to go. So did the water buffalo sandals. So did the wraparound muslin shirt and the woven poncho. She had to trash the glasses. And that hair. She might, I thought, end up being pretty. She caught me looking at her. I mouthed "thank you." She blushed and shrugged, managing to knock *The Female Eunuch* onto the floor. When I stood up and bent over to pick up the book, Harlan slammed a sneaker down on top of it.

"Hey, your favourite position," he said.

"Fuck you." I yanked the book out from under his foot and passed it back to Rose.

Mr. Cuthbert handed out permission slips for a field trip to Fort Langley in two weeks. We all groaned.

MY PARENTS WERE liberal intellectuals. They both taught at the university. They advocated for human rights, attended anti-nuclear rallies, went through a swami and guru period when the house smelled like sandalwood all the time, and had dinner parties attended by artistic guests where I sat quietly taking mental notes to use as ammunition.

When I was fifteen, my mother got it into her head to have a serious talk with me. I knew what it was going to be about the minute she introduced the conversation by telling me that I was precocious for my age and that some people might get the wrong idea. Harlan said "homo"; my mother said "precocious." They both added up to the same thing as far as I was concerned: oh brother. At least with homo I knew where I stood. Precocious was shaky ground.

I sat at the kitchen table resting my chin on my hands, watching my herbal tea grow cold in a homemade mug from my mother's pottery phase. After a weak preface, she struggled with a sketchy central theme and hedged around the focal issue toward an inconclusive conclusion, the brunt of which concerned my being careful not to get into cars with strange men. I was certain that I wasn't getting the meat and potatoes of her point, but the smell outside the restaurant was enough. Fortunately the phone rang. As I went to answer it, she offered her assurance that if I did happen to get into a car with a strange man, she and my father would still love me.

Poor Mom. If she only knew.

One rainy night the previous April, I was on my way home from a Joni Mitchell concert. I had to hitchhike because I'd lost my bus transfer and didn't have any money left. I got picked up almost right away by a guy driving a '72 Olds Cutlass. He was old, maybe about thirty, but good-looking. There were baby things in the back seat. He wore a wedding ring. He put a hand on my lap while he was driving and asked me if it bothered me. I said no. He turned down a side street that led to the edge of the university woods and parked in a secluded spot where he gave me a blowjob and jerked himself off. He thanked me when he dropped me off around the corner from my house and I told him it was no problem.

I hitchhiked a lot after that.

MY LOCKER WAS right inside the door to the smoking steps. It was lunch hour, and they were crowded. I put away my books, took out my knapsack, and stepped outside. There was a brief lull in conversation followed by a couple of titters while I walked down the steps. Then some grade eights resumed telling each other Monty Python sketches. If I heard "This parrot is dead" one more time, I was going to kill myself.

A slight rise in the ground on the school side of the field formed a knoll above the baseball diamond where a couple of cute, shirtless grade twelves played catch. I sat down on the grass against the concrete gymnasium wall to soak up some sun and watch them. I wanted to be by myself to think about Phillipe, the reason I'd been home alone on a Saturday night with a new haircut and a bottle of dye. Even worse, watching a repeat of *Midnight Special*. Even worse than that, with Yes and Edgar Winter. The woman on the TV commercial had said, "A little colour is a little pick-me-up." It was funny how little pick-me-ups could quickly become big put-downs.

"Hello."

I looked up. It was Rose.

"Hi."

"Mind if I join you?"

I did but I said, "Go ahead."

She put down her lugubrious handbag, spread her poncho on the grass, and sat. She smiled at me. Politely, I smiled back. She brought out a sandwich in wax paper and carefully unwrapped it. She methodically smoothed out the wax paper, then lifted the sandwich to her mouth. It was gigantic, two slabs of dark grainy bread with a perimeter of a pubic mattress of alfalfa sprouts.

"Wanna bite? It's cream cheese," she said.

"No thanks, I've got my own lunch."

"You're not eating."

"I'm not hungry."

It was probably a good thing since I wanted to reduce my waist to a size 27 down from 28 so I could buy a keen pair of satin pants at Le Chateau. I had to save up two more family allowance cheques to make the purchase so I still had some time to reach my goal.

"You shouldn't let those idiots get to you," Rose said, munching on her sandwich. She brushed the hair falling into her face behind her ears. "What do they know? Male hormones. They'll be the death of us."

"They don't get to me."

She swallowed and looked at me. "You don't have to be so defensive. I'm on your side."

"I didn't know I had a side."

"Fine. I just meant I don't care if you dye your hair orange. Or purple or green for that matter. Even though your natural colour's much more flattering if not so ... spectacular." She threw her arms into the air to express drama. "I don't understand, though, why you're doing what women have spent the last few years fighting against."

"I haven't really thought much about it," I said. It was gross how everybody thought my fashion statement was a gender manifesto. Why couldn't the world take a big pill and lighten up?

Rose finished her sandwich and neatly folded up the wax paper, putting it back into her handbag. She pulled out an apple and crunched into it. I stayed silent and stared at the guys playing catch. I was trying to insinuate that our conversation was over, but the hint sailed right over her head far into the woods behind her.

"I have an uncle who's gay," she said, her mouth full of apple. "He's my mother's older brother. They're English. They were born there but they came here when they were little. He lives back in England now with his boyfriend. I stayed with them in London this summer. My mother told my uncle to keep it a secret from me. She didn't know his boyfriend was living with him. To say my parents don't approve would be an understatement. But my uncle didn't. Keep it a secret, that is. Like they could hide it. I'm not blind, well, not with my glasses."

"How come you don't get contacts?"

"I wanted to. But I can't because I've got a hereditary astigmatism in my left eye. All the worst things are inherited. I think the nineteenth-century determinists were right, don't you?"

I shrugged my shoulders. "I don't know. I don't even know who they are."

"Well, trust me," said Rose. "They were on to something, at least on a psychic level. But people inherit the good things too. Like my handbag you keep staring at. I inherited it from my Great-Aunt Daisy."

"Daisy Esterhazy?"

"I know. Unbelievable, huh? It's this superstitious thing in my father's family to name every girl after a flower. They should've been consistent and named the boys after vegetables. Aunt Daisy was a homesteader on the prairies, a pioneer woman of great intensity, passion, and reading. She never married and she did the accounting for my great-grandfather's seed company. I carry this around with me in respect for her memory. It took me a while to reconcile her early feminism to my family's rampant capitalism, but she was a product of her times."

She reached into her prodigious satchel and produced a plastic baggie of nuts, raisins, and seeds. "I also carry it around because I've got a lot of crap."

I forgot I wasn't supposed to be hungry and took a handful of trail mix when she offered me some. Rose had just strung together more sentences than I'd heard her utter the entire time I'd been cognizant of her existence.

"My uncle says England has a homosexual tradition, especially if you include Ireland. Like Oscar Wilde. Half the men in

England who aren't gay sound gay, the educated ones anyhow." She threw her apple core into a nearby bush. "How come gay men act like they're the only people with interesting personal lives?"

"I'm not gay," I said.

"Fine with me. No big deal."

"Okay, I'm gay, all right? Happy?"

"Like I said, Trevor, I'm not blind. You'd like London. You'd fit right in. Everyone there thinks they're David Bowie. I saw someone with a pair of platform shoes this high made of clear plastic, with a live goldfish swimming around inside, at a pub my uncle took me to. I had a beer. He's coming here. Do you want to meet him?"

I wondered what I'd do with a fruity old Brit. I envisioned him with a ton of pancake makeup on his face, enormous spidery eyebrows, hair combed and sprayed into a bouffant, wearing a velvet pantsuit and trying to get his hands down my pants. Gross.

"I don't know," I said. "I guess."

"I thought you'd be more enthusiastic. I wasn't going to go. Not by myself."

"Go where?"

"The concert. David Bowie. You know, skinny guy, red hair, androgynous? Sings a lot about outer space? People like you are nuts about him. Don't ask me why. What did you think I meant? It's for his new album, *Diamond Dogs*. I've got a backstage pass."

"No way. Get out."

"Uh-huh." Rose folded up her trail mix baggie and put it back into her handbag. I noticed the handles. They were dark wood, mahogany maybe, and had a brilliant patina.

"My dad is on the board of the Pacific Coliseum," she said. "We'd get to meet David Bowie."

"That's fantabulous! Meet him? Like really meet him in person! I'd kill to go."

"November fifteenth."

"I can't believe it." I could feel my pulse racing as I calculated family allowance cheques to figure out if I'd have enough time to get those satin pants before the concert.

We sat in silence for a little while, watching summer's chilled rump waddle past the horizon. A lazy bee wavered in the air and landed unsurely on my knapsack. Nullified by the lateness of the season, it didn't react when I tried to wave it off, so I killed it. It was a matter of survival. I was deathly allergic.

Rose sighed theatrically.

"What?" I asked.

"Fort Langley," she said.

"I know!"

"There's no God," said Rose.

I couldn't entirely agree. I was in heaven as we spoke, millions of miles away in another world where I was mentally assembling my wardrobe for Bowie's concert. I imagined the luxury hotel suite where I would be whisked along with David and his entourage — and Rose, thanks to my persuasion — to a post-concert party. David would don a satin kimono like some cat from Japan, smiling sadly for the love he could not obey. There'd be champagne. Someone well-hung would pass around a polished mirror with thin lines of snow-white sand and a tiny silver spoon, like the party I went to with Phillipe. It would probably be the Bayshore Inn, but maybe the Four Seasons.

"He's so bourgeois," said Rose.

"Hunh?"

"Mr. Cuthbert."

I sighed like Twig the Wonder Kid as I pressed my space face close to Lady Stardust and imagined Life on Mars. I was lost in a Moonage Daydream. Dancing with spiders from Mars.

"Oh, yeah."

SOMETIMES I'D INVENT places to go just to hitchhike. One Sunday in April I settled on Stanley Park. The first car, a middle-aged woman in a Volvo, took me as far as Davie Street where I got out and started to hitch again. I noticed a few guys about my age, a couple who were quite hunky, hanging around on the sidewalk for no apparent reason. They looked bored. A snazzy Eldorado pulled up and a man who was about forty offered me a ride. I hopped in. I almost choked on the smell of aftershave. He asked me how much and I said how much what. He said, "Cute. I won't go above fifty." I told him fifty sounded okay and wondered what would happen next.

He took me to a hotel in a gritty neighbourhood in the oldest part of the city between Gastown and Chinatown. The room had a moth-eaten bed with no bedding or pillows, a card table, and an unfolded folding chair. There was a shared bathroom down the hall. The window overlooked an alley across from the back entrance to a Chinese restaurant, providing a smell of fish and spices that offered the guy's aftershave competition. Everything was spruced up nicely by a red plastic rose in a white plastic bud vase on the card table.

He told me he wanted to watch me masturbate. While I did, he kept sniffing out of a little brown bottle and saying, "Oh yeah!" The other aromas in the room were overpowered by a smell like old socks. It was kind of gross. Then he went down on me. He gave me fifty bucks when it was over, and I was on my way. The next day after school I went to Eaton's and got my mother a nice blouse for Mother's Day.

Three days later, I sat in the waiting room at the free clinic clutching my number tag and trying not to be recognized. They called my number. The doctor asked a bunch of health questions while he examined me. "Yes, no, yes, yes," I answered angrily; he could have gone a bit easier with the Q-tip. He left the room, came back with a bottle of antibiotics, and sat down beside me.

"Have you had any homosexual encounters?"

The way he said it, I half expected to hear melodramatic 1950s B-movie music over the PA system, but it kept playing Carole King. I didn't say anything.

"Older men?"

I shrugged. "Not as old as you."

"Have you got problems at home?" he asked, putting a hand on my lap.

"My parents didn't give me gonorrhea, if that's what you mean."

He laughed and told me I was precocious.

When I was about to leave, he told me he had a son about my age. "Be careful," he said. "Your folks love you."

"I know."

Why did I have a guilty feeling in the pit of my stomach, like I'd committed a crime?

A FEW WEEKS later summer vacation started. I was taking silk-screen classes at the art college downtown a couple of evenings a week. One night after class, it was so nice out, I decided to walk for a while before I hopped onto the bus. I took some side streets I'd never been on before. I came across a group of people smoking in front of an open doorway through which loud music blared. A mirror ball shattered short, sharp splinters of light onto the pavement. I stuck my nose inside and saw men dancing together. A brass plaque on the doorway said: FACES Private Club. A guy with shaved eyebrows, platinum-blond hair, and glitter on his eyelids sat behind a small window in the entranceway. He sized me up. "Too young! Out!" He pointed to the street.

Back outside there was a wolf whistle and I turned around to see a tall, heavily made up, overdressed woman staring at me. She smiled and blew me a kiss.

"Hi there little Mr. Handsome," she said. "Why don't you come on over and give Mrs. Robinson a great big kiss. Maybe she'll let you graduate."

"No thanks," I said but stuck around. My parents let me stay up late once to watch *The Graduate* on TV with them, so I knew who Mrs. Robinson was. Plus, I'd never seen a drag queen before. Now here was one right in front of me in the flesh — and heels. I was captivated.

Mrs. Robinson walked up to me.

"You aren't trade, are you?"

"Pardon me?"

"Girls, the chicken tonight is tender but she's definitely not for rent."

A couple of guys standing nearby laughed.

"*Et moi, j'aime beaucoup le poulet.*" Mrs. Robinson put a muscular arm around me. "And I think the chicken wants to fly the coop."

I didn't know what the hell Mrs. Robinson was talking about, but he seemed to find himself hysterically funny.

Mrs. Robinson took me aside and said, "Girlfriend, let me give you a few pointers."

Mrs. Robinson was a gold mine of information although I hated the way he kept referring to me as girlfriend. He spent half an hour telling me everything I needed to know about where — and how — to pick up men. I had no idea Vancouver was so busy.

One Saturday night I swabbed myself in my dad's Old Spice, lied to my parents that I was going to a party, and set out to investigate Mrs. Robinson's agenda. First, I went from bar to bar: the

616, the Castle, the Ambassador, Faces again, the Thunderbird, the Shaggy Horse, Playpen South, Playpen Central, Uncle Charley's, ticking each one off the list as I got turned away. Not being legal posed a ginormous problem. I couldn't get access to men in bars. I had to revert to nature to find a boyfriend.

I went to the Fruit Loop. Mrs. Robinson told me that nothing much happened there until midnight, so I hung out in a café on Davie Street where I had one coffee after another and read a new issue of *Rolling Stone* that had a feature interview with David Bowie in it. It was by William S. Burroughs, who I'd heard of because my parents had some of his books. There was a picture of the two of them. Bowie had an eyepatch and looked like a cross between an old movie starlet and a pirate. Burroughs was an old geezer with criminal eyes. He looked like somebody who could shoot someone.

At one minute after twelve I went to the convenience store beside the café and bought some breath mints.

The Fruit Loop was a nighttime cruising area around a semicircular parking lot by a beach in Vancouver's West End. The cruising continued along adjacent walkways that led beneath the Burrard Street Bridge. I was nervous but excited. There were several parked cars and dozens of men milling about.

I saw Phillipe almost right away when he was briefly lit up by headlights as a car swerved into the parking lot. He stood in the shadows smoking a cigarette against a tree. He was gorgeous. I went up to him and asked him if I could bum a cigarette, which was stupid because I didn't smoke, but it was the only thing I could think of to say. He lit it for me, and when I started to cough like an idiot, he smiled and asked me if I was certain a cigarette was what I wanted. I couldn't stop coughing so he pounded my back. Tears were streaming down my face by the time my fit subsided.

Phillipe lived in a one-room bachelor apartment in a high-rise. It was a couple of blocks up the hill from the Fruit Loop. From his window I could see a dim, dark glimpse of English Bay through the uneven tunnel of buildings; a stream of cars along the avenue; beach, shoreline, bay. Moonlight pierced a crack in the clouds. The waves glimmered like stars, as though the world had been turned upside down.

He gave me a beer and we sat side by side on the edge of his bed, practically the only furniture in the apartment. There was a chrome and Formica kitchen table and two chairs. Dumbbells pinned down a frayed corner of the green shag rug. Most of his belongings were stored in plastic milk crates. The walls were coffee and cream. Sparkles twinkled in the ceiling plaster. The closet door was missing. His clothes were neatly hung up, shoes tidily arranged underneath. On the floor by his bed was a stack of paperback books: poems by Walt Whitman, *Howl* by Allen Ginsberg, and a couple of books in French by Marie-Claire Blais, who I'd never heard of.

Phillipe told me he was eighteen, from Montréal, and that he wanted to be a poet. He'd run away from home to escape his "asshole family" when he was sixteen and thumbed his way to Vancouver. He'd been a hustler for a while, then got a student loan to go to a vocational college where he was studying to be an electrician so he could support his poetry. He had curly chestnut hair, big brown eyes, and porcelain white skin.

I looked around at the posters on his walls. There was a black light pirate ship, Van Gogh's Sunflowers — *Tournesols*, Phillipe corrected me — a "Today Is the First Day of the Rest of Your Life" poster that I guessed was supposed to be ironic, and President Nixon with a Pinocchio nose.

Phillipe saw me looking at it and said, "Janis Joplin, she was cool, eh? In that song she said that freedom was another word for nothing left to lose. Now Nixon's just another word for nothing left to believe. What an asshole."

I loved his accent. "Did you make that up?"

He nodded.

"You are a poet."

"Not really. Not yet. One day."

Phillipe put his arms around me and asked if I minded.

"No."

Why did people keep asking me if I minded what I wanted?

We kissed. One thing led to another. I was nervous at first, unsure what to do, so I let Phillipe take control. His hair smelled like sandalwood. His body was lithe, athletic. His touch made me feel safe. Later on I was nestled against his chest while he sat up in bed and smoked a cigarette. Phillipe put the lid on the Crisco and shoved it back under the bed. I'd never be able to watch my mother bake again without laughing or being grossed out.

We spent weekends hanging out with each other after that and talked on the phone every day. Doreen, my older sister, kept asking me what drugs I was on because I was so happy. I invited Phillipe over to meet my family. He passed my Leftist Parents' Good Housekeeping Seal of Political Approval. They'd been opposed to the War Measures Act in 1970. When they found out he saw the tanks roll through Montréal and that his father was arrested as a suspected FLQ member, they thought Phillipe was great. I'm sure they knew what was going on between us, but they could hardly have said anything about it given some of the hectic characters they'd introduced me to.

Then, on the Friday evening before I ruined my hair, I went over to Phillipe's as usual. There was an envelope with my name on it pinned to the door. I opened it up. Inside was a note on foolscap that said, "Went back home. Sorry. Take Care. P."

That was all. On my way out I ran into the building superintendent. He said, "If you see that friend of yours tell him to steer clear if he knows what's good for him. He owes me four months' rent."

"He does?"

"Yes, he does. Wanna settle up for him?"

"No," I said. "He can settle up for himself."

I ran out the door so he wouldn't see me crying.

STAIRWAY TO HEAVEN is the longest song in the universe. Rose made me play it all the way to the end on the 8-track as we sat parked in my parents' station wagon. They let me drive it because they'd just bought a second car. I looked in the rear-view mirror and adjusted the cap I'd bought to replace my father's hat, trying to tuck as much of my brassy orange hair beneath it as I could.

"You'd think she'd get tired or have a heart attack with all that climbing," I mentioned. Rose told me to shut up.

We were going to the Roxette to see a gay movie Rose's uncle had told her about. *Death in Venice* was playing right around the corner from the skanky hotel where I caught my venereal disease. Rose made me show her the outside of the hotel on our way to the second-run movie theatre. I'd told her all about it. I'd told her all about everything. It was Friday, a week since Phillipe's disappearance. Rose had said that I was better off without him anyhow. "Poets can be unstable." I told her he could die for all I cared but she thought I was being melodramatic.

Rose and I had ended up having lunch with each other every day that week and were, I guess, starting to become friends. She was so different than I'd thought. Of course, it's hard to tell what someone's like if they never open their mouth. Now Rose was talk talk talk.

The Roxette was on the main drag of the Downtown Eastside, a sad, Skid Row part of town. We stood in a short line outside watching an old man throw up on the curb. He took a swig from a bottle in a paper bag and wobbled into an alley. A couple of women wearing too much blue mascara and country singer hairdos walked by. By the time we got to the ticket booth I didn't want to watch a movie even if it was about homosexuals. The street was too interesting. But Rose dragged me inside.

The concession in the dank, musty-smelling lobby served fruit juices, coffee, homemade baked goods, and vegetably things. We got ourselves a coffee. Rose picked up a flyer from a stack on the counter advertising a rally at the American Consulate to protest nuclear testing in the islands off the Alaskan coast. Milling around were a few people my parents' age: elbow-patchy, tweedy men with unkempt hair and women not wearing makeup, some college students, and a group of effeminate-sounding men. I maneuvered Rose close to them so I could hear what they were saying. One of the men, who was well built and very good-looking, kept looking at me, and I kept looking back then looking away. He finally excused himself from his friends and walked over.

"Well," he said. "If it isn't little Mr. Handsome."

I was mortified. If Rose's grin was any broader, it would have knocked off her ears.

"Rose, this is —"

"I know who it is," said Rose, sticking out her hand. "You're Mrs. Robinson. Pleased to meet you."

He looked confused at first, then suddenly started to laugh so loudly that everyone in the lobby turned and stared. Two of his friends exchanged a knowing whisper and one pointed at me. I wanted to kill myself.

He took Rose's hand and kissed it. "*Enchanté.* In broad daylight and theatre foyers that aren't triple x, I'm known as Lyle. Rose. What a lovely name."

"Thank you," said Rose, beaming.

Lyle looked at me. "I'm afraid your friend here never disclosed his real name to me."

"Trevor," I said. My voice broke for the first time in three years.

A man with an Afro came into the middle of the lobby and announced that the movie was about to start.

"Here you go, Trevor," said Lyle. "My card. Call me sometime. I'd better go back and join my friends. You can't leave those old queens alone too long. They start off talking about you behind your back and you never know when the stabbing will begin."

"Wow," I said, looking at the card he'd given me after he'd gone.

"What?" Rose asked.

I showed her the card.

"General Manager, Vancouver Opera," Rose read. She looked at me. "He's gorgeous, Trevor."

I took Rose's arm and packed her and her handbag into the auditorium. We made our way down the aisle and sat in creaky, uncomfortable seats covered in ripped velveteen.

"You should call him," said Rose. "I think he likes you."

"He's not really my type."

"You're joking," said Rose. "He's one of the best-looking men I've ever seen."

"But he wears dresses and makeup. I just don't think it's, you know, very sexy."

"If you don't think dresses and makeup are sexy then why do you keep telling me to wear them?" Rose remarked.

Fortunately for me the lights dimmed. Curtains parted on the battered Art Nouveau proscenium and the movie started. *Death in Venice* was pretty boring. Nothing much happened. It wasn't very realistic. Dirk Bogarde played an aging, ill composer who arrives in Venice for a much-needed rest and falls into a nagging obsession with a beautiful, untalkative boy named Tadzio. He stalks, Tadzio glances; he stalks a little more, Tadzio glances a little more. It was basically an all stalk, no action movie. One more ounce of pastel cinematography or Mahler soundtrack and I was ready to kill myself.

We got a running commentary from an older couple sitting behind us who thought that *Death in Venice* was supposed to be an Agatha Christie whodunit. They'd recently visited Europe, Venice included, on a package tour.

"Oh look," the woman said to her husband, "there's St. Mark's Square with all those pigeons." A little later, when their enthusiasm about the film was on the wane, the woman commented, "I think he has his eyes on that boy."

The movie ends up with Dirk Bogarde getting a complete makeover, which he doesn't hesitate to unveil at the beach in the middle of the day, in full view of Tadzio, who seems more interested in doing artistic hand movements while standing ankle deep in sea water. Then Dirk Bogarde's hair dye runs, and he dies, presumably of embarrassment.

Rose rolled her eyes when I gave her my film review on the sidewalk after the movie was over. She said, "Don't you know anything about European homoerotic expression and metaphorical construction?"

"It depends."

"On what?"

"On what that means."

I had a sneaking suspicion that if hard-pressed for a clear

explanation, Rose would cave and admit she didn't have the faintest idea either. Over the last few days, I'd discovered that Rose carried around a little invisible phrase book of comments by her fruity English uncle. Sometimes she could translate them, sometimes not.

"Oh, forget it," she said, proving my theory.

We went up the block to the Yangtze Pearl Café where drug addicts were supposed to hang out and sat in a booth at the front by the window. The proprietor, an old Chinese man, shuffled up to us with menus and after a quick look we ordered milkshakes. We maintained a vigilant lookout for underbelly in the sputtering red neon glow of the greasy spoon's malfunctioning sign. The action on the sidewalk along East Hastings Street didn't disappoint.

Across the street two greaseballs shoved each other back and forth, shouting. A police car pulled up. Two cops got out to intervene. On our side of the street a bored-looking girl about our age in a fake fur bomber jacket and platform go-go boots tried to look like she wasn't hooking. She turned her face away from the traffic and pulled a small plastic baggie from her leather jacket. She sniffed from it, put it away, then faced the traffic again.

"Youth was Dirk Bogarde's fatal flaw," Rose informed me.

"I think not having a very interesting story to be in kind of sealed his fate, if you ask me," I said, keeping an eye open for junkies.

The proprietor returned with our milkshakes.

"Don't you think it was sad?" Rose asked me. "I mean. Dirk Bogarde spent his whole life in the pursuit of beauty and in the end, it killed him, because it was flirtatious but out of reach."

I took a sip of my milkshake and said, "You think that Tadzio is supposed to represent beauty?"

"Yeah."

"Hunh. I just thought he was wimpy and irritating."

"But don't you think it's even sadder then if Dirk Bogarde thought he was chasing after beauty and it was really just a figment of his imagination, that it was there inside him all the time?"

I shrugged. "I don't really care what happened to some old European guy a million years ago. That's the kind of film my parents go to and think they know something new about the world. Who needs ancient history? I'd rather see a movie about, I don't know, that girl out there."

I pointed at her. She was leaning into a car window.

Rose sighed. "Trevor, you're supposed to look at the subtext of *Death in Venice*, not just what happens."

I drained the last of my milkshake and said, "What's the point of subtext if it makes a story boring? Why not just tell it like it is?"

"Duh," said Rose. "Then it wouldn't be art."

"Then art is a pile of shit," I said. "Art isn't telling the truth."

The old man slapped our bill on the table.

"You pay. I close," he said.

We paid, left the Yangtze Pearl, and I drove Rose home.

THE NEXT GREY Monday morning Rose sat on the railing beneath the concrete awning over the smoking steps waiting for me. Her hair dripped and her poncho was soaked through. The day was torrential. *Death in Venice* seemed a world away. A group of kids stood on the grass nearby under umbrellas, having a last smoke before the nine o'clock bell. They briefly looked over their shoulders at me and were strangely quiet. Rose seemed worried.

"What's wrong?" I asked.

Rose stood up and heaved her handbag over her shoulder. Her glasses were all fogged up. "I just wanted to be with you when you saw."

"Saw what?"

"Come on," said Rose, taking my hand.

We went inside. When I saw it, at first, I thought it was kind of funny. Then, when it sank in, I wanted to pound the shit out of somebody.

"Trevor, where are you going?" Rose asked.

She scrambled down the hall after me. I shoved people out of my way. I found Harlan by his locker with Mike and Sammy. I grabbed him and pinned him against his locker. Harlan was taller, bigger, and stronger than me, so it must have been an adrenalin rush that gave me the strength to hold him there. Mike and Sammy went to grab me, but Harlan motioned them to stay back.

"Don't, Trevor," said Rose.

Harlan smiled the smug smile I hated. "I didn't do it," he said.

"Yeah, right." I slammed his head against the locker.

"Ow! I didn't, you stupid faggot."

He'd stopped smiling. His face was turning red. I slammed a fist into his stomach.

"Trevor!" Rose shouted.

Harlan swung back at me, pounding my right ear with a fist. I heard a loud ringing. He shoved me onto the floor. We started to wrestle. Somehow, I got on top. I went insane. I took his head and started to bang it against the floor. He jammed his knee into my nuts. I groaned and rolled over onto my back. He thrust a fist in my gut, and I did the same back. I knew I was getting hurt, really hurt, but I couldn't feel any pain. I heard the nine o'clock bell in the distance.

Suddenly two strong hands grabbed me by the rib cage and pulled me up onto my feet. I found myself face to face with Mr. Cuthbert.

"That's enough," he said.

Harlan was struggling with Mike and Sammy. Rose stood there looking helpless. Half the school had congregated to stare.

"Now shake hands and apologize, the both of you," said Mr. Cuthbert.

I stretched out a shaky, tentative hand and so did Harlan. We shook, but my heart wasn't in it. I think we both mumbled something stupid. As we were hauled off to the principal's office, I felt my body start to sting in several places and noticed a bruise on my right arm. My ear was still ringing. We were sentenced to two hours of supervised detention after school for the entire week. They called our parents.

My locker door was totaled. Harlan had attached the HOMO milk cartons with industrial strength glue. The school janitor had to replace it. He threw out the old door before I could remove my *Aladdin Sane* David Bowie poster taped on to the inside. I was pissed off. Just once in my life I wanted to be consulted before someone did something that affected my entire existence. Every day from three to five I had to sit in an empty classroom with Harlan, while the principal or vice principal sat at the teacher's desk doing paperwork and drinking coffee. I reread *Lord of the Rings* for the third time. All Harlan did every single minute of every single detention was stare at me. Whenever I looked up from my book, there he was, lasering me with a creepy look.

My parents grounded me for a month, which meant I wouldn't be able to go see David Bowie. I was mortified. I begged and pleaded with them to let me go to the concert, but they were intractable. I made plans to sneak out. It wouldn't be difficult at all. Since my bedroom was on the ground floor, all I had to do was be very quiet and leave through the garage door. My parents grounded me on the honour system. They trusted me.

They were so dumb.

"THOSE ARE PRETTY strong opinions for someone your age," said Mr. Cuthbert when he handed back my essay on the Cultural Revolution.

Everybody was a critic.

"What kind of opinions am I supposed to have? I'm sixteen, not mental," I said, crabby from a fight I'd had with my parents at breakfast. "A-plus?"

"Maybe strong was the wrong word to use. I meant mature."

He put his hand on my shoulder and gave it a squeeze. An electric shock went through my body. I started to get a hard-on.

"Well done, Ms. Esterhazy," he said, handing Rose her essay. She sat beside me, by the window.

"Thank you, Mr. Cuthbert," said Rose, smiling sweetly, looking for her mark. "A-minus?" she said under her breath, looking crestfallen.

We were on a school bus in the parking lot about to leave. Fort Langley loomed on the inevitable horizon. The weather was bleak. It was cold and dark. A light, misty rain fell. The sidewalks were treacherous with slimy leaves.

I had on my bulky Cowichan sweater, patched jeans, and hiking boots — a subdued outfit that contradicted my mortifying scare-do. The roots were beginning to show dramatically. I wanted to dye it back to blond but I couldn't afford the hair dye. My parents wouldn't give me an advance on my allowance. Over breakfast they said something boring about responsibility and how adults must live with the choices they make. I pointed out that adults could make a choice to dye their hair back to its natural colour because they had money, but it got me nowhere. They laughed and exchanged a know-it-all look like they did when they first saw my orange hair. I told them that if I saw that look one more time, I was going to kill myself. My father suggested I should play another record.

"Do it, do us all a big favour, kill yourself," Doreen said as she came into the kitchen.

Now we all got to hear her two cents' worth. My sister, who was a year older and in the graduating class, said that she was sick of sticking up for me at school. She said that if I wanted to stand out in the crowd, the crowd was bound to notice, and I'd better learn how to deal with it. My parents said Doreen was right and that she'd never been given any special privileges where money was concerned. I told them that if they said, "Why don't you get a part-time job like Doreen?" I really would kill myself.

"Promises, promises," Doreen said, eating peanut butter out of the jar.

I told her she was gross and informed my parents they didn't love me. I slammed the door on my way down to my bedroom in the basement where I put on *The Rise and Fall of Ziggy Stardust and the Spiders from Mars* at full blast. I didn't turn it off when I left for school. They wanted another record, they got it.

All I wanted was a little respect but all I got was criticism. My essay, for example. I showed Rose the encyclopedia of comments on it.

"I know." She showed me the A-minus she got for *The Big Leap Forward*. "He did the same to me. I hate teachers who give you a good mark then tell you everything you did wrong. It's so Catholic."

I didn't know what she meant but nodded my head in agreement.

"But I guess it makes you think." Rose added. I just kept nodding.

It was a long drive to Fort Langley, over an hour on the highway up the Fraser Valley. There wasn't a view to look at because the mountains were covered in clouds. I'd already seen it dozens of times, so I wasn't missing anything. The fort, built for fur trading and the gold rush, was a part of pioneer history from the previous century. It was the only thing resembling history anywhere close to Vancouver, which was why every couple of years you were thrown into a bus and shipped there for yet another grim trudge from one lecture in a gloomy log building to another. By now I could likely have hand-churned butter, shoed a horse, and given Hudson's Bay blankets to Indians in exchange for a province all at the same time in my sleep. Rose was reading, so I took *Lord of the Rings* out of my knapsack and started to read too.

A spitball hit the back of my neck. I looked around. Mike and Sammy were a couple of seats behind me. Harlan was across the aisle from them. They stared out the window looking innocent, except for Sammy's glass eye which was boring a hole into Cheryl Johnson's ponytail. I went back to my book.

"Ow!" Rose exclaimed. She reached into her nest of hair and struggled with a wad of chewed-up paper.

I turned to her and said, "We could start our own fucking space program with all the rocket scientists on this bus."

The girls behind us laughed.

A couple of minutes later another spitball whacked my left ear. I turned around to say something but before I had a chance Mr. Cuthbert loudly announced, "The scope and clarity of rear-view mirrors on buses are amazing. Certain people might be interested to find out that we don't do spitballs in my class. We don't do that either, Harlan."

Harlan put down his finger and snickered.

It was taking longer than usual to get to Fort Langley because we were slowed down by the horrible weather and congested traffic. We were still in the suburbs, not even halfway, when Harlan, Mike, and Sammy started doing Cheech and Chong for each other. Along with the Dead Parrot sketch, if I heard Sister Mary Elephant one more time, I'd kill myself. It didn't seem to bother Rose, though. She was buried in her book, transfixed by *The Edible Woman*.

Nothing could have looked drearier and more uninviting than the fort's rain-smothered log barricade and its surreal gun towers rising above us as we trouped off the bus onto the soggy gravel parking lot. We were herded through the front gate and corralled in the centre of the fort's quadrangle, where the grass was quickly being overtaken by squelching mud. Fort Langley employed retired senior citizens to conduct the tour. A tall woman with a bony face, a large nose, and thick grey hair wound up in a bun welcomed us. She had a British accent and was unbelievably cheerful. She wore a sensible beige pantsuit with the legs tucked into knee-high rubber boots. We were given tour itineraries and told to line up in pairs. Our first destination was the blacksmith's shop.

"Uh-oh, horse-hoofing," I whispered to Rose.

We were at the very back of the line. While no one was looking, we snuck away and went into the Governor's House. It was a large, ramshackle wooden building supposedly considered a mansion in its day and had been home to the people who'd once controlled the province. The rooms were sealed off by low-hanging chains. Do Not Touch, the signs read. Rose and I seemed to be the only ones in the building. An eerie silence descended upon us as we walked from room to room and peered beyond the chains. Occasionally a floorboard groaned. On the second floor, I stepped over the chain that blocked off the master bedroom.

"Come on," I said.

Rose looked uncertain. "We'll get in trouble."

"We're already in trouble."

Rose tentatively put one leg over the chain, then the other, and she was inside the out-of-bounds, old-fashioned bedroom with me. A board creaked loudly as we walked over to the window.

"It's okay," I said.

Rose came up behind me and put a hand on my shoulder as

we stared out the window. The house was on the highest point of land in the fort. Through the grey we could see the river, the hills, farms, and trees spreading across the valley and, a few miles away, the dim mountains. I thought about the view from Phillipe's apartment and suddenly had a strange feeling, as though part of me was missing, was somewhere else far away.

Rose went over to a wooden dresser where there was an enormous porcelain water jug hand-painted with a design of delicate wildflowers. It was cradled in a large basin with edges sculpted like a flower petal. She picked it up.

"It's heavy," she said and put it back down. She breathed in and out deeply. "I love that smell, the smell of settled wood. I bet it smelled this way when someone still lived here. A room like this needs people to live in it. Now it just feels like a tomb."

I sat down on the edge of the large bed, a mattress of straw supported by a mesh of rope secured to four large wooden poles. The thick, faded, hand-stitched quilt sank beneath my weight. I lay down on it. My head floated on a cloud of goose down pillows. Rose put her handbag on the floor and lay down beside me.

"It's a fairy-tale bed," she said.

I told Rose about the fight with my parents.

"Whether you like it or not, we need to get a job," said Rose. "We're vassals, victims of economic dependency. We don't have any freedom because we can't pay our way. We need to be emancipated. So long as our parents control the distribution of wealth, they can dominate our choices."

"We're only sixteen," I reminded her.

"But we're the future," said Rose. "The imminent collapse of the economic unit called the nuclear family has got people in power frightened of social and cultural change."

I rolled my head toward the ceiling. "Where'd you pick that up?"

"In a *Ms.* magazine article in the school library. It's our duty to get a job at the bottom of the inverted pyramid that makes up capitalism, where the blue collar carries all the weight. Then, when we get closer to the top, we can start educating people. The workers of the world will thank us."

"The workers of the world aren't even paying attention," I said. "Besides, I don't want to work to change the world. I just want to work so I can dye my hair back to its original colour."

"It's a start," said Rose. "Let's go downtown on Saturday and start looking for part-time jobs."

"Okay." I stared up at the wooden beams on the ceiling.

Rose was quiet for a minute or two, then said, "My mother asked me something strange the other day."

"What?"

"I think she thinks we're going together. Of course, she doesn't know anything about you, it's none of her business. But when I mentioned your name the other day, she asked me if you had big feet, and when I said I didn't know she had this weird smile on her face."

I laughed. "It's subtext, Rose."

"Oh," she said. "OH!"

"I haven't heard it about feet before. But I've heard big nose, big hose."

"You're disgusting."

"How about big feet, large meat?" I suggested.

"Gross."

"Broad back, big snack."

"Oh, I know," said Rose. "Here's one. Long finger, long stinger."

"I know I know I know — long shin, big as sin."

"How about, break the rule, stay after school?" Mr. Cuthbert stood grinning in the doorway. Rose and I sat up.

"Hi, Mr. Cuthbert," said Rose. "Sorry."

"I hate to break up your poetry salon, but your presence is requested in the Map Room," said Mr. Cuthbert. Mortified, we stepped over the chain and followed him back into bleakness.

DETERMINED TO DEFY my parents, and inspired by Rose's dissertation on the merits of economic independence, I devised an income stream so that I could afford a David Bowie ticket. There wasn't enough time to get a part-time job, so on a Saturday afternoon, I went downtown to where I'd been picked up by the guy with the aftershave several months earlier. I hung out until a car stopped and an old man asked me if I was looking for company. I made him pay me fifty bucks to suck me off in his car in an alley. Then I went and bought my ticket for *Diamond Dogs*. I didn't buy the satin pants.

The night of the concert was cool and starry. My parents went to a dinner party, so sneaking out was kind of academic. Rose and I arrived early. We elbowed ourselves to near the front of the line at the Pacific Coliseum. I wanted to scout out a spot on the concert floor close to the stage. Standing outside, we ended up smoking a joint with some other early birds. I wasn't used to being stoned and for a while I looked up at the sky and got lost in the stars.

We were like lemmings to the sea when they opened the doors of the Coliseum. We found a place at the front, right at the centre of the stage. The concert was sold out. A sea of people swelled up to the rafters. A huge screen rolled down and they showed a Salvador Dali art film, which didn't make too much sense, but I liked it any how. When it was finished, people started to chant. "Booo-weee. Booo-weee," they screamed over and over again. In the bleachers, they stamped their feet. The lights began to dim.

Everyone started holding up lighters, candles, and matches. I looked around the Coliseum. It sparkled like a giant birthday cake, or a funeral, or a galaxy. I asked someone for a match. They passed it to me. I lit it and held it up.

The match burned down to my fingers, but I didn't put it out. I wanted to feel the fire against my skin. A deafening surge of cheering almost blasted me to the ground. David Bowie came onstage. He looked fantastic, but he was smaller than I expected. I squeezed Rose's hands with excitement. Then, because I was stoned, I had a thought. What if Harlan wasn't the one who put those milk cartons on my locker?

"This ain't rock 'n' roll," David Bowie shouted, as he launched into *Diamond Dogs*. "This is genocide!"

The crowd went hysterical.

The Hidden History of Gangsters

I WAS CHANNEL surfing in the Sea of Happiness. Except for Big Helen, I was alone in the hotel bar, nursing a Bloody Caesar. I munched disconsolately on the celery stick and thought, the more you try to bite out of life, the more fibrous strands you're likely to get caught in your teeth. The remote was like a prosthesis, appended to my wrist, switching stations in time with my pulse. The war, a soap opera, the weather channel, more talk about the war, snow, a sitcom rerun, more war, more snow, country singers whose mothers don't know they're lesbians, heroes of the war. Big Helen put my sandwich on the table.

"You want malaise with that, baby?"

"Malaise. I don't need malaise. My God, woman, look out the window," I said, pointing. "It's all around us."

"Baby, I said mayonnaise. And that ain't no window, that's a TV."

I came to my senses and sure enough, I was waving the remote at the wall screen television.

"Sorry."

"You better settle on what you want. You gonna wear that thing out."

I laughed self-consciously. "Yeah. I guess you're right. Got a toothpick, Helen?"

"Sure, baby."

She handed me a red plastic toothpick in the shape of a swordfish and plunked down a clean ashtray. Concord Hotel, it said, in lettering that made me think of zoot suits, swing music, and victory in Europe.

"Thanks."

"Uh-huh."

I'd come here looking for happiness. When did I turn into a spectator, confusing what I saw with what I felt?

MONSIEUR DELACROIX AND I arrived the day after the war ended. We had both lost our jobs, taken our separation pay, borrowed Monsieur Delacroix's sister's convertible, and driven the long drive to Chicago. When we crossed the border at Detroit, there were yellow ribbons on all the cars on the highway. Except ours. At truck stops, on turnpikes, at gas stations, in all the towns, big yellow bows welcomed home the troops. Just past Gary, Indiana, Monsieur stuck in the Judy Garland tape. "Chicago!" she belted out as the silhouette of its tall skyscrapers came into view on the horizon. For a split second I thought I saw a huge yellow bow tied to the very tip of the top of the Sears Tower. It was a trick of the light. Out came the sun, a gold-plated knife cutting through the platinum winter clouds. We laughed, rolled down the rooftop to let the icy wind whip our hair, and took the first exit downtown. No one noticed. Safe, at last.

BIG HELEN TOOK my empty glass, wedging her large hips between tables. She brushed against my cigarette. Ashes flew.

"Gee, Helen, sorry."

"Saw'right, baby. Saw'right."

Big Helen — that was how she introduced herself the first time we walked into her bar — had taken a real shine to me and Monsieur Delacroix. And we to her.

"You boys are ... different. Where you from?"

"Toronto," we said together. "Canada," I added.

"Oh, honey, I know where Toronto is. Hear it's a lot like Chicago."

"Yeah," I said. "It's a lot like Chicago."

Big Helen's stacked bracelets rattled as she put down our drinks. She navigated the bar escorted by an armada of eye-popping accessories. Declarative rings. Demonstrative necklaces. Defiant earrings. Jewellery circumnavigated the shorelines of her body, bobbing and swaying as it lapped against collar, cuffs, and the contour of hemlines. Her bijoux were beacons in the dimly lit cocktail lounge. Anchored in darkness, they suddenly floated to the surface, twinkling briefly as she passed beneath tiny pot lights in the ceiling. Their lustre seemed to emanate from somewhere deep in time and far away in space. I imagined them breaking free and forming galaxies.

She flipped back her dreads and waved a finger when I tried to pay for our drinks.

"On the house, baby. I need to build me a better clientele. I don't have enough people of refinement coming here yet. I need to create a buzz." She said "refinement" in a snooty, old Hollywood movie voice. "I'm workin' it, though. If you know what I mean."

We did. And she was right. No one worked it like Big Helen.

MONSIEUR DELACROIX AND I had been here some time. We planned to stay till the money ran out. We liked it here. And what was there to go back to? A life of crime? No one had work anymore.

The big TV screen reminded me of Monsieur's Theory of Elevators, which had been going over and over in my head since I sat down.

Wide awake, after stumbling in from the bars at four a.m. our first night on the lam, I couldn't sleep. Monsieur Delacroix sawed logs, clear-cutting his way through giant redwoods.

In the drawer of the bedside table, I found the usual Gideon and a book in Korean that seemed to be something Buddhist. Left behind, no doubt, by one of the many pay-by-the-week Korean students staying here to learn English. We'd run into a couple earlier on the elevator. I'd experienced my usual moment of doubt but hid my fear of heights from Monsieur. He thought I was ridiculous. Technology of any application lifted his spirits, particularly if it also lifted Monsieur Delacroix. Especially if it made him higher than a kite. He lived for the moment, worshiping machines and motion. Monsieur Delacroix treated life like an adventure movie, munching popcorn through its ups and downs.

The students had chips and Coke from the lobby vending machines. A break in their homework, I guessed. I stood in one corner. Monsieur stood in the other corner on the same side. Each student took a remaining corner. They were very nice to us. We smiled and said hello to each other.

"Tourist?"

"Yes."

"American?"

"No, Canadian. Toronto."

"Ah, like America!"

"Yes, like America."

We stood at opposite sides of the elevator, smiling.

"Nice night."

"You have a nice night too."

The elevator door closed. Monsieur Delacroix turned to me.

His mouth lemon-sucked itself into a tightness of concentration.

"Have I ever explained my Theory of Elevators?"

"Your what?"

"My Theory of Elevators, dear."

"Wait," I said. "My notebook."

We got inside our room, and each cracked open a beer. Monsieur kicked off his black-and-white-checkered sneakers and sat down on his bed. On the opposite bed, I lotus-positioned and cozily lap-topped.

"In an elevator, if there are two people, they will form a perfect line," Monsieur Delacroix announced, playing absently with a strand of hair. "One will stand against the left wall, and one will stand against the right wall. If there are three people, they will form a perfect triangle. One at both the right and the left wall, standing away from the door, and one right in front of the door as close to it as he can get. If there are four people, you have a perfect square, as you witnessed. Each will take his own corner. If there are five, all corners will be taken, and there will be one right in the centre, so you have a possibility of lines, triangles, and squares."

"Lines, triangles, and squares — oh my!" I said. "What if you're by yourself?"

"You're free to stand where you wish, but you'll try to abuse the privilege. You'll nonchalantly lean against one wall, then the next. You'll cross your legs, fold your arms, maybe even close your eyes. You'll turn the light off, and then back on. You'll fiddle with the fan. You'll carve your name into a wall. You might even carve some pornography if you're interesting. You'll contemplate Emergency Stop. But ..."

"But?"

"But! Your freedom is an illusion. No man can bear to go up and down alone. When you share the elevator, you worry ... What to say? Where to look? How to cover up a smell? You worry about the spread of germs, and what another's cough means. But when you are alone, nagging away at the back of your head, you start to think to yourself ... you begin to worry ... what if the cables snap?"

Monsieur Delacroix helped himself to another beer and let out a self-satisfied sigh.

"Now it's time for our facial," he said. And got out the Aloe Vera Five-Minute Masks.

I wondered if he was right, that people trapped in a box can't form a circle and join each other. What about the guy I'd met?

"WANNANOTHER?"

Big Helen's large bosom was inches away from my face. She smelled of salt and citrus.

"Sure. Thanks."

A serial killer famous for stashing the body parts of twenty-five victims in the pipes underneath his house was giving an exclusive interview. He said he wished he could turn back the clock. A revered newscaster, known for hard-hitting, take-no-prisoners reportage, furrowed his brow and asked the serial killer if he regretted what he did. No, he replied, he just wanted to turn back the clock. Then he said, "Regret what?"

"Same? Hot?" Big Helen segued her heft through the flip-top counter and reached for a glass. She had her paws on the Tabasco. I jumped in before it was too late.

"A little less this time," I said. "But you're starting to get it. Don't be shy with the celery salt though."

First time I ordered a Bloody Caesar, Big Helen drew a blank.

"You mean a Bloody Mary."

"No. A Caesar. With Clamato not tomato juice. It's practically Canada's national cocktail."

"I don't know 'bout that. I just can't wrap my head round

putting clams in your juice." She put the drink on a fresh napkin that had a picture of a hula girl on it.

"Where's Mr. Delacroix today?"

"Monsieur Delacroix hasn't come home yet."

"He's bad. Good bad. But bad."

Big Helen laughed. She went behind the bar and started to cut up limes for the late-afternoon crowd. I changed channels to a game show.

I felt cables snapping all around me.

"THE MEAT PEOPLE are buried in Graceland," he said.

We were on the El, grinding toward downtown from the night before. He to school, me to my digs. He pointed out the window as we clattered over a graveyard straight out of Charles Dickens. Unwieldy tombstones and crooked memorials loomed among leafless trees sprouting in brown grass. Blue sky cheated through breaks in a thin skin of filmy clouds.

"The Smiths, the Oscar Meyers, they're all buried in Graceland Cemetery," he said.

We rattled over the bones of meatpacking and the remains of railways. A cemetery with a life of its own.

"You can get a tour."

Why didn't he just tell me? I had all the clues. They followed him around like breadcrumbs. He avoided the topic even though what I knew about him — everything in his apartment, what he ate, how he made love — broke his scam and made me hurt for him even more. I loved an out-of-step con artist. I wanted to tell him I knew. I wanted to tell him so I could break down. That he wasn't a criminal. That he wasn't alone. The only person he was conning was himself. If he needed a fall guy, I was it. I could write myself into his story if he gave me the opening lines. It was his gambit.

"You can get a tour?" I said, trying to sound enthusiastic.

"Yeah." He dimpled in a boyish smile and glanced at me.

His innocent face belied the instinct of a felon. He was unable to sit still, his knee was up and down, all over the damn place. I could show him how to hold on to stillness if he let me. His books were loose on the seat beside him: Environmental Studies. I took his hand and squeezed it, long enough for the suit across the aisle to rustle his paper and give us a dirty look. He blushed and withdrew his hand. I took it back, and he let it stay. He sighed.

"But only in the summer," he said. He said "summer" as though it were a distant place, somewhere he'd never visited. "I've never taken the tour," he added.

"What about the gangsters?" I asked, as Graceland receded into the narrow end of perspective's funnel. If anyone knew, he would.

"Huh?"

"You know. Al Capone. The Roaring Twenties. The Saint Valentine's Day Massacre. The stuff Chicago is famous for." I'd been looking around for monuments to the criminals who gave Chicago its glamour. My snooping for some history of the crimes that made it a great city had not turned up any leads. It was perplexing.

"Oh, that." He looked out the window and curled his lip. "That's the past. Who cares?" He brushed me off with a wave of his hand, as though he were clearing the air of a bad smell. We lurched into a station. He quickly got up, dropping my hand. I wanted to give him a hug, to tell him. I knew why he wouldn't let me put my tongue down his throat.

"This is where I have to get off," he said.

"Oh," I said. "Too bad."

The suit was staring so I pulled him back down and kissed him right on the lips before he had a chance to stop me like last night. My head filled with jazz. Did the kid hear too?

"You shouldn't have done that," he whispered. Dazed, he stumbled to the door. "Tomorrow?"

"Yeah," I said, with a reassuring smile. "Tomorrow."

I watched his tight little backside merengue off the car. It was touching how he thought he could fool me. He was so young that everything he did was a fingerprint. And I was an expert at detection. The train kicked out onto the trestle. We clattered by repeating brick walls and dark windows, like in a cartoon.

I wanted to know where they buried the gangsters. There must be a museum.

THE SEA OF Happiness is in the Concord Hotel. The hotel has nothing else in common with the supersonic jet but a name. The speed of sound is irrelevant in the Concord Hotel, if you're escapees like me and Monsieur Delacroix, trying to outdistance the speed of shame. We were vigilant, looking over our shoulders to make sure shame wasn't tailgating us like a second-rate detective. So far, we'd been smart and quick, committing crimes and leaving evidence. On purpose. We imagined that shame was stuck at the scene of a felony, smoking a stogie as it scratched its double chin. Clueless, it overlooked the obvious.

The rooms at the Concord Hotel are forty dollars a night for a double with TV. But there's no cable or converter, just a dial you turn by hand and fuzzy reception. You get two hard beds, a closet with a broken door, red, orange, and yellow striped curtains and bedspreads, a cockroach in the bathroom, and Monsieur Delacroix snoring his head off beside you. The walls are paper thin, so if it isn't Monsieur keeping you awake, it's the TV above, people having sex in the next room, or an occasional bout of glittering repartee up and down the hallways.

"Motherfucker!"

"Give it back faggot!"

"Come get it bitch!"

Stuff like that.

The Concord Hotel was built in the 1920s. Mr. Maharaj on the graveyard shift told us. You could tell it was stylish then. A marble lobby in deco lines. Brass rails. There was probably someone to shine your shoes while, fedora doffed, you read your *Chicago Tribune*.

Nowadays, the marble is cracked, and the brass is tarnished. But there is still life in the Sea of Happiness.

You get to the bar through a doorway in the hotel lobby, past a wall mural of piccolo-playing mermaids, whales with trombones, giant clams propped open like grand pianos with musical notes coming out of the keys in wavy lines, and lobsters with eyes winking at the end of long stalks, playing their claws like castanets, all dancing at the bottom of a Day-Glo ocean. The Sea of Happiness is spelled out in interlocking sea horses. Inside, the ceiling and walls are draped with purple fishing nets encrusted with blue plastic starfish and pieces of pink and yellow coral. There's a stuffed marlin over the service area. The tables are covered in plexiglass embedded with shells: oysters, periwinkles, sand dollars, conches, nautiluses, butter clams.

"Hey, Canada."

"Hey," I replied.

It was the roadie I liked from the Shriner Circus. Part of the reason Monsieur Delacroix and I patronized the Sea of Happiness was the Shriner Circus. The show was in town, and the bar was a hangout for some of the roadies. We were quite taken with two of them. Monsieur Delacroix preferred a mastiff who looked like something from the World Federation of Wrestling, with thick blond Viking hair, and thighs that could bend steel girders. I liked a guy Monsieur Delacroix called Trailer Park. He had a taut, sinewy look, ready to snap. Like he'd been in juvenile detention and learned a few tricks you'd like him to teach you. He had hurtin' eyes, variegated according to the light, and a tattoo on his right forearm featuring an eagle, an anchor, a trident, and a pistol. "Navy Seals," he'd explained one night when he saw me staring at it, offering nothing further.

The roadies came filing in and crowded round the bar. They all smiled at me. I was regular now. I smiled back.

"Where's the French dude?" Trailer Park asked.

I shrugged my shoulders. The roadie winked and gave me thumbs-up, then turned to his big friend. I wasn't in the mood to talk. I needed to think a bit more, work my way around/through the feelings. I was thinking about the young man I met. He told me about his brother. He never said a thing about how proud he was, though, or what a fine thing his brother had done for his country. There was a scream in his eyes as he told me. All I saw when I looked at the good-looking roadie was that same scream in the form of a smile, coming at me like a fist.

I surfed. Channel after channel, people congratulated themselves on the war. Military strategists were talk-showed into celebrity status. Children got a quick fix of living history, watching the war on TV, with commentary. Right and wrong were being re-established. People had stars in their eyes, and stripes.

"You okay, baby? Another drink?"

"No thanks. Not now, Helen."

Sometimes I think too much, so I surf. It calms me down, the regular rhythm of waves, as they crash and disappear. To me, the ocean sounds just like the snow on a station after sign-off.

I WAS HAVING an out-of-body experience at Vortex when I met him. The club had comedy nights on Tuesdays, called America's Funniest Homo Videos. I perched on a stool against a wall in the video room. It was so dark when I first came in that I couldn't see a thing except the enormous screen and a bank of monitors hanging from the ceiling. Earlier, on the roomy dance floor in the front of the club, the outgoing Miss Gay Chicago did a show to promote the upcoming coronation of the new Miss Gay Chicago. She lip-synched to several disco standards, accompanied by a chorus of brick shithouses wearing leopard-skin G-strings, and a laser show.

It took a while for my eyes to adjust. They were showing old *I Love Lucy* segments, Buddy Cole monologues from *Kids in the Hall*, stuff from *Saturday Night Live, Men on Film, The Golden Girls,* Joan Rivers, the best Alexis moments from *Dynasty*, that kind of thing.

When I arrived with Monsieur Delacroix at the beginning of the evening, we went straight to the karaoke bar at the back. Monsieur got up and sang "D.I.V.O.R.C.E." to me. Everyone stared. First at Monsieur Delacroix, then at me, then back at Monsieur Delacroix. He had a mushroom cloud of blond hair and radiated charisma. On the flip side, he couldn't sing and was dressed from head to toe in beige. But people love a somebody-done-me-wrong song. They'll overlook anything for a good cry in their cups, even pitch.

After, we had a drink, then Monsieur Delacroix headed off to the baths. I stayed. Monsieur Delacroix's taste for anonymous sex verged on the pathological. I used to be like that, but I'd changed. I had become a romantic, looking for picket fences through the poppers. I liked a little mystery, having something more to take off than a white towel. That's all people wear at the baths as they perambulate through its dusky corridors, searching from cubicle to cubicle for semaphores of invitation, imagining they are free.

A white towel conceals a multitude of crimes. It contributes to the myth of democracy, like McDonald's. It's the Big Mac of sex. All we want in life, it seems, is to be quick. You walk into the baths, you remove your clothes, you put on a white towel. You are Everyman going undercover. Sans identity, you are guilty of nothing. No past, no class, no language of your own. Nobody knows who you are or what you've done. The discourse of the baths is strict and linear. How could I trust a place that takes the sex out of words, the freedom out of speech? I liked to flirt with my tricks, confuse them with circles of rhetoric, ensnare them with a jazz riff of amorous maybes. But Monsieur Delacroix liked to draw lines. Which was why you'll find him in his little box, his stomach on a pillow, white rump raised to whoever is interested.

My rocks had been offed at the baths more times than I could count. I had had a good time. A lot of fun. A few laughs. But in exile my tastes had turned to more exotic pursuits. I was on to new things. I was after new blood. The kind the heart pumps. The kind that courses through your brain and lets you make mistakes. I wanted out of all the boxes. All around me, cables were snapping. I wanted to know what someone wore when they were on the outside, see how they deceived the world. A pose is a pose is a pose. In the baths you can pretend to be anyone you want to be. I didn't care who you wanted to be. I was hungry for who you pretended to be when you were on the outside. In hiding. Then I wanted to strip search you visible with love. Uncover what you did wrong, and then spread you against the fence.

Monsieur Delacroix liked things he can measure, things he can count on. For me, the baths were about the law of averages, and I was ready for a lot more than average.

When my pupils had expanded suitably to survey the crowd, I did a trick scan, hoping my tracking beam of pheromones would collide with another's, and beautiful music would happen. I was in wide-beam mode that evening.

He made his move.

"Hi," he said, playing coy to the hilt. A bit awkward though, not very slick.

I stared. He was a babe.

"Hi."

He was younger than me, dressed like a college kid. Jeans, topsiders, a button-down shirt. An awkward bang of thick auburn hair fell into his eyes. He swept it away with a goofy gesture. His eyes sparkled, big, oval, and bright, bright blue. He had a toothy smile as Midwestern as a cornfield on a clear day. I was smitten. The Gershwin brothers poured a tune in my ears. A sentimental lyric and a haunting refrain oozed through me. Some of it spilled out of my eyes. My brain turned into a cocktail shaker of good spirits. Infatuation and alcohol have the same effect on me as nostalgia. They're all about forgetting where you are, right now. You feel like you remember something good, only it's better than it really was.

"Can I buy you a drink?" I asked.

"Yeah, sure. A Coke. I don't drink."

"Sure." I waved over a waiter and ordered a Coke and a beer.

He leaned into me with his pelvis, inserting a leg between mine. He put a hand inside my open jacket, on my chest, right above my heart.

"I'm not usually like this," he said. "It feels good."

"Feeling's mutual," I replied.

"How old are you?"

"Thirty-two."

"Wow!" he exclaimed. "You don't look it."

"Thanks. And you?"

"Twenty," he said proudly. "I'm in college. You're not from here, are you?"

"No," I said as our drinks arrived. "I'm from Canada. Toronto."

He took a large gulp of his Coke. "I've never been there before," he said. "Everyone says it's a lot like Europe."

"Yeah," I said. "It's a lot like Europe."

"Wanna play cops and robbers?" he said.

"Gotta gun?"

"Yeah," he said, putting my hand on his crotch.

Sometimes you just look at a person and know. It's too late to get away. But who was chasing whom? Where were the handcuffs?

BIG HELEN PUT down a fresh drink.

"From your friend over there," she said. She didn't approve. "A boy with your looks could get his pick. You could do better."

Trailer Park raised his beer at me. I raised my drink at him.

"How's your wife, sugar," Big Helen said loud enough for everyone to hear.

He gave her a tight smile. "Fine. Usual. Y'know."

She narrowed her eyes and said to me through her teeth, "He pockets his ring when he sees you. Don't go with him. He's trouble."

"Thanks. Don't worry. I won't."

Big Helen looked doubtful.

It was after five. The Sea of Happiness was packed. I felt claustrophobic and changed the channel. I watched a commercial for a suburban discount store that sold furniture suites and home entertainment centres. Chicagoland's finest selection of more things to put in a box.

MONSIEUR DELACROIX AND I had been waiting for Mr. Wright. God's house is in Oak Park. And you can't move the furniture.

One afternoon, we took the car and sped along the freeway past the tall buildings, past the projects, through the suburbs, out to the quiet land of perfect houses. The studio and home of Frank Lloyd Wright was serene. You can get a tour. A retired schoolteacher, with steely grey hair tied back in a braided ponytail and wearing a tweed skirt-suit, took us and a red-faced cabinetry sales representative from Indianapolis through the hard, tranquil rooms. Monsieur Delacroix had proved forward-thinking by pocketing his tape measure at the last moment. The architect's paean to right angles pleased him. Or rather, the artifice did.

"There are no consistent, unswerving lines in nature, darling," he said as he measured corners and crossbeams, recording geometrical conclusions in his scribbler. "Gravity bends light and twists sound. Wind wavers spider silk. We think we're all standing on solid ground, but we're not. The horizon curves. We can't see it, but even seemingly flat terrain is slightly bent."

"Um, that's one way of looking at it, I guess," said our tour guide, turning to me. "Does your friend always talk like this? He's got quite the way with words."

"Sometimes his way with words is better when he keeps them to himself," I replied. I abruptly changed the conversation by pitching a few questions about Mr. Wright's private life.

The married Mr. Wright had had an affair with another woman, with whom he eventually fled. He left his home and the other homes he'd designed, impeccable boxes you don't want to sit in for too long. They are low and flat, wide and square. The placement of tables and chairs validates the lines. You can go from one room to another because the lines lead you on, but there are no curves to allow you to stray.

"What's this table made of?" asked the cabinetry man.

"Walnut," replied our guide.

"That's not walnut, that's oak," the cabinetry man said accusingly. "What's this chair made of?"

"Teak."

"No, it's not. It's rowan."

Monsieur Delacroix rolled his eyes and put his arm around my shoulder.

"He left all this to fuck in Europe," I said.

"No circles, that's why," sighed Monsieur Delacroix, putting away his tape measure. "We should all leave to fuck in Europe."

"But what about that museum he designed in New York?" I asked. "It's round."

"No one lives in a museum, dear. That's where we bury people."

Monsieur Delacroix dropped me off downtown where I'd arranged to meet my new friend. He declined my invitation to join us. He was impatient with my affairs of the heart. He told me I was wasting my time. Whose time was I supposed to waste?

HE WAS BROODING in front of the public Picasso, a scarf wrapped tightly round his neck to fend off the wind. There again was that perky bum. I was happy to see him. I walked right up to him, and against a swell of saxophone music, with a slight undercurrent of strings, I took him in my arms and pried open his mouth with my lips.

"No," he said. "Don't."

"Yes," I said. "I must."

And did.

"But why?"

"Because I know. And I'm not afraid."

We spent the fading late afternoon walking through streets of the oldest skyscrapers in the city, the Louis Sullivans and others dating to the turn of the twentieth century. Things got high when they started to build with a skeleton of steel girders and beams. Before, they laid a solid foundation and built as high as they could go with layers of gradually tapering bricks. Now, things were suspended in the air. Glass and concrete hung from the sky. Chicago was a cluster of dangling testimonials. Lest anyone should forget where the money came from.

"I want to go to the top of the Sears Tower," I said.

The only way you can get rid of your fear of heights, they say, is to go somewhere high. I had nothing to lose. I was already falling.

"Okay." He put his arm around me. We didn't care if people stared.

First, we had to sit in a little theatre through a film of Oprah Winfrey telling us how great Chicago was. It included a brief history, the old melting pot chestnut of races and religions living happily together. It eulogized Frank Lloyd Wright, extolling the virtues of the city's architecture. No gangsters. Some children with their parents sat beside us so I put my hand on his lap and felt up his leg. The kids stared. The parents frowned. How would they answer the questions that were bound to come? I had effectively upstaged Oprah Winfrey. This wasn't in the history lesson.

When the elevator arrived to take us up, the parents held back their children to wait for the next one. We were alone. He held my hand all the way up. I was holding on for life. His knuckles were white when we got to the top. He told me I looked cute in the face of death and smiled. There was much more to what he said than he knew. He meant my fear of elevators. He could have been talking about his own death. He could have been talking about mine. I was worried about the both of us.

"They have backup cables," he said. "It's all in your head."

Twilight kissed the horizon with crimson lips, rubbing up against the black, velvet night. We stood on the observation deck of America's second-tallest building and watched the city turn itself on. We were like two street urchins looking at a sea of candlelit cakes in a bakery window at closing time. I put my arm around him. I wanted to write a saxophone sonata for him. I wanted to rob a bank, get caught, and tell the world on TV: I did it for him. I didn't want to get back on that damn elevator alone.

"How come no one here talks about the gangsters?" I asked.

He slipped a hand into my back pocket. I liked that.

"The place where the Saint Valentine's Day Massacre happened, it's an old folks home now," he told me.

"But aren't there any museums?" I asked. "You know, to keep a history of the gangland slayings, speakeasies, prohibition, mob rule. That stuff."

"Not that I know of." He leaned into the window and pressed his nose and lips against it. He left the imprint of a squashed kiss.

"People here aren't proud of it. They want people to come here. They don't want people to be afraid. They want people to think it's not like that anymore."

He wiped away his kiss with the sleeve of his jacket. "Crime is a part of the past. That's where they want to keep it."

"But it's the most exciting thing that's ever happened here."

The poor kid turned to me with a dead serious look on his mug. "There's something wrong with me," he said.

"I know." I gave him a peck on the cheek.

He cleared his throat. "No. You don't," he said, angrily.

Making love is a little like arithmetic. You're the sum of his parts, he's the sum of yours. You're both trying to find equal signs. It's easy to add things up incorrectly. The night before, when I went home with him, it had been 100 per cent hand-in-glove. Almost. At Vortex, we flirted and tried to find out if our bodies would fit together like a pure equation. We tried things on to see where they fit. My hand there, his head here, that kind of thing. I like big feet — you've got big feet. Do you like to get rough? Me too. He wouldn't let me kiss him, though.

I drank more beers; he drank more Cokes. At first, I wondered if he was religious or alcoholic. I started to piece things together when we went to his place. Typical student digs, not much furniture: a Mac on a desk, a few ramshackle bookshelves, stereo and VCR. Framed architectural renderings were scattered on the walls.

A black-and-white poster of Louis Armstrong took up almost all of a door to the kitchen. No plants. There were humidifiers in every room, steaming with an antiseptic smell. Sure, it was late winter, it could get pretty dry with the heat cranked up. But every room? I noticed that the windows were sealed with tape.

"Music?" he asked.

"Sure."

He looked a little embarrassed. "I've just got jazz stuff."

"Fine by me." He put on a Chet Baker CD.

He didn't have any booze, so he offered me a coffee. He only had instant.

"I don't drink it," he said, and made himself herbal tea. When I asked for milk for my coffee, he told me he only had powdered creamer.

We twisted up together on the futon sofa, and I tried to neck with him, but he kept moving his mouth away. He seemed tense. Okay, I thought, a hang-up of some kind. So, I told him to take off his shirt, and gave him a massage until he relaxed. He had a slender physique, slightly muscular but natural. His skin was incredibly soft. There was something very sweet and vulnerable about him that reminded me of someone, but I couldn't remember who. There was that nostalgic feeling again. His flesh and warmth were intoxicating. His body, naked, took me out of time.

He got up to go to the bathroom. I snooped in the kitchen. Sure enough, not a single dairy product in his fridge. Nothing that could succumb to bacteria. Nothing that could turn and become toxic. An army of natural vitamins — no preservatives — commandeered the shelf above the sink. If I could've thrown something and broken glass right then and there, I would have. But he hadn't said anything to me, so I had to pretend I didn't know.

We fooled around on the sofa for a while, no kissing, then

headed for the bedroom. I stopped for a pee on the way. I flushed, then noticed a Rolodex on the toilet tank. It was a calendar, and each card included the date, the day of the week, and an inspirational saying, from Gandhi to Louise Hay. He was infected.

"You're very passionate," he said some time later, in bed.

He winced, still sensitive, as I removed his condom. I tried to prevent any of the fluid from spilling, and gingerly deposited it into a small plastic trash can, where it landed with a wet thud beside the one I had used earlier. I sealed the airtight lid and crawled back into bed.

"Thanks," I replied. He'd flopped over onto his belly, with his head nestled in the crook of an elbow. I brushed my hand back and forth along his back, thinking of his illness. Wondering if I should say anything.

"That's nice," he said, opening his eyes and looking at me. He had long lashes. I'm the one who should be sick, I thought. I'm of an age.

He turned over and put his head on my chest. I wrapped my arms around him. We both stared at the ceiling. A humidifier puffed mistily in the background. Outside, a car passed, its motor decaying into the distance.

"Who's that?" I asked, pointing at a framed picture on his night table of a handsome guy in an Air Force uniform, beside an inhaler for asthma. Was it his lover? Was he still alive?

"My brother," he said. "He got killed in the war. Shot down."

"I'm sorry," I said, stunned. "Were you close?"

"Yeah. Pretty close. It was just the two of us. Stupid fucking war." He pressed himself more tightly against me, putting his arms across his chest and taking my hands so that we were joined together like a Möbius strip.

"You've got beautiful eyes."

"I'm sorry," I repeated softly in his ear.

He craned his head and gave me a confused smile. "But you do, really, have beautiful eyes."

"Oh. Thanks."

I had been imagining his brother flying over that distant desert, his plane plummeting in a spiral of flame, a corkscrew of fire twisting into barren dunes. "Was he by himself?"

"No. They don't fly alone anymore, not with the planes they've got now. There were half a dozen guys." He played distractedly with my fingers. "It's no big deal. They're all heroes."

He pulled the photograph down from the night table and stared at it. "He's a hero." He looked at me. "At least that's what the official letter said."

"How old was he?"

"Twenty-two." He smiled. "All he ever wanted to do since we were kids was fly."

"I'm afraid of heights," I said.

"So was he."

BIG HELEN TOOK a load off and sat down at my table for a quick break. She had a soda water in her hand. She watched TV with me. *Love Connection.*

"What do you make of the war?" I asked her, flipping to a rerun of a 1970s sitcom.

"Baby, I got my own wars." She slipped off a shoe and rubbed her foot. "Three of 'em, sitting at home. And they're hungry. Excuse me while I go sing for their supper."

One of the roadies was at the bar staring at her impatiently.

"I'm coming, baby. Don't get your pants in a bunch."

Monsieur Delacroix sashayed into the Sea of Happiness,

looking odd and drawing attention. He headed for my table in a straight line.

"Hey, Frenchie!" yelled Trailer Park.

Monsieur Delacroix tossed him a Queen Elizabeth wave and parked his butt beside me. He didn't look too good. His eyes were pink and puffy; his complexion was pale.

"Rough night last night?" I asked mercilessly.

"The worst, my dear, the worst," he declaimed. "We've been here long enough. I think it's time we went back."

"I'm not going," I said, and flipped to MTV. "Holiday." An early Madonna song. I'd left a Depression behind me in Toronto. I wasn't going back.

"But it's only meant to be a holiday," implored Monsieur Delacroix. Then he noticed the look in my eyes. "Oh, my dear, you haven't?"

"I have."

Big Helen came to the table with Monsieur's cocktail and a package of pork rinds, his favourite snack. He ripped it open and munched. He offered me some. I declined. I've never been one for pig fascia deep-fried in oil. I thought about the bones beneath the ground at Graceland.

"I suppose that means I must go alone," Monsieur Delacroix said softly, looking at the wall screen.

"Yes," I said.

Madonna was telling everyone it could be so nice.

"WHY DIDN'T YOU tell me?" I asked. "I was wrong. I'm sorry."

We were on the observation deck. He stared eastward to the lake, or where the lake would be if you could see it. Night obscured the horizon.

"No one believes me. They leave," he said. "It's like being a convict or something. Hey, this is America. Guilty until proven innocent, right?"

"I guess so," I said, feeling more ebullient than I had in years, despite my mistake. I was a little guilty about my selfishness.

"The *Geraldo* show called me up to be a guest, like I'm a freak show."

I kissed him on the mouth, this time with my lips closed. Now it was okay. I understood.

"Sometimes, even if they believe me, they leave," he said. "They get a taste of danger, then go. At least I can't give it to anybody. That's the only good thing about it."

I figured that it must be lonely. I thought about those who feed on loneliness, draw their energy from it, and depart. A trench coat in the shadows, a hat with the brim turned down, a wolfish smile. The cockteaser: shame.

"Is everyone where you come from like you?" he asked.

"No. No one knows who they are where I come from," I joked. "I suppose I don't really have a place of my own, yet."

We walked to the elevator door.

He had told me the truth. At some point when his components were being mixed together, his DNA got dizzy and put its foot down. Born with a suppressed immune system. Genetic. He was allergic to practically every natural thing in his environment; almost all microscopic organisms and agents that produce or sustain life could kill him. Sealed windows. No preservatives. No bacteria or pollens. Even protected, he was at risk. He'd spent his whole life looking over his shoulder. I wanted to be his bodyguard.

"A crime against nature," he called himself.

"You should be proud," I told him.

"What?"

"Nature's been overrated ever since we invented it. It's a big cliché." I mimed a fake yawn. "Boring."

The elevator door opened. He took my hand.

"You're a healthy sign that nature's falling apart at the seams," I continued. "Write a book about it. You'll make a mint. And go on *Geraldo*. Do all the talk shows. People want something new."

We stepped onto the elevator. The children and their parents, who again had been standing behind us in a nervous state, decided once again to wait for the next one.

"It won't be easy," he said. "Are you sure?"

"Yeah," I replied, "I'm sure." The door closed and I put my arms around him. I planned to eat him up alive, to swallow his eyes, his lips, his tight little ass, his blood, to consume every inch of his flesh so that it was buried deep inside me, undetectable and beautiful and alive and safe. He could go outside through me.

"Later, you might regret it," he said.

I looked at him. We were alone in the elevator, which had begun its descent. "Regret what?"

Why God Forgives Our Sins

"TREVOR NEEDS CONSTANT looking after. That's why his friend's here," says Flo. She's set up the board in the living room to watch the late-night news while she irons. "You be nice at supper tomorrow. Not a peep, understand. He's got enough on his plate without you."

"I wasn't going to say anything," Murray mumbles.

He uses the remote to turn the volume of the TV up one green dash and adjusts the brand new La-Z-Boy to half-recline.

"It's a surprise. I thought it'd cheer you up," he'd said, running up behind Flo as she stood at the front door in her baking apron, telling the delivery men they'd made a mistake.

It cheered her up all right. In the three weeks they've had it, she's only been able to sit on the La-Z-Boy when Murray's at work, when Flo hasn't got time to. She's the one who needs cheering up but he's the one with the bad back. At least he's passed the point of playing with the controls. For the first few days it was up and down, up and down, up and down. Murray is gadgety. Their toolshed is overpopulated with 1-800 junk. Flo could live without all the miracle products that make life better. Frozen orange juice took two minutes. They got that juice machine, and it took five. When Murray ordered the book of home remedies,

Flo wondered what was wrong with doctors and aspirin. She was vindicated when Murray got a horrible earache. He wanted to call the doctor, but Flo handed him the book of home remedies. It said to use a blow-dryer on a low, warm setting. They didn't have a blow-dryer, so they had to buy one. In the end it didn't work because Murray had an infection that required antibiotics. Flo's become more suspicious of products that force you to make do with what you have.

"I was born in the Depression," she'd told Denise in Tablewares. "I don't want to die in it."

Flo raises her voice to compete with the news. "I mean it," she says. "I don't want to hear anything out of your mouth that'd make them uncomfortable."

"I said I won't say anything. I'm fine about it."

"I know how you feel. Keep it to yourself."

"Dammit Flo, I said I won't say anything."

Flo leans over. She frowns at his use of language but doesn't bring it up. There are worse words. She knows it's her. Flo knows she shouldn't push him like she does. She just can't help herself these days. Sometimes she hears her own voice and wonders, who's that?

"Sometimes you get hotheaded," she says, her voice muffled, lost in the laundry hamper. She stands up and puts the laundry on the ironing board. "Sometimes you find it hard to keep your opinions to yourself. They're coming for turkey, not lip."

Murray gives up trying to watch the TV and turns the volume back down. The line of green dashes shrinks from view.

"Have I got to spell it out?" he says. "O.K." He spells out the letters in the air.

"They're out here from Toronto because the doctors don't give him long," Flo mentions.

"Doctors can be wrong."

"Listen to Mr. Home Remedies." She presses down the iron. A cloud of steam billows up. "Em says he's got skin cancer, but inside him, on his linings. It's a rare kind normal people don't get."

She stops pressing, puts down the iron, and starts to fold.

"They say it's something to do with a deficiency of cells. Your body can't fight day-to-day things we don't even think about."

Flo puts the serviette she's been folding on a pile with the rest and pulls up a section of tablecloth. "I'd like to see you with AIDS," she says. "That'd be a sight. You're a handful with a cold."

She mists a section of tablecloth with a quick spritz of unscented spray starch, pressing the iron down and across. The steam smells nice as it lifts the scent of fabric softener into the air, not of Mountain Fresh Pine Forest as the label claims, but just like every other liquid fabric softener Flo has used, like cotton candy. Fabric softening then starching might seem like one step forward, two steps back, but Flo likes the sweet-smelling table you get from a little extra effort. Murray gets after her for making things twice as difficult for herself and tries to get her to use scented starch. She tells him life wouldn't be twice as difficult if he'd lay off those gadgets. Besides, Flo finds the scented starch too cloying. She prefers the subtler smell of fabric softener leftover once most has been steamed out.

Flo got into the habit of ironing late at night last January soon after she retired from the Famous Food Floor in the department store up at the Heights. Her retirement was early due to their closing down the chain. Ironing is a thoughtless activity to take her mind off not sleeping. Murray stares at her and keeps silent. The sports report sails by.

"Em says he's dropping weight like there's no tomorrow," says Flo. "It'll be his last visit, that much is for sure. And Doreen's out from Toronto too. Em says she's been like an angel to her brother through all this. Poor Em. I don't know how she copes with it all. They may be liberal minded, they may be educated, but you can't bury where you come from in books. Who you are is who you are. Thirty-three years old. Honestly, I don't know any more."

"Jesus Flo," says Murray. "You made me miss the scores. Happy now?"

The news has moved from hockey to a women's rowing event in China. Murray takes a swallow of beer. The bottle's empty. He puts it back on the TV table and pushes the table aside. He flips until he gets the FOX station from Seattle. Three women with big hairdos and tight clothes vie for dates with two muscular young men who have perfect teeth, long hair, and no necks. The men answer skill-testing questions about their love lives. Their lips move but nothing comes out. Murray keeps flipping. Flo gives him a disapproving look from the ironing board, his language again. She yanks at another large section of tablecloth, spreads it out over the board, and presses. Flo has a sense of rhythm and weight with an iron. She rarely goes over the same spot twice.

"His friend's name is Ian," Flo says through a cloud of steam. "Em says he's artistic, so mind."

Flo irons everything, always has, even underwear. It threw Murray for a loop when they were married. But he was happy about it when the bus company moved him into middle management after twenty-eight years in the garage. He showed up every day with the whitest, crispest looking shirts at branch office. Flo was glad to be rid of the coveralls headache. Nothing ate grease like it said it did. The switch from coveralls to office clothes didn't come soon enough for her money. People commented. Flo didn't like to take credit. She pointed out the good cut you could count on with an Arrow shirt. Collars like that don't happen overnight, she'd say. All the same, she was pleased by the congratulations. Not a wrinkle gets by Flo.

"He's from Newfoundland," she adds.

"An artsy-fartsy Newfie who's light in his loafers," says Murray. "There's gotta be some kind of grant for that."

"Oh you."

"Now it's out of my system. You're safe."

"Em says he's a hockey fan."

"That's no surprise," says Murray. "Half the coaches are up-the-bum."

"I give up."

"Jeez, Flo, lighten up. Can't you take a joke? Fags have got a sense of humour like anyone else."

"I suppose you've been down at the local gay bar soaking up culture. And don't say that word."

"Now I give up."

"Fine." Flo starts to work on the tablecloth edges. It's an old one from storage. Parts of it are worn so thin she can see through it when she holds it up to the light. She'd normally never dream of using it for company. But with a pad underneath, and her table setting, it'll do fine. It's worn out from being her favourite for years. When Trevor and Doreen were kids, they often stayed with Flo and Murray so Em and Jack could get away. Trevor liked to help set the table, especially the tablecloth. It's got an embossed pattern of leaves and branches winding in and out. Flo would walk into the dining room and find Trevor with his knees up on a chair, tracing the outline of the leaves and branches with a finger as though he were following a path. It was a maze, but he never backtracked, he kept moving forward. Flo would put down whatever she had in hand and do the same thing on the other side of the table. It was a race.

"I'll get there first," Trevor would say excitedly, meaning the far end of the table. He always did. Flo let him.

"The way you talk you'd think I never saw a queer before," Murray says. "They're all over the TV for Christ's sake."

"That's what I'm talking about. That kind of language," says Flo.

She drapes the finished tablecloth over the back of Mum's wingback. She unplugs the iron, puts it down on the floor, sets the ironing board upright, and starts to close the legs. "Queer. That's a fine how-do-you-do, your own nephew dying of AIDS." She snaps the board shut.

"That's what they call themselves," says Murray. "They call themselves queer."

Murray readjusts the La-Z-Boy. He needs to for his back. Every half hour. The doctor told him. The chair doesn't just go up and down and turn. He can change the pressure at the small of the back to follow the curve of his spine. A change in posture makes all the difference in the world.

Flo looks at him like he's gone nuts. "Not all of them. Not the ones like Trevor. Just the active ones call themselves queer," she says. "We saw it on *Sixty Minutes*, remember?"

"You don't know what you're talking about. You mean activist," says Murray. "Not active."

Despite following doctor's orders, his back begins to act up. It does that whenever he gets into an argument with Flo. She has a way of painting herself into a corner and him with her.

"I do too know what I'm talking about. And I know what I mean," Flo insists, picking up the iron and ironing board. "I mean to make sure you don't spoil a perfectly good Easter supper with anti-homosexual words like queer. Just keep an eye on that mouth of yours."

"All right," Murray grumbles, "I'll try to watch what I say. Now can I watch my program in peace?"

"Do what you like," says Flo, going to put the ironing board away. "Lord knows I'm wasting my breath," Murray hears her say, her voice faint as she disappears through the doorway to the linen cupboard.

Murray turns up the volume on the TV, so he won't miss the sports recap. Flo's back in the room just as it's about to begin. She takes the tablecloth off Mum's wingback and folds it over her arms. She thoughtfully sinks into her left hip, the one she's favoured since they put a metal plate in her right hip to compensate for bone erosion. Flo stares at Murray. He pretends not to notice, hoping she'll give up and go away. It's useless. Flo settles into her long-term stare, the one that won't let up until he lets her have her say.

"What?" says Murray.

"You know, they might vote different," remarks Flo. "Don't get on your Reform Party bandwagon. You know what they say about company. Don't talk about sex, politics, or religion. Years ago, Em and Dad used to go at it tooth and nail when she was at the university and visiting home for the holidays. It ruined it for Mum and me. You and Em aren't any better when you get a couple of drinks in you, fighting about how to solve the world's problems. So put a zipper on it. Sex, politics, and religion don't have a thing to do with Easter."

"Okay," Murray agrees.

"Promise?"

Murray has missed the entire sports recap. He turns off the set and gets up from the La-Z-Boy.

"Promise," he answers wearily.

He follows Flo into the hall as she goes to the dining room to set the cloth, to save time in the morning. He heads into the bathroom. He doesn't bother to close the door while he pees. Flo sticks her head out of the dining room.

"Em says they've got earrings," she yells.

"All the earrings in the world and they won't ever be as pretty as you," he yells back.

"Snake charmer," Flo says under her breath and goes back to laying out the tablecloth, pleased.

Flo, as usual, doesn't go to bed with Murray. After spreading the tablecloth and folding the serviettes origami-like into swans the way Denise did during one of the Famous Food Floor's Friday lunch-hour home hospitality demos, Flo takes her sleeping pill. The doctor tried to make her take pills for depression, but Flo wouldn't have any of it. In the end she agreed to the sleeping pills.

Not working makes her sleepless. Flo couldn't get a job after the Famous Food Floor. She tried, even at the new Walmart across from the Heights. No one said so but they really didn't want to hire a woman over sixty to do cash.

Flo doesn't really need a job. They're set. As well as her antiques, Mum left them some money when she died. There's Flo's severance, Murray's earnings until he retires in a couple of years, plus their pensions. She eventually passes out in the La-Z-Boy with the TV on.

She wakes up to an infomercial for a ball of wax that can remove unwanted body hair. The room is milky with dawn. She opens the curtains and blinds and turns off the TV. Flo gets dressed in an old pair of Murray's pajamas, a dressing gown, and slippers, then goes into the kitchen where she puts out milk and cat food for Whiskers. The old tabby slinks out of his lair beneath the dining room sideboard and pads into the kitchen. He slurps his meal, arching his back like a drawbridge. Once everything is gobbled up, he slips back beneath the sideboard.

Flo checks on the Butterball she put out last night. She generally prefers a ham at Easter, but she has a freezer full of turkeys she's looking for ways to get rid of. The wives at Our Lady had a raffle for Save the Children, and Flo, who bought two books of tickets because she couldn't sell them all, won the second prize of ten Butterballs. She has half a mind to give the rest away to the food bank people.

"I've got enough to think about without too many turkeys getting in the way," she'd told Murray.

The bird is nicely thawed. She fills it with bread and raisin stuffing, massages sage and garlic into the skin, and sticks in bacon strips with toothpicks. She places the turkey into a well-greased roasting pan and slides it into the oven. Flo is one for slow cooking, breast up. The Butterball taken care of, she puts a sweater on over her bathrobe and steps through the sliding doors onto the back porch. It's going to be a fine day. Not a cloud in the sky. Dew sparkles on the grass. Their place has a view of the bridge into New Westminster and the Sky Train monorail crossing the Fraser River. The mountaintops a few miles north are amber, the soft morning sunshine reflecting in what little snow is left.

Their large yard slopes down a gentle hill to a chain-link fence. Beyond it, a new subdivision of pink and beige monster homes dwarfs the strip of postwar bungalows like Flo and Murray's. The massive houses are built to the very edge of their properties, with three-car garages and giant staircases rising to second-floor double front doors of elegant wood.

All the large trees have been chopped down. A couple of the gardens are planted with a hardy kind of palm tree. Flo misses the Douglas firs and cedars that used to tower over the landscape wherever she looked. The palm trees are exotic but don't belong. They remind her of the time she and Murray RVed down south. With the exception of some bamboo, Flo's made a hobby of nurturing local flora, and her green thumb has left its print throughout their yard. She looks over her garden bursting with spring and feels proud. Flowers bloom everywhere and most of the shrubs and trees are more than halfway to full leaf. She must remember to give Em some clippings. And advice. Clippings without advice would quickly become compost in Em's incapable hands. Flo got the green thumb in the family. Em got the kids. Murray and Flo tried their best for several years. Sluggish ovulation was the verdict.

There's no shortage of family next door. Mr. Hsiang's father is in the middle of the yard pretending to be a stork or heron or crane, or some other kind of long-legged bird. He stands on one leg with the other extended behind, arching his arms like graceful wings. Mr. and Mrs. Hsiang have six children. The three remaining grandparents live with them. Denise calls it "Hongcouver." Flo's heard other people at church call it that too, and they don't have a friendly tone.

The old man sees Flo and stands up properly. He smiles and nods his head, spreading an arm over the landscape to indicate the grandeur of the morning.

"Lovely day," says Flo.

"Yes, very lovely," says the old man. "Tai chi," he explains, smiling as he folds himself back into the shape of a bird. There is something comforting about the old man's movements.

Flo makes a mental note to ask Em what clippings she'd like and goes inside.

Her hip feeling up to the three-block walk to Our Lady, Flo decides on eight thirty Mass. Murray likes to sleep in, so she's quiet as she pulls underclothes out of drawers and one of her church suit dresses from the closet. She remembers earrings from her jewellery box, and the Chanel No. 5 Trevor and his friend sent her last Christmas. She washes up, then changes in the living room where her things are spread out.

Flo looks up from buttoning her blouse at the framed portrait of Jesus exposing his sacred heart above the La-Z-Boy. She crosses herself. Jesus smiles, winks at her, and gives her thumbs-up. In the time it takes to blink, he's regained his composure of distant compassion. Flo puts it down to the sleeping pill. The pills often leave her feeling not quite right. She slips on her jacket and shoes. On Tuesday she'll call the doctor and have him prescribe something different.

Flo walks to church as briskly as her hip will allow.

Denise is two pews up. Her hyperactive six-year-old wriggles in his suit. Denise swats the side of his head.

"Ow!"

"Jason, haven't I told before why God forgives our sins?"

"I don't care."

"Because Jesus didn't squirm."

"Jesus is a toilet face."

"Shhh!"

"Toilet face, toilet face, toilet face, toilet face — Ow! Let go!"

"You behave. Now take this and put it in the basket when it comes by. Not in your pocket like last time."

"Toilet face."

Flo knows what a lucky boy he is. Two years ago, a lump in his back was diagnosed as cancer. Denise was scared because her husband had passed away with stomach cancer. (There was talk of toxic waste in the ground where he grew up in Ontario.) Fortunately, the boy's lump was benign and operable. Her son had begged and begged Denise to keep the lump and she finally relented. After the operation, they put it in a jar of formaldehyde for him to take home. He made his mother print a label on masking tape. MY CANCER, the jar said. He brought it to his kindergarten Show & Tell and it was such a success that he received invitations to birthday parties for the rest of the year.

Flo catches Denise's eye and waves. Denise waves back. She's back at community college studying computers. A much younger woman than Flo could do that. Flo envies her. The mass begins. Flo makes a point to tell Denise about the serviette swans.

After, outside in the warm sunshine on the steps of Our Lady of Immaculate Conception, Flo thanks the priest and goes to the bottom of the stairs to wait for Denise and her boy.

"Hi there, Flo. Happy Easter."

"Happy Easter, Denise." Flo bends down to tousle the boy's hair. "And what did the Easter Bunny leave you?"

The boy pulls his head away. "There's no such thing as the Easter Bunny." He races off into the parking lot, spinning and kicking and humming the *Power Rangers* theme song.

"They grow up fast these days, don't they," Flo comments. She watches him playfight invisible monsters.

Denise lights up a cigarette. "Yeah, they sure pick things up quick," she says. "He'd only be disappointed sooner or later, so I set him straight about stuff like the Easter Bunny."

Flo smiles and reaches out to touch the woman's arm.

"I just wanted to tell you that I folded my lumps into swans for supper tonight like you demonstrated that time," says Flo.

Denise isn't listening. She's staring off at her son. She throws her cigarette on the pavement and grinds it in with her shoe.

"Jason," she shouts, "you stop that!"

The boy stands in the parking lot exit, pounding his fists on the hood of a car trying to get through.

"I'm telling you! I'm going to swat you into the middle of next week," Denise yells as she runs after him. "Bye Flo!" she tosses back.

"Goodbye," says Flo, concerned.

She watches the small boy in front of the car, his eyes closed and hands clenched as he collects all his superpowers together to cover himself in the protection of a mechanical dinosaur and crush his enemy to death.

On her way home, Flo realizes that she told Denise lumps instead of serviettes. She doesn't have time to ponder why. Not with what she sees when she turns onto their street. Although it's only ten and they aren't supposed to arrive until noon, Jack and Em's minivan is parked in front of the garage. Jack and Em are on the porch with Doreen. Murray stands with the screen door halfway open, blurry eyed in his bathrobe. Running on the lawn toward Flo is an old man she's never seen before. He's frail and thin, dressed in loose-fitting clothes and bedroom slippers. His wispy, longish hair strays from his head. He carries a bunch of tulips in his hand. Flo figures out they must have been torn from her garden. They trail soil. A good-looking young man wearing a black leather jacket chases after him. The old man approaches Flo, raising the tulips above his head.

"A diadem of flowers to anoint the Queen of Heaven!" he cries rapturously. He places the tulips at Flo's feet. Flo stands there, not quite sure what to do as the old man sinks down on his knees and clasps her legs.

"You must be Florence," says the young man in the leather jacket as he catches up to them, holding out his hand to Flo. He's a little out of breath.

"Ian," he says, smiling.

Flo takes his hand and shakes it. He's got a pansy voice, but his grip is firm. A fairy nice fella, Murray would say, like he did that time about the waiter at the Old Spaghetti Factory.

"He wanted to come early," Ian explains. "He gets impatient. Sometimes you've got to humour him."

Flo looks at him, then down at the old man at her feet.

"Trevor?" she asks.

"We are saved!" her nephew shouts with elation. He starts to cry. "At last, we are all of us saved!"

THE KITCHEN IS filled with the harmonious twang of cheated lives. The radio on top of the fridge is tuned to Flo's country station.

Flo bends over the oven to baste her Butterball, tapping a foot to *Achy Breaky Heart*.

"He's still normal most of the time but he has moments," Emily says to Flo's backside. She takes a sip of Chardonnay.

Flo stands up, closes the oven door, and puts the turkey baster on a folded tea towel on the counter. She presses her hands into the small of her back, kneading the muscles with her thumbs.

"I'm going to have a moment if this bird doesn't step to it and brown," she says.

Different people throw themselves with abandon into different things: drinking, the track, sometimes love. But Flo's Achilles heel is a possible breakdown in the timing and composure of a well-laid spread. When Murray chides her, Flo snaps that good food never put anyone in the drunk tank or the poorhouse. She's mute on the consequences of overindulged love.

A twin set of porcelain roosters bookend *Fanny Farmer*, *Joy of Cooking*, and the entire Company's Coming series on a special section of counter space. There are also several photo albums containing years of clippings from *Canadian Living, The Vancouver Sun*, and the local community newspaper. Her crab and Tabasco/mayonnaise puffs, cheese curls, Nanaimo bars, lemon squares, and all-time favourite The Devil Made Me Do It Double Fudge Brownies are among the many prized baked goods she serves up at church functions, prompting more than one person to approach her with catering offers. Flo always declined, thinking it unchristian to take money for something that gave her enjoyment.

"Women like that Martha Stewart ought to be ashamed," she'd said to Murray. They'd been watching the "It's a good thing" woman on TV one recent winter evening. "I read in *Cosmo* that women are having Martha Stewart breakdowns trying to keep up. Imagine."

"I think she's a super babe," Murray had remarked.

"Oh, talk your age. She eats men like you for breakfast, in a hollandaise sauce she won't shut up about for half an hour."

Flo takes off an oven mitt and picks up her wineglass.

"Ian and Doreen have adjusted to it," Emily continues. "Jack and I are learning to. Books and counselling don't really prepare you. But being around Mum in her last years has."

Flo swallows an urge to mention prayer and washes it down with wine. She gives her younger, thinner, smarter sister a thoughtful glance.

"It's just like Mum in a way," says Flo. "Though she called you and me a lot worse than the Queen of Heaven. Once she lost the last of her marbles no amount of soap could clean out that mouth. I swear it got hard to believe Mum housekept a rectory all those years after Dad died."

Emily smiles and drains her wineglass. "Dad was the reason Mom went off like that, Flo, we both know that and there's no pretending we don't. All his carrying on. She just let go of all the stuff she'd bottled up about Dad all those years and took it out on whoever came close: you, me, the nurses, whoever. It doesn't take illness to drive a person mad. So long as you've got families, you've got madness. They fuck you up."

"Em!" Flo tries to conceal a half smile as she blushes.

"That's from a poem I teach my first-year students. Come on, Flo, if anyone knows about family fucking you up it's you."

"I think you'd better check the speedometer on that wineglass," Flo says sharply.

"Sorry."

"The past is the past. It was the Irish in Dad. They can't settle."

"That's what religion does to people."

"That's it, Em, get on your high horse. Take advantage of the Irish to find fault with religion."

There's a moment of silence for Ireland as Emily goes to the fridge, takes out more wine, unscrews the cap, and pours them both a full glass.

"Truce," she says, passing Flo's glass.

"Truce."

They clink and sip.

The potatoes and yams begin to boil over. Both women put down their glasses. Flo hightails it past Emily to the stove and turns the elements down. Then she goes to the fridge, removes the thawed peas she'd brought in from the freezer in the garage, handpicked from her own garden last season. She gives the turkey another quick baste. Emily has found her way to the sink where she starts draining iceberg lettuce, which she rips into boat-sized pieces. Flo bites her lip watching her sister deposit the hopelessly large lettuce into a salad spinner.

"Use Mum's crystal bowl. It's on the sideboard," she says.

Emily retrieves the heavy cut glass bowl. She almost drops it. It lands with a thud on the countertop. She fills the bowl with spun lettuce, then rummages in the fridge's crisper, producing tomatoes and green onions.

"Where are the carrots?"

"I used up the last in my Jell-O mold," answers Flo.

Emily sees it wiggling on a tray on the shelf in the fridge — red, translucent, and fish shaped, with raisins, shaved carrots, and miniature marshmallows.

"Score!" shouts one of the men downstairs. Jack, Murray, and Ian are in the basement watching the rec room black and white.

"Religion is helpless, Em. Even at Easter it can't stop the playoffs," says Flo, sighing at the stove as her peas rattle in a Silex pot.

Ian appears at the top of the basement steps. "It smells fabulous up here."

"I hope you're hungry," says Flo.

"Famished beyond belief. I need to get us men some more barley pops."

Flo furrows her brow.

"Um, beer."

Flo points at the fridge. "Help yourself."

"Thanks, Florence."

"Uh-huh."

"Who's winning?" asks Emily.

"Can you believe it, Toronto. For a change. Isn't that fabulous?" He pulls three beers out of the fridge and dashes back down the stairs.

"He's not very shy, is he?" says Flo after Ian's left the room.

Emily laughs. "No. But he's fabulous."

"ACCORDING TO THE ghost of Liberace, who appeared before an eighteen-year-old waitress in an all-night donut store in South Dakota, Rock Hudson has turned straight in the afterlife." Trevor shows Doreen Flo's *National Enquirer*. There's a picture of Rock Hudson looking emaciated, the same image that was all over the media when he died of AIDS, as well as one of the flamboyant piano player in an outrageous stage costume featuring rhinestones, ostrich feathers, and fur trim.

"Can you imagine?" says Trevor. "If there was ever proof of extraterrestrials amongst us, this is it."

Doreen sits in front of the La-Z-Boy massaging Trevor's feet. She inspects the picture. "Someone I know used to wear platform shoes with seven-inch heels, red satin pants, and a skin-tight T-shirt that said Surrender Dorothy in sequins."

"That's different."

"Exactly what everyone else I knew said."

"Hah-hah."

Outside the living room window, nature resurrects itself, waking up and stretching with greenery. The slanted light of early evening provokes a scandal of leaves. A slight breeze stirs. The leaves flap in and out, a coy toss-up of new life. In and out. It seems to Trevor that his life has become little more than a series of ins and outs. In and out of the hospital. In and out of bed. In and out of doorways he's too feeble to open by himself. Needles and tubes shoved in and pulled out of his body.

"Get this. It's a quote from the waitress," says Trevor. "'I'm putting out some fresh dutchies when I look up and there's Liberace staring at me. He tells me about Rock. Then he disappears, just like on *Star Trek*.' Ow!"

"Sorry. Too hard?"

"Just a bit. I'd turn straight too, given a choice between that and a dead Liberace."

Trevor folds the paper and puts it on the floor.

"Your uncle and I saw Liberace crossing the street in Palm Springs that winter we went to Southern California," says Flo from the doorway. She steps into the room and rests a haunch on an arm of Mum's wingback. "Diamonds on every finger. Flashy clothes. In broad daylight too. He did it long before your Elton Johns."

Trevor and Doreen give each other a look.

"Sorry about earlier, Aunt Florence," says Trevor.

"I don't know. Queen of Heaven sounds pretty good to me," says Flo. "It'll give me some poker chips when I get there. If I get there."

Trevor doesn't say anything. He only believes in God or heaven when he's having one of his dementia episodes or when the morphine peaks.

"Holy Jehoshaphat, it's hot in here," says Flo. She stands up and goes to turn down the wall thermostat.

"I turned it up for Trevor," Doreen mentions quietly.

"Oh." Flo stops awkwardly mid-stride, unsure of where to put her hands, unsure of what to say next. "Well. I just came in here to tell you kids dinner'll be ready in ten. I guess I should have asked you, Trevor, if there's anything you can't eat."

"Just food."

Flo returns to the kitchen and Trevor adjusts the La-Z-Boy to organize his pills. Doreen passes him his cup of juice from the TV table. One by one, he pops a pill into his mouth and swallows a sip of juice until all eight pills are gone. Then he sits back and closes his eyes, relaxing into Doreen's massage. Between the worlds of pain and peace is the purgatory of being alone. Sometimes Trevor finds himself standing at the brink of an inevitable horror like *The Incredible Shrinking Man*, who faces an expanding cosmos until he becomes so small, he is beyond the range of the most powerful microscope.

TREVOR SITS AT the head of the table where he can see through the door into the kitchen. Doreen sits beside him. He absent-mindedly circles the outline of a leaf on the tablecloth pattern with his finger, round and round and round. Flo, humming a country song, bustles back and forth ferrying plates, bowls, and sauce boats, some to the sideboard, some to the table. Smiling absently, Emily drifts in with a pair of salad forks, bumps into Flo, and deposits them by the salad bowl. When they're both out of the dining room, Doreen turns to Trevor.

"What's with them?"

Trevor nods his head in the direction of the kitchen and Doreen leans over so she can see. Two empty wine bottles sit on the counter.

"They're half cut," Trevor says.

Flo re-enters with a condiment tray, moving her shoulders in time with the kitchen radio. She puts it down and leaves. Trevor watches her go to the top of the basement steps.

"Turn off that hockey. Supper's on!" she shouts.

Murray, Ian, and Jack shuffle upstairs. They bring their hangdog expressions into the dining room and sit down where Flo tells them to: Murray opposite Trevor, Ian between Trevor and Doreen, and Jack beside Emily's empty chair. Flo and Emily bring in a few more things and sit down. Flo, mindful of her hip, takes a seat close to the kitchen door, where it will be easier for her to be up and down.

"What am I thinking?" Flo exclaims. "I've left the Jell-O mold sitting on the counter, along with my head."

Flo returns with the wobbly fish and sets it down in front of Trevor.

"Aunt Florence, you haven't lost your touch," he says, avoiding eye contact with Doreen. "It's, well, lovely."

As usual, Flo has made too much food. Vegetables vie for space alongside the turkey and dishes containing an assortment of Flo's homemade bread, pickles, and preserves. An enormous butter pat skis down a mountainside of whipped potatoes. Green peas. Orange yams. Ochre mushrooms. Scarlet tomato chutney. Ruby-red cranberry sauce. Thousand Island dressing basks pinkly in a crystal bowl.

Doreen pours everyone wine.

"Who's going to carve?" Flo asks with a self-satisfied glow from the spread she's delivered, and a touch of vine leaf. "Since grace is out of the question," she adds with a stern look round at the heathens.

Murray and Jack argue about who'll perform the honours.

"We'll flip," says Emily, holding up a penny. "Heads or tails?"

She's always been a settler of things, ready to dispense justice from her change purse. When Trevor and Doreen were kids, disputes were settled this way. Who would rake the leaves? Who would take out the garbage? Emily was a shrewd diplomat. She let the loser keep the coin. Trevor's father chooses tails and loses.

"I don't want it," he says grumpily when Emily offers him the shiny, new penny.

"Oh Jack, really," Emily says. She exchanges an aren't-men-something look with Flo. "Take the damn penny."

The buzz of an electric knife cuts through the room as Murray slices the turkey's plump breast. Trevor watches him carve. He has always found his uncle sexy: the short brush cut that shows his scalp, the tattoo on his sinewy forearm, the way he lights his Export As with a lighter that looks like a beer bottle.

"White meat or dark?" Murray asks Trevor first.

"White meat, please."

Everyone turns to him and smiles.

"White meat for Trevor," announces Murray.

"He always did like white meat," murmurs Flo.

"He's never been fussy about dark meat," Emily chimes in.

Doreen catches Trevor's eye.

"I'll have a drumstick," Doreen says.

"Doreen always did like drumsticks," says Trevor.

Doreen dollops potatoes onto Trevor's plate. He shakes his head at peas and points at the mushrooms. The clatter of people passing plates and bowls seems to be taking place outside somewhere. Satellites of chewing noises and small talk circulate the table like the hum of tiny flies. Trevor sits in silence, staring at his plate, not touching a thing.

"You all right, son?" asks Jack.

"Trevor, honey?" Ian is looking at him.

"Yeah. I'm fine," says Trevor. "Fine."

Emily looks at Jack. Murray looks at Flo. Doreen looks at Ian. Trevor looks at Whiskers. The cat is at his feet, on the prowl for turkey.

"Can I?" he asks Flo.

"We don't usually feed him from the table," says Flo. "But what good's a rule without an exception."

Trevor gives Whiskers a piece of turkey from his plate, then another, then another. The cat leaps into his lap and curls up, purring.

Ian leans over and gives Trevor a peck on the cheek. "Love you."

Doreen looks at Trevor. Emily looks at Flo. Jack looks at Murray. Whiskers looks at the turkey.

"Ian was quite the hockey player in university, he tells me," Murray announces to Flo, to break the ice.

"When I was at Memorial," Ian remarks through a mouthful of potatoes.

"His wrists might be limp, but his ankles are firm," Trevor mentions.

"Trevor!" His mother chastises him with a glance.

"I was into figure skating when I was a kid," Ian says. "That couldn't be said about too many boys in Corner Brook at that time. The only guys who got away with being sissies were the priests."

Ian chuckles and takes a sip of wine. Murray showers Flo with an I-told-you-so stare. She glowers.

"My older sisters took figure skating, so I wanted to, too. My folks hoped it'd be, y'know, a phase or something. When it wasn't, they put me into hockey, thought it'd be an antidote. I spun circles around those guys. They didn't know what to make of me. And let me tell you, them changing rooms. Enough to make a good Catholic girl like me blush right through her knickers."

He winks at Trevor. "But Corner Brook was Corner Brook. It wasn't very fabulous. They say still waters run deep but let me tell you, backwaters run deeper. I left, went to school, kept on with the hockey, the skating."

"He was on the Olympic figure skating team," Doreen pipes in.

"My folks changed their tune when I came to Halifax with the Disney on Ice tour. The whole fam damily showed up from Corner Brook and regions farther afoot."

"Do you still skate?" asks Flo.

"I just teach now. The last skating gig I had was Legends of Hollywood on Ice at Canada's Wonderland. That's where I met Trevor, on a free day for PWAs. I guess it was, what, five years ago now. About that."

Everyone turns to look at Trevor as though a curtain has parted. Suddenly Trevor feels the spiny fish attacking. He throws Whiskers from his lap. The cat scrambles beneath the sideboard. The spiny fish lives in his stomach. Trevor had hoped it wouldn't show up tonight. He has to stop it from getting bigger. He breathes deeply and slowly. There is a brief jab of pain, then the spiny fish disappears into the shallows. Trevor excuses himself and goes to the bathroom.

It's nice to be locked in. The white tile floors and yellow walls are spotless. Each tile reflects a shadowy Trevor. TV-commercial-fluffy towels wrap themselves around chrome racks. There's something safe about bathrooms. It's the one room that doesn't judge you. He kneels before the toilet, a posture of habit. To his right is a wicker basket piled with copies of *Chatelaine, Good Housekeeping*, and *Canadian Living*. And an *Atlantic Monthly*. His mother must have left it behind. On top of the toilet tank sits a box of tissue covered with a poodle cozy knitted from synthetic yarn, with a pom-pom tail and googly eyes.

The spiny fish expands. It punctures him with reckless, hysterical fins. He bends over and throws up. He flushes. Trevor flips down the toilet seat and sits, placing his head between his legs to regain his equilibrium. The tile seems to echo his heartbeat. He slowly raises his head. He gets up with difficulty. Supporting his weight on the sink, he leans closely into the mirror. The Kaposi's sarcoma is beginning to take hold outside as well as inside him. A fine purple web of cancerous skin is starting to show on the bridge of his nose. The spiny fish reaches the shoal of Trevor's endurance again. He vomits in the sink.

There's a knock at the door. "Are you all right?"

"I'll be out in a second, Aunt Florence."

"That's okay, you just take your time," she says. "There's pie."

TREVOR LEANS AGAINST Flo, looking out through the Emergency Room window at the dark street. He rests his head on her shoulder. She strokes his hair. Suddenly the street lamps switch on. When he was little, he used to squint to make rays of light come to him. He thought that if he collected all the light he could, one day he'd turn into the most powerful person in the world. He starts to do that now, squinting to capture the light. And hold on to it. He takes his aunt's hand. Flo caresses his forehead the way Ian usually does. He closes his eyes.

After dinner, everyone had herded downstairs for coffee. The 1950s Wurlitzer jukebox Murray got at the bus company's annual charity auction was lit up. It revolved in a sequence of red, orange, blue, and green. The windowless room was like a rainbow. The jukebox was stacked with old 45s, which they played for a while until Murray persuaded Flo to sing for them.

She sat down at the 1-800 electric keyboard and started to sing "Goodnight Irene." Her voice was not unpleasant. She was about halfway through when Whiskers came padding down the stairs.

The cat headed straight for the centre of the room, made a terrible noise, arched its back, and then threw up all over the rec room carpet. Flo had to stop singing to clean up the mess. The cat continued being sick until there was nothing left to be sick with. Shivering, it huddled under the hutch where Flo kept her good crystal, fine china, and a miniature Versailles of porcelain figurines resplendent in Rococo regalia: women wearing beribboned hoop skirts and floral bodices, holding flirtatious fans; men in frock coats and breeches, turning a leg to show off stockinged calves; and oh, the wigs and hats! Whiskers rallied for another surge, this time with an anterior trajectory.

Not too long after, Doreen started to complain about cramps, followed soon after by Emily, Ian, and Jack. They excused themselves, Doreen to the upstairs bathroom, Emily to the one in the basement. Jack and Ian dashed out the back door. Flo, Murray, and Trevor could hear them being violently ill. About half an hour lapsed. Everyone was still sick. Flo said she thought they should all go to the hospital, which wasn't too far away. She wanted to drive but Trevor pointed out that she'd had too much to drink. Feeling a little better now, he was the only one sober and not sick. So, with Trevor at the helm of the minivan driving, Flo beside him praying, and the rest in the back clutching their guts, they headed to Surrey Memorial.

Trevor opens his eyes again and sits up. "When did you learn to play the piano, Aunt Florence?"

"The truth?"

"Why not the truth?"

"I've never told this to anyone. Not even your Uncle Murray. Only your mother knows."

"Only my mother knows what?"

She tells him. When Flo was sixteen, she was pregnant. Her mother sent her to a special place for girls in her condition, far away. Delivery complications left her barren, but the baby survived. It was a boy, but she never got to see it. It was given up for adoption.

"They had a piano there. At the house," says Flo. "The woman who ran it taught me how to play. Piano lessons took my mind off things."

"Who was the father?"

Flo doesn't say anything. She stares out the window.

"Jesus," Trevor says under his breath. "I'm sorry. I'm so sorry."

Flo smiles and sighs, taking a tissue from her purse to dab her eyes. "You're sorry. That's a fine thing. With everything you've got to deal with."

"Something I've learned, Aunt Florence, is that one person's tragedy does not cancel out another's."

The night nurse comes up to them.

"It's not life-threatening," she says, smiling. "Just a bad bout of staphylococcus. It should pass by tomorrow. Was there something they all ate in common?"

"Oh, my Lord, the Butterball," Flo exclaims. "I'm going to phone those people tomorrow and give them a piece of my mind."

The nurse shakes her head. "It's not from the turkey itself. It's from the person or people handling the food. It's a common bacterium. Most of us carry it."

"Oh," says Aunt Flo.

"The best advice I can give you is to give them lots of water and try to get them to rest."

The whole family camps out at Flo and Murray's. After everyone's been settled in makeshift beds, Flo and Trevor go down to the den where Flo has laid out bedding on the sofa for Trevor.

"Aunt Florence?"

"Yes."

"Will you play something for me?"

"Are you sure? You look exhausted. Don't you want to get to sleep?"

Trevor gets beneath the covers and puts his head on the pillow.
"It'll help me sleep," he says. "It'll take my mind off things."
Flo starts to play *Moonlight Sonata.*
"That's beautiful," Trevor says drowsily.
"Oh, I don't know," says Flo. "I'm no Liberace."

The Emperor's New City

THE LATE-DECEMBER RAIN pounded Pussy's cab as it pulled up to the curb. She paid the driver a handsome tip, collected her umbrella and shoulder bag, and swung open the door. A puddle glistened beneath the street lights, its surface slick with oil. Pussy watched its fragile rainbow fade into fragments as a party limo rolled by, strafing decibels and basslines.

"Excuse me, driver. Can you pull up a bit?" she asked.

"Yes, ma'am. Um, can you close your door?"

"Of course."

The cab jerked forward, hitting the pothole and spraying the sidewalk.

"Hey, what the fuck!" someone shouted in a dimly lit doorway.

"You sure you want off here?" the driver asked Pussy. "This isn't really a neighbourhood for someone like you."

"This is the only neighbourhood for someone like me," she said, staring at him in the rear-view mirror. "Or was," she added.

"All I'm saying is that the Downtown Eastside isn't a safe place for a beautiful woman. Especially with what's been going on. You've seen the news, right?"

"Don't let the Burberry, Gucci, and Cartier fool you, sweetheart," said Pussy. "I worked the street here for a while. It's not safe for any woman."

Pussy noticed the driver staring at her legs as she stepped onto the sidewalk. Wishing she hadn't tipped him so well, she slammed the door, pulled up the collar of her trench coat to keep out the chill, then bent down to the driver's half-open window.

"Here's the tea," she said, opening her bag to show him a hunting knife. "I've got bear spray too. Oh, and this." She rummaged around her bag and pulled out a spool of polypropylene rope. "No woman's ever safe. And the women around here, their troubles really start when they get into a car, and that car drives away. So, you ask yourself this, sugar. Are *you* safe doing what you do when someone like me who's packing what I'm packing gets into your cab ... and could take you from behind?"

The perplexed driver couldn't shut his window fast enough. Pussy pulled a cigarette and lighter from her purse as she watched the cab swerve into the busy Friday night traffic. The driver couldn't know that the knife and rope were professional tools, specialties for some of her clients. Not the bear spray, though. She'd gotten that from Estelle.

PUSSY ESPERANTO STARTED out as a professional name, after she moved to Toronto to be anonymous and live completely as a woman while she spent a year preparing for her reassignment surgery. Her boy name had been George. Now her passport and provincial ID said Georgina Gavreau. That was her legal name, but she wanted a pseudonym for her work, or rather a *nom de plume*. Her classified ad in *The Toronto Sun* said, "Pussy Esperanto, The Universal CXXX." They wouldn't print the last three letters: proof yet again, said Pussy, that "people always draw the line when it comes to cunt."

Pussy went online before most. She was always forward-thinking, even when she was still George. George was born and raised in a small mill town up the coast outside Ocean Falls. His mother slipped away into the night when he was twelve and went back to her reserve near Peace River. George's father was a mean drunk. The reserve was no great shakes either, but their father was white so they could call the cops if he showed up on reserve land uninvited. George and his sister Estelle stayed, partly because of school, also because they were Métis. That was when being mixed meant you didn't have official Indian status. Not seen as Indigenous, not seen as white, George and Estelle weren't seen at all. They lived in a no man's land. All they had were each other.

George idolized Estelle, who was several years older. She looked out for him. Life there was tough on an effeminate boy. But when George was fourteen, Estelle left for a job running a bar up in Whitehorse. Things got worse for George. At sixteen, tired of getting the shit beaten out of him, he fled south to Vancouver and hustled, first as a boy then as a girl, and did drag in the clubs. He took martial arts — tae kwon do — to protect himself.

He stopped doing drag for a while to finish high school on the dole. Then he hooked as Georgina to pay for college courses. Always one with a book on the go, he started a journal. He knew that one day the truth would be his meal ticket. Over time, George faded into the background, a phantom pain at first. Then a ghost. And finally, a stranger.

Pussy hit the motherlode with her ad in *The Toronto Sun*. The city was full of straight men on the down-low. "They don't call it Hogtown for nothing," Pussy would later say on the promo circuit.

Then the recession hit. Now even sex workers had to go vertical and specialize. Value added and all that stuff. Pussy hit the nail on the head with sadomasochism, bondage, and discipline.

All that hitting, slapping, and making someone lick your boot had caught on like wildfire. It was safe sex. It had an artistic edge too. Pussy was all for art and safety. She became a dominatrix.

No one who knew her was too surprised when she wrote a memoir based on her experiences. A shelf in her apartment was crammed with her journals. She often read from them to friends. Everyone agreed that her writing was excellent, especially after a couple of joints. She sifted through her journals for the best parts, changed the names of a prominent media magnate, a former provincial leader, and a famous hockey player, among others, and out popped a book. The book people convinced Pussy to keep her professional name because it got attention. They said it would sell books. It did. *The Indelible Woman* became a bestseller.

It wasn't enough money for Pussy to hang up her whip and fuck-me pumps.

"Prostitution pays better than art," she told her friends. "The general public appreciates it more."

The book was published internationally, selling out in Japan, Germany, and several former East Bloc nations, even making it onto *The New York Times* bestseller list. American sales had gone through the roof after some evangelists in Cincinnati held a book burning that made the U.S. news, propelling Pussy to cult status. Her publicity tour was electric.

There was a new print run too, and it flew off the shelves like hotcakes. Pussy said this was a good thing because "no one wants to see my remainders on a discount table." *The Indelible Woman* snagged Pussy more pots of money when the book people sold the rights for a TV movie to an American cable company with a studio in Vancouver. They were going to call it *The Pussy Esperanto Story*. She was thrilled to the now-much-talked-about tits. But then all that shit went down with Estelle, the thing with the bear.

PUSSY'S LIGHTER WAS dry. "Hey, hon, got a light?"

"Pussy?" The figure in the shadowy doorway stepped into the light.

"Thumbs?"

"Guilty as charged," he chuckled, lighting her cigarette.

Pussy was surprised to see Thumbs A) out of jail and B) away from his usual place down by the Orange Door, a gentleman's enterprise. When he was younger, Thumbs worked in the Alberta oil patch. Two fingers on his left hand were severed in a machine accident. Then, working as a rodeo hand in the bucking chutes at the Calgary Stampede, he crushed the pinkie finger on his right hand while he was adjusting a bronco's flank strap. A tall, burly Cree guy from Manitoba, he first showed up selling along the strip, around the same time Pussy started working the street. He was clumsy at first, constantly fumbling with his product and dropping it.

"Dude, you're all thumbs!" people would tease him. The nickname Thumbs evolved, and stuck.

"I got out last week," said Thumbs. "Two years, can you believe it?"

"But you're still holding?" Pussy asked. "No big life changes?"

"The trust fund never came through. You know how that is," said Thumbs, laughing. He shrugged. "A guy's gotta make a living, Puss."

"But this isn't your usual spot."

"I'm diversifying my distribution network. And I adjusted my stock so that it's more risk-averse," he said in a put-on snobby voice. He took a drag from Pussy's cigarette. "Just weed now. They don't care so much about that these days. They're after the hard stuff. Need anything?"

"No. Thanks. But you take care of yourself. I'm off to the Smith. They're throwing a going away party for me."

Thumbs stopped and stared as a dark grey van drove slowly by. The driver wore a hoodie and dark glasses, not a good sign after nightfall.

"What is it, Thumbs?"

"That grey van, it seems to be around a lot," he said, keeping his eye on the van as it rolled away. "Like almost every time someone disappears, that van's been around. Like the night before last. I seen Ginger that evening, but not since. No one has. I seen the van that night too. Funny thing is, it's got different licence plates every other time. You know, so people don't get suspicious."

Thumbs stared at the van, moving his lips as he quietly repeated the licence plate number.

"I'm recording them," he said. "Whenever I see that van. Maybe someone will want to know sometime, like the cops or something. Or maybe not. You never know. I'd write them down, but" — he chuckled, holding up his hands — "well, memorizing them is faster and easier."

"I get it," said Pussy. She took a long drag from her cigarette, making smoke rings as she exhaled. "Do you think it's the Farmer?"

There were rumours of a guy with a farm in the Fraser Valley not far from Chilliwack, who picked up women and took them to wild parties on his property. People said that all kinds of crazy shit went down, but no one offered specifics.

"Could be," said Thumbs. "Then again, maybe not." He sighed. "You're going away? Where?"

"Away from this," said Pussy. "To something else."

"That sure sounds cryptic."

"You know me, Thumbs," said Pussy. "Always a woman of mystery."

Thumbs laughed. "No lie. Hey, before I forget, I read your book when I was inside. Four times. I got it right here." He stepped back, dragged a rucksack from the doorway where he'd been standing, and pulled out a well-thumbed-through paperback. "I folded back the page corners of my favourite parts. Okay, the parts with me in it. Can you sign it for me?"

"Sure, sugar." Pussy grabbed a pen from her shoulder bag. It was encrusted with Swarovski crystals.

"That's quite the pen you got there, Puss," said Thumbs.

"That's because the pen isn't just mightier than the sword, Thumbs, it's *fiercer*. You take care of yourself, baby. Things around here are changing. Maybe for the good but probably not. Anyhow, there won't be room left for the likes of you and me once the developers are done."

Pussy gave Thumbs a kiss on the cheek, adjusted the strap of her purse, swivelled on her Louboutins, and strode into the neon-lit drizzle of Hastings Street.

Thumbs opened the book and looked at what she'd signed on the first page. "All my love, dearest Thumbs. Pussy Esperanto, The UC."

"THERE'S NOTHING REAL about real estate," Estelle had said to Pussy once. "There's nothing estate about it either. All you're buying is space between walls. All you're buying is air."

Pussy thought about what Estelle said as she looked up at the cranes and girders ascending from the street, towering over faded, two-bit hotels all dressed up with fancy names by the owners who built them way back when, although even then they were little better than last chance digs for worn-down people with worn-out shoes: the Empress, the Astoria, the Balmoral. Not that the names of the new condos going up were any less misleading, according to the development signage: Arcadia, the Olympus, Xanadu. Pussy marvelled at all the pretty little coffins rising high to heaven, soon to house the gods of a new century, and witnessed around her the sacrifices in play paving the way for their arrival.

She paused at the chained door of the shuttered Smilin' Buddha, the carcass of a former strip joint turned punk palace. She strolled by the boarded marquee of the old Pantages Theatre, once a vaudeville mainstay; then a burlesque venue; then an art cinema; now a crack house — at least to those who knew where the loose board in the back alley was. Dives were disappearing all along Hastings, yet the street itself was getting more and more crowded. People had pitched tents among the dealers and sex workers. Fly-by-night stalls and market spaces had popped up amid the syringe caps and used condoms. Pussy wondered what anyone would want with old 8-track or VHS tapes, a Baywatch lunch box, one left shoe, a Super Mario fanny pack, lamps without shades, or a game of Monopoly with missing pieces.

The shadowy scaffolds hovering overhead were impervious to the tents below. The city was expanding upward and outward, laying down the groundwork for snazzy condos, swanky restaurants, luxury lofts, and chic "retail destinations," razing the past and scattering the peasants. Or burying them. The cops and developers had dreamed up a gimmick called broken windows policing. If you removed visible elements of criminal activity from the street, and then added a fresh coat of paint, everything would be hunky-dory. Expensive new buildings with sky-high cribs that cost the moon would change the character of the neighbourhood for the better, they said. Because no one in a penthouse ever committed a crime, no one in a townhouse with all the mod cons ever pushed dope, no one in a condo with world-class views ever overdosed, and no one in a designer loft ever pimped out their bitches.

Pussy stopped for a moment at the Wall of Tears, a stretch of plywood nailed to the facade of an old welfare hotel being converted to fancy live/workspaces. It was covered in photographs of young women, with names and contact numbers.

Women were missing, that was how the news put it. As though they'd been misplaced. Or had disappeared, like in a magic show: here one minute, gone the next. Poor women. Native women. Trans women. Desperate women from desperate places, smuggled across the border, then abandoned by the men who had brought them here. Women from ruinous homes in small, hope-starved towns, side-eyed by society and called trash. Nameless women no one cared about, except for everyone who knew them. Some were drugged. Some were beaten. Most were forced to work the street because what else was there.

It wasn't a mystery if you lived in Canada's poorest postal code. You knew different. Abducted and probably killed, that's how you'd put it. You knew that a lot of those young women had fled well-to-do homes in the suburbs. You knew their names. And you knew what they'd left was sometimes worse than where they landed. Pussy sighed when she saw that someone had put up a picture of Ginger.

Before turning onto Abbott and hitting the Smith, she stopped at the window of Model Xpress, where she used to buy her thigh-highs. On display beyond her reflection was footwear aplenty for every kink, from gold pleather zip-ups to schoolgirl Mary Janes.

Around the corner, a block down Abbott, at the corner of Pender, was the Smithmore Hotel, known as the "Smith" by locals. It straddled the derelict cusp of Chinatown where brick and limestone warehouses and walk-ups were waning in the wake of glass and steel high-rises. The city had recently declared the Smithmore a heritage building, so it was safe from demolition, plus the hotel got a subsidized facelift. Before that there was a joke about which was a bigger dump, the Smithmore or the Smithrite dumpster beside it.

Now the Smith had become respectable, looks-wise. A big American science fiction TV series used it as a location for an episode set in a conservative Midwestern town, which gave the patrons a good laugh. But the clientele didn't change too much except for the occasional A-gay who gym-bodied his way into the hotel foyer via a recommendation in *OUT* magazine, which promised a view. This claim might have been said to be a bit of a stretch. If you stood facing north in the middle of the one-way street outside the lobby door while the light at the adjacent intersection was red, and if there was no traffic on the five consecutive cross streets, you could see the waterfront, a few tankers, and the mountains rising over the buildings on the North Shore.

The Smithmore had been Pussy's "office" for a few years. It was still pretty much a dropping off point for sex workers, street kids, queer tourists on the cheap, and people on welfare. Or a picking up point if you think about it. A democratic community of eyes peeled for cops looked out for the safety of the guests and the guests' guests. Fire escapes and other quick getaways were hospitably indicated upon registration, with a special mention that on each floor the showers were to be found at the far end of the east-west hallways. Toilets were separate. Try to hide your stash there and you were out on your ass.

Most of the main floor was a gay club, which was divided into three sections. There was a dance floor with a stage for drag shows, a karaoke bar, and a bar where male strippers performed.

Truth be told, they weren't technically exotic dancers. They were rent boys on the hustle. Yet sometimes the production values were entertaining. Everyone still talked about a kid from Kamloops whose specialty was a *Star Wars* theme. He'd dress like Darth Vader and do suggestive interpretive dance moves with a plastic lightsaber while he disrobed. One time he was so high after his set that he ran out onto the street buck naked but with his Darth Vader mask still on, waving around his lightsaber and shouting like a maniac, clearly feeling the power of the dark side. The cops chased him three blocks before catching up with him.

Car lights twinkled red and amber on a nearby viaduct as Pussy approached the bar. Graffiti and concert posters layered the fence around a construction site. A lone seagull screeched, scraping the darkness like a fingernail on slate. Pussy could smell the sea a few blocks away.

She reached the club's main entrance and swung open the door. Dance music pounded briefly until the door whooshed shut, silencing Destiny's Child and relinquishing the night to the tap-tap-tap of a drainpipe and, in the distance, a wailing siren.

IF THERE WAS a *Roget's Thesaurus* for slap and tickle, Estelle would be prominent among the list of synonyms for diesel dyke. Not too long after Pussy headed east, Estelle hauled her ass down to Vancouver from Whitehorse to thaw out. Her heart had been chilled by an icy breakup. The two-timing femme she'd lived with for years had run off with a bush pilot.

Years of managing a tough Yukon bar paid off. Almost right away she landed a job as a bouncer at the Smith. She also maintained the Smith's security in exchange for a room of her own, "which is all," said Estelle, "a woman really needs." That and the money she stuffed in her mattress.

As a bouncer, Estelle had the gift. One look from her could stop a scrap. Sometimes, though not often, Estelle had to use brute force. It wasn't a good idea to let her calm manner fool you. Something hot slow cooked inside her and it wasn't pretty when the lid came off. Brass tacks, though, she detested violence of any kind and felt badly when she had to deck someone for losing it.

It took Estelle a long time to get over the woman in Whitehorse. Sometimes, in the wee hours of the morning after the bar closed, she would stand in that spot in the centre of the road and stare toward the mountains, smoking a cigarette. It was quiet then, no traffic, no anything. Just a faint clicking sound as the traffic light changed.

A port city is a city of drifters and summer is the driftiest season. Summertime saw the Smith grind down to a slower pace. This being the case, Estelle decided to take up tree planting and find a replacement for her two months' absence.

Pussy was Estelle's replacement. Thanks to her tae kwon do, the bar was in good hands when she came out from back east on her bike every summer. Pussy liked escaping the Toronto humidity. Taking over the reigns from Estelle was Pussy's way of keeping a hand in the community. Like Estelle, she didn't give airs. And like Estelle, she believed you've got to remember your roots. Even if they were dyed platinum like Pussy's. Mind you, one or two of the Bay Street business types she serviced were none too pleased. No one delivered a spanking like she did. Her attitude was, "What are they going to do, call the Better Business Bureau?"

Like clockwork each June, Pussy arrived on her Harley with her laptop and lingerie packed in a custom Harley Davidson tail bag strapped to the back of her bike. Last summer was the same as the years before; the journey had become a kind of ritual. The sun was beating down hot and dry. Estelle could hear the Harley humming blocks away. Around the corner zoomed Pussy in a great big blur of black and chrome, a road warrior Cleopatra. Pussy Esperanto could wear a Hawg like jewellery.

She pulled up in front of the Smith, parked, took off her red spangly helmet, and dazzled everyone waiting for her by the hotel entrance with a blinding ear-to-ear grin, showing off her new teeth that the made-for-TV movie paid for. Pussy wasn't big like Estelle, she wasn't as tough, but she wore a lot of black leather. Sometimes that's all that's necessary.

Estelle gave Pussy a bear hug and helped her into the hotel

with her things. After she'd settled in, they retired to the bar for a cocktail catch-up with some of the regulars. Everyone wanted a piece of Pussy, fussing for her attention, telling her what they'd been up to for the last ten months.

"Hey, Pussy, you hear about ...?" "Hey Pussy, those teeth come out?" And so on. She'd radiate a smile at whoever was speaking like they were the only person in the room. Heads got to spinning from all that Toronto glamour.

The next morning, Pussy helped Estelle pack up her pickup. A small group congregated to wish Estelle well and see her off.

The tree people would've made Estelle a saint if they could. Her first summer, Estelle held the all-time provincial record for tree planting. She had a knack with a plunger, the whatsit they use to shoot saplings into the ground. She had a finesse. Something to do with angle and twist. No one could match her. The logging people left their scars on the land and along came Estelle to soothe the forest with a balm of new life.

Most of the time she was assigned to a camp on Vancouver Island but this time she ended up at a harvesting location deep in the Kootenays. The team comprised seasoned hands except for a kid called Jace. Estelle didn't take to Jace, and he didn't take to her. Jace was a skinhead from a small Okanagan town, thick-headed and thick bodied too, with a swastika tattooed on his left upper arm and a Canadian flag on the opposite arm.

"Butt-ugly squaw," Estelle heard Jace mutter under his breath as she passed by him the day she arrived.

For the next few weeks, she kept her distance to keep the peace. A summer storm broke her resolve.

A heavy rain fell the night Jace tried to get into Estelle's pants. It'd been like that all day, and they hadn't planted a single tree. Conditions were impossible. The mud on the slopes was ankle-deep. The planters stayed in their tents. Estelle played solitaire and napped. Just after nightfall, she heard someone trying to unzip the flap of her tent.

"Who's there?" she said, not in the mood for company.

There was no answer. Just clumsy fingers fumbling with the zipper.

"Who is it?" Estelle tried again. "Go away."

"Aw shit!" came the reply.

Estelle heard a thud, a bottle falling on the ground.

"Go away," she said again.

The fumbling fingers finally got lucky. The flap came open and in slipped Jace, drenched from head to toe and stinking of rye. Estelle smelled weed too. Whatever sense he had when he was sober, if any, was gone. All he was now was a slobbering bundle of animal needs with hungry eyes. Estelle sat up and leaned on her elbows.

Jace whipped out a knife and pointed it at Estelle. People make a mistake of looking at the blade when someone waves a knife at them. It's psychological; your eyes want to go for it automatically. Your attacker counts on it. It's a little like hypnotism; it sets you off guard and you lose that moment or two of quick thinking that could make all the difference. Estelle had seen more than her fair share of knives. She didn't give it a second glance. She kept her eyes on Jace nice and steady. He circled the knife at her, acting the tough guy. Anyone who'd been around could tell that Jace didn't know what he was doing. Too many movies.

The fumbling fingers went to his belt. He unbuckled it, popping the button at the top of his tight jeans. Down slid the zipper. His jeans fell to his hips, revealing the waistband of his tighty-whities. Jace wobbled as he tried to keep his balance. He jerked to a surprised standstill, looking around for a minute like he didn't know where he was. Then he focused in on Estelle with swimming eyes.

"You're going to lie there and take it. If you make a sound, I'm going to slice you open," he said. "You butt-ugly squaw fuck."

Estelle stared at him.

"Did you hear what I said?"

She stared.

"Say something bitch!"

Estelle stared.

"Okay. If that's how you want it, it's how you're going to get it."

It was like someone feather-tickled Nature herself. Nobody in the camp had ever heard a laugh like that before. They came running to see what the joke was. In no time there was a crowd around Estelle's tent. Someone opened the flap and inside was a spectacle no one was going to forget for a long, long time, at least not until the drinks dried up or the story was overtold. There was Estelle, smiling away with a knife clenched between her teeth, as cool as a cucumber, holding Jace, three sheets to the wind, in one hell of an arm hold. What tipped the iceberg was seeing Jace with his pants wrapped around his knees.

Estelle spit out the knife.

"Have a good look everyone!" she said, laughing so hard there were tears in her eyes.

They did. They all had a good look. No one could believe it. It was unreal. Couldn't be. But it was. No bigger than a thimble.

"Four inches full mast, I reckon," Estelle announced.

Seems that the minute Jace lowered his drawers and Estelle got a front-row view of the show, she bust a gut. Caught off guard by the ridicule of his manhood, Jace suddenly got self-conscious and tried to cover up, dropping his knife. Estelle had the knife in her mouth in a second, and Jace in a nice, firm lock. For the rest of the encampment, until the end of tree planting, Jace was known as Thimble Dick. He steered clear of Estelle from then on.

The weather turned hot and dry after that night, and stayed that way for weeks. Estelle planted saplings into the slopes like there was no tomorrow. She was on her way to beating her own record. She could smell the thousand-dollar bonus that would top off her earnings. Only one more week to go.

Man and Nature do a dance and take turns leading. No one knew that better than Estelle. The last week of August, they were working on the side of a tall mountain with a peak that stayed snow-covered all summer. People were sparse in this part of the Kootenays. There wasn't a town for fifty miles. The mountain looked across a valley with a turquoise lake. It was man-made, the result of flooding some thirty years earlier when they built a dam for hydroelectricity. Invisible to the eye, forgotten ghost towns from the gold rush days rotted hundreds of feet below the surface of the lake. People from all over the world had come here in the eighteenth century to find fortune, some so desperate they had nothing to lose but lost it anyway. For many, the road to hope led to dead ends. They went missing. Now their boardwalks, saloons, and shanties were disappearing too, drowned by progress and obscured by history.

One night over whiskey by the fire, the planters tried to outdo each other with tall tales about prospectors. Someone had gone into the bush alone and never returned. Had they lost their way? Did they freeze on a glacier? Did they slip from a rock? Were they mauled by a bear or eaten by wolves? Only the Kootenays, the mountains themselves, knew the answers. Maybe while planting they'd discover a skeleton clutching a satchel of gold. It was an unsettling thought, being all alone in those mountains where anything could happen. Estelle said that as they tried to outdo each other with scary stories, you could almost hear the lake below moan with the ghosts of drowned fortune hunters. She couldn't get to sleep that night.

The next day, overtired, Estelle forgot her sense. Maybe that's why she wandered so far off from the others, losing track of time and distance. The land had become parched from lack of rain. Twigs, bracken, and dried-up moss crackled under her heavy boots as Estelle worked the slope. She'd just about run out of saplings and would have to get back to camp to replenish when she realized she hadn't heard a human sound for almost half an hour. She looked down the slope, and across it. No one. She yelled but there was no reply. This didn't shake her. Estelle had a sense of direction. She'd find her way back. But she was hungry, real hungry. As luck would have it, she found herself standing by a dense thicket of salmonberries. She grabbed a few and sucked them back. She reached for more and that was when she heard the sound that made her heart skip a beat. You couldn't mistake a sound like that. She was up Shit Creek without a paddle.

One of the deadliest things alive is a grizzly sow cornered with her cubs, or thinking she's cornered. An animal driven by hunger, say a wolf or cougar, is one thing; if you're hard to get, it just might pass. Not a grizzly, she's driven by something else. Estelle hadn't packed her bear spray because she couldn't find it the day she left, so she lay still playing possum. But there was no fooling the bear. She came up close and snuffled, then raised herself sky-high on her massive hindlegs. She took a swipe at the air before swooping down, enormous jaws wide open. It was one clean bite beneath the elbow, tore Estelle's forearm off right at the joint.

They never found her arm, but they found Estelle in time to airlift her to Revelstoke. They'd fanned out into the bush when they'd realized she was late returning. It took about an hour before one of the guys shot up a flare that sent everyone running. It took another hour for the helicopter. She was lucky to be alive with the blood loss. It almost defies believability that Estelle had the wherewithal to rip a strip from her clothes and use her teeth to tie a tourniquet before she passed out, but she did. The doctor put it down to shock. He said shock for a short spell can clear your mind like nothing else.

"If there's a God, that's it," Estelle said later. "God's a shock that saves your life."

PUSSY PAID FOR Estelle's prosthesis. She was a real crutch for Estelle to lean on those first few weeks of rehab. After she'd flown up to the Interior to collect Estelle's truck, Pussy decided to stick around for a while and help with things until Estelle came out of her depression.

Estelle wasn't herself. She wouldn't visit the bar. She couldn't pull it together. To be a bouncer you need two real arms, she said. Not one, two.

"This is a salad tong," she said, holding up her prosthesis, "not an arm."

People say you can break the body, but you can't break the spirit. Seems that in Estelle's case, one good swipe did both.

Pussy had a few tricks up her sleeve. She knew what's what when it came to being between a rock and a hard place. It saddened her more than she could say to see Estelle all bunched up inside herself and squeezed to death by misery. Given Pussy's unique circumstances in life, she'd learned to look on the bright side of disappointment by changing the rules and breaking the mold with a new blueprint. Original model or newly reconstituted, there are people who like to put you in your place for being a woman, as she explained in her first book. Pussy was transgender, not a martyr. Her body was her living. She needed to defend that privilege.

Back when she started taking her first tae kwon do classes, the other students stared at Pussy like she was a three-ring circus. But they were quick to realize that they had a prodigy on their hands. Pussy could jump, spin, and kick her way around everybody.

"You already understand the chi," the master had told her in front of the class, meaning Pussy's balance of body, breathing, and spirit.

By the time of Estelle's accident, it'd been nine years since Pussy had taken up tae kwon do. She was almost ready to earn her *yeedan*, second-level black belt. Pussy decided it was time to take Estelle in hand and navigate her back to a sense of herself by using her knowledge of the martial arts, and reverse psychology.

A couple of months after the accident, Pussy and Estelle were sitting in Estelle's room heating up water for instant coffee in the microwave. Estelle was down-in-the-mouth, rubbing what the doctor called a phantom pain where her artificial arm was now. Pussy was a regular Chatty Cathy, making jokes, small talk, and whatever came to mind to cheer Estelle. Nothing Pussy said struck a spark. Estelle stared out the window like a zombie. It gave Pussy the creeps. It wasn't until the ringer on the microwave went off and Estelle got up to make their coffee that she saw Pussy standing in her tae kwon do outfit.

"What's that getup for?" she asked glumly.

"Nothing," said Pussy, giving Estelle a brush-off voice. "Here. Would you tie the belt for me?"

Estelle looked at her and held up her prosthesis.

"Sorry. I'll do it myself. You can't keep using that as an excuse, Estelle. You've got to start getting used to it."

Estelle scowled, dolloping a spoonful of instant coffee into two mugs. She handed one to Pussy.

"Where're you going in that?" she asked.

"Just downstairs," Pussy said nonchalantly. "Thanks. Mmm. Good coffee."

There was a knock at the door and Estelle opened it to find one of the regulars from the bar standing there grinning. She was wearing a tae kwon do outfit too, with a white belt.

"Pussy here?"

"Yeah, she's here," Estelle said, looking suspiciously back over her shoulder at Pussy as she opened the door wider.

"I'm just on my way down," Pussy trilled. She breezed past Estelle, pausing quickly to say, "I'm giving some of the girls a class. We'll be in the bar if you want company."

A minute later, Estelle strode down the hall to the fire exit door and marched down the stairs. Nothing happened in this hotel, in this bar, without Estelle's knowledge. If they thought that just because she was short one arm that they could put her out to pasture, she was going to show them they were dead wrong.

Albert, the rake-thin old queen who'd been working the hotel's front desk for years — ever since retiring his legendary drag career as Ida Dunnit — was watching *The Young and the Restless* on the portable black and white he kept on the counter for slow periods. He had no idea what was going on, but later he told everyone that he knew something had hit the fan when he saw Estelle's face. She barreled across the lobby to the entrance to the bar and stopped cold in her tracks when she saw the cardboard sign perched on an easel. In big black letters it said: "TAE KWON DO. The best defence is Self Defence. Let's take back our streets and lives! Classes with Pussy, Tuesdays, Wednesdays, and Thursdays, 5:30 p.m. sharp." Someone had crossed out TAE with a felt pen and scribbled DYKE above it, so it said DYKE KWON DO.

Estelle slowly walked into the bar, passed the coat check, and peered around the corner at the dance floor. The place was packed. News about the classes had spread like wildfire. And it wasn't only women. There were almost as many men in the class.

Gay bashing was getting worse. A group called Canadians for Safe Families had set up shop in some rundown offices down the street. The organization's website deployed a kitschy cacophony of maple leaf flags and Biblical quotations to highlight its convictions. But it didn't look like there were too many families involved. It seemed to be mainly young and middle-aged men with chips on their shoulders, who got their kicks from hanging out in gangs and beating the crap out of people outside bars, clubs, bathhouses, and cruising spots. The cops were never around when they were needed. They made a big deal about setting up a community policing unit with an outreach bus and anti-bashing flyers. But the thing is, someone bludgeoning you with a baseball bat is unlikely to stop even if you hand them an informative brochure.

The serious nature of Pussy's tae kwon do class hadn't stopped a couple of queens from showing up wearing festive workout looks. "If I'm going down, I'm going down looking fabulous!" one of them announced, curtseying to applause.

"That's what she said," someone yelled at the back, and everyone groaned.

Estelle joined the others sitting in rows facing the stage where Pussy stood. Behind her on an easel was a picture of General Choi Hong-hi, founder of tae kwon do.

"Always remember that the best way to deal with an attacker is to run or scream or do both," Pussy told the group. "Tae kwon do is a Korean form of the martial arts. The martial arts are a skill to be used only in extreme situations. The weak person must develop herself, the blind person must learn to sense her opponent's moves, the person who is crippled or disabled" — she looked right at Estelle — "must learn to compensate for her inadequacies. That is the philosophy of the martial arts."

The first class was a little awkward for all concerned. There were plenty of nervous giggles and people felt foolish they would fail. Pussy introduced them to the first in a long series of training movements, which in Korean are called *hyung*. You could see the jokes coming a mile away about who was "well *hyung*" and who wasn't.

Within a few weeks, Estelle had taken to tae kwon do like a fish to water and was soon swimming in chi. Pussy was right, Estelle's confidence boomeranged back.

Over time, the classes became so popular that they had to turn people away. One night, Pussy took to the stage after class, looking like she had something important to say.

"It's not enough just to defend ourselves," she said. "We need to reclaim our neighbourhood. Estelle and I — Estelle, would you stand up ..."

Estelle stood up begrudgingly, half-heartedly waving her prosthesis at the group. She didn't share Pussy's love of the spotlight.

"Estelle and I talked about it, and we think that we need to do more. We need to start our own vigilante group and start patrolling the streets around here. We all know the cops won't change anything. But we can."

There were murmurs of agreement throughout the group. This was followed by an impromptu meeting that lasted well beyond midnight because everyone had an opinion. It took more than an hour to establish the meeting's agenda. Then there was a testy discussion about parity, resulting in the decision that everyone present would each have five minutes to voice their ideas and concerns. They finally had something like a charter and, even better, a name. And fashion.

The media started paying attention when Pussy Patrol hit the street wearing hot-pink sweatshirts emblazoned with a big black maple leaf on the back and front, and the group's name in reverse pink. Photos and videos of Pussy Patrol policing the Downtown Eastside arm-in-arm in groups of four started to pop up online. What with Pussy's reputation in the literary world, journalists were soon lining up for interviews with her. Newspaper articles featured a PR photo from Pussy's publisher of her showing off her new teeth.

The publicity garnered its fair share of adversity. A transgender sex worker — and even worse, a writer — leading militia-style posses of people embracing an alternative lifestyle through the streets of our fair city was not tickety-boo with everyone. There was an influx into the hood of even more thugs eager to protect Canadian families. Some brought knives. Someone, a gun.

"SAY MY NAME, bitch!" said Feng, taking a pause from ticketing hangers to give Pussy a pose for the ages. Destiny's Child's "Say My Name" was playing full blast on the sound system. "God, I love this song!"

"Well smell you, Beyoncé," Pussy shouted above the din as she shook off the rain. She tossed her trench coat onto the coat check counter. Not her bag, though. She never relinquished her bag.

"We all know I'm a Kelly," said Feng. "You're the Beyoncé, mother."

Feng was one of Pussy's un-asked-for drag daughters. His drag name was Fu Ling Yu. Feng's parents owned the city's most celebrated Chinese restaurant, and other ones in Calgary, Ottawa, Toronto, and Montréal. He'd been studying business at UBC because they were grooming him to take over the family company. Then one day his mother discovered something in the pocket of his jeans while she was micromanaging the housekeeper's attempt to do laundry: a room key attached to a tag that said Steamworks Baths. He'd forgotten to hand it back when he'd left the tubs the night before. His mother looked it up online.

Feng's parents were bigwigs in the Chinese Baptist Church. Later that day, he returned from class to find his packed bags on the front porch and the locks changed. That night, Pussy found Feng drunk and distraught at the bar, so she got him a room at the Smith and convinced Estelle to give him a job cleaning. One day

Estelle heard him singing while he was cleaning rooms. She called Pussy on her cell.

"He's singing fucking opera!" said Estelle. "Real good too. I think. I don't know. But it sounds dope."

It turned out that Feng had studied opera growing up and had an amazing counter-tenor voice. It took some convincing, but Pussy finally persuaded him to perform at the bar one night, and it's a good thing she did because the kid was a natural.

People still talk about Fu Ling Yu's debut. She started her set in Kabuki drag, singing "Un Bel Di, Vedremo" from *Madama Butterfly*. Feng was hesitant at first because he was Chinese, and *Butterfly* was Japanese. He was concerned about cultural appropriation, not to mention cultural dyslexia.

"Darling, *Madama Butterfly* is an opera by a white male Italian based on a short story by a white male American," Pussy told him. "She is a figment of the white Western male gaze, girl. She's a fetish. Her existence *is* cultural appropriation. So, play with it!"

Which is exactly what Fu Ling Yu did, after asking Pussy to explain what "male gaze" meant. Her high *geisha* drag was impeccable, and disturbing. She held a whip (from Pussy's collection of professional play toys), which she cracked loudly against the stage floor throughout the aria. At the end, she pretended to bite her lip while biting down on a capsule of fake blood, which streamed down her chin. Then she smeared her makeup and removed her kimono for a shocking reveal: a nude illusion bodysuit with gold chains and locks wrapped around her limbs and torso.

"Do you think you can get Roger to turn the music down, at least for now?" Pussy asked Feng. "I can't hear myself think."

Feng picked up the phone and dialed the tech booth. "Hi, Roger. Can you turn down the music? Our Lady Pussy needs to collect her thoughts." He replaced the receiver. "There. Done.

Oh, and by the way, I've got some not such good news. The Boys are in the management office."

"The Boys?"

Feng bit his lower lip and nodded.

"Rasputin and Bitchface?"

"Uh-hunh, 'fraid so."

The Boys were the Smith's owners. They were a couple. Sergei and Roland had both grown up in nosebleed sections of the city. Roland in the rarified country club air of landscaped, spit-level, modernist homes clinging to the mountainside in show-offish West Vancouver. Sergei in starchy Shaughnessy with its boulevards, mature chestnut trees, and vintage street lamps.

Pussy started the nickname Rasputin for Sergei. It was meant ironically because his family were Russian aristocracy who fled the Bolshevik revolution. Over time, they built the largest chain of car dealerships in western Canada and developed a portfolio of properties that included the Smith, which Sergei had inherited. His partner, Roland, was younger, forty-five going on twenty-one thanks to an unrestricted regimen of cosmetic procedures, which gave him permanent resting bitchface, hence his nickname among the Smith's staff. Also, because he was gratingly high maintenance.

The ambience in the management office was funereal. Rasputin, Bitchface, Estelle, and Roger — who co-managed the Smith with Estelle — sat around a 1950s chrome and Formica kitchen table that served as an improvised boardroom table. Estelle looked fit to kill.

"I'd guess that someone farted or died but from the look on all your faces I'd say someone did both," said Pussy as she sat down between Roger and Estelle.

"These fuckers are selling the Smith," said Estelle, never one to mince words.

There was a large binder in front of Sergei, which he pushed across the table to Pussy.

"What's this?" she asked.

"They made us an offer we couldn't refuse. And I'm not getting any younger. So, I'm winding down and selling off most of my properties," said Sergei. He grabbed Roland's hand. "We want to spend more time together."

Pussy opened the binder. Her heart sank. "You sold the Smith to Roydall Developments? The Smith is becoming condos?"

Arthur Roydall was the city's most powerful real estate developer and marketer. He made an international name for himself as the "Prince of Pre-sell" because he practically invented the concept of pre-selling condos before they were completed, or even started. Every building he touched turned into a luxury condo, leaving the previous renters out on the street.

"They're turning the bar into a tapas restaurant?" Pussy asked as she flipped through the binder. "And there's going to be an oxygen bar? What about all the people who live in the hotel, and all the patrons who think of the Smith as community?"

"Well, that's all nice and kumbaya, but you can't sell community," said Sergei.

"But you can sell air," replied Estelle.

The bar was starting to fill up. The music was louder. The waves of laughter and conversation grew in volume.

"We'll wait till tomorrow to tell people," Pussy said to Estelle. "Let's give them one last night."

Estelle and Pussy both got up to leave. On their way out, they slammed the door.

THE NEXT DAY, in interviews and quotes on radio, TV, online, and in print, Albert from the front desk was all over the news. He was a key witness to what had happened. He was relatively unscathed compared to most of those trapped in the bar because the perpetrators had entered through the bar's street entrance, not via the hotel lobby. The minute Albert heard shots and the first screams, he fled out onto the street, dialling 911. But by the time the cops and ambulances showed up, the damage had been done: four dead, fifty-two injured, one missing, and everyone else royally fucked up.

"They were wearing balaclavas, black balaclavas, and were dressed completely in black," Albert told a scrum of microphones and cameras. "I think it was mostly men, if not all men, because of their voices. I didn't hear any female voices. They were shouting so loud, you could hear them from the street, even above the screaming. They were calling people all kinds of names, names we all know so they don't bear repeating. Some of them had guns, some had knives, and some had machetes. Machetes! This wasn't random. This was organized. Planned. It was purposeful."

As an emergency worker walked him away, sobbing, in the background you could see police tape, people being carried out on gurneys, a hushed and horrified crowd gathering beyond the barricades, and the staccato strobe of endless ambulance lights.

THE PERSON MISSING was Pussy. She got to the guy with the machete too late. Estelle's neck was severed almost in half. Pussy wrested the machete away, knocked him to the floor, and pulled off the balaclava. She kicked him in the head, and he passed out. Then, somehow, she made it out onto the street, and started to walk aimlessly in a daze.

It was late. The rain had stopped. The moon was out. The cars along Hastings were few and far between. The trade was gone. The dealers were gone. Tarps were sealed, the cardboard shacks closed and curtained. It was just Pussy, by herself, standing in front of Model Xpress. She held a brick in her hand, from the construction site down the street. She was in her stocking feet, her high heels carefully placed side by side on the sidewalk so she could run faster.

Pussy felt the weight of the brick in her hand. She felt its fate. More than a hundred years old, from a warehouse built along a train track long since torn up and paved over, the brick was scarred from years of commerce, eroded, no longer able to withstand the tensions of time or pressures of progress. Its surface had corroded to a dark oxblood red, as though stained by sacrifice.

Pussy lifted the brick to her lips and kissed it, leaving a bright red imprint on its decay. After checking to see that there was no one around, she raised it up above her head, swung back her arm, then hurled it with all her might, shattering glass. She didn't wait for the alarm to sound. She grabbed her shoes and hightailed it down a nearby alley. She turned a corner at the next side street and continued to run until she couldn't run any longer. She stopped beneath the awning of a closed restaurant, put on her shoes, pulled a smoke from her purse, and tried to figure out what she should do next.

That's when the van pulled up.

IN THUMBS'S EXPERIENCE, the cops never listened to anything someone like him had to say, but that didn't stop him from trying. Every week he made his way to the police station to attempt to persuade someone — anyone — to consider his van sightings and list of licence plates. And every week he was told not to interfere with their ongoing investigation of women missing from the neighbourhood, even as more and more women disappeared. It wasn't just Thumbs; they weren't willing to hear from anyone in the community, or outside it. Some parents had showed up with theories, clues, and evidence concerning their disappeared daughters, but they were ignored too. Now that Pussy had gone missing, Thumbs was hellbent on trying yet again.

The officer at the front desk rolled his eyes when he saw Thumbs shuffle up to the counter. "Not now, Thumbs. We're up to our eyes with the attack at the Smith. I don't have time for your nonsense."

Thumbs whipped out Pussy's book from his coat pocket and shoved it in the officer's face. "Yeah, my friend was there. And now she's gone!"

"Get that book out of my face, Thumbs. Yes, we know Pussy Esperanto is missing. She's kind of famous. Which is making this whole thing an even bigger headache."

"Why?" asked Thumbs. "Because now everyone's looking at how you guys fuck everything up? Now you can't pretend that you're doing something when you're not."

"Calm down, Thumbs. And let's use our inside voice, okay?"

"Check out a grey van with this licence plate, asshole," said Thumbs, stating the number from memory.

"We're done here, Thumbs," the officer said quietly as he feigned being busy with paperwork. "Go home."

"We're not fucking done here! I'm not going anywhere until you fuckers get off your asses and do something!" shouted Thumbs.

Being shoved into a crowded cell wasn't the outcome Thumbs had been hoping for, although this wasn't the first time this had happened after one of his heated exchanges with law enforcement. He found himself a spot on a bench and looked around at his cellmates, some he'd seen here before, some not. He kept his eye on a kid slumped on the bench across the cell. He was solid, tough-looking, dressed in a black tank top and black jeans. There was a nasty gash on his shaved head.

"Jace! Jace Gilley!" shouted a cop at the cell door. "Your counsel's here. C'mon. Step it up."

When the kid got up, Thumbs noticed that he had a swastika on one arm and a Canadian flag on the other.

THE VAN WAS heading east out of the city, flying along the freeway past hilly suburbs, sprawling subdivisions, big box strip malls, industrial parks. Eventually, here and there, farms. And in the distance, the looming mountains. They were going to somewhere near Chilliwack. He had property there.

"I have a farm," he told Pussy after the van rolled up to her and she leaned into his window. "More of a compound really. Five acres. Some animals, but mainly machine work. And lots of partying. Lots."

"Sounds exciting," said Pussy. "Want some company?"

"What's your name?"

"Ginger," Pussy answered. This seemed to discomfit the driver, for a brief second.

"Well Ginger, hop on in!"

The van drove by a new condominium development at the very edge of the city. A large sign promoting the virtues of the cluster of tall, slender, glass high-rises with matchbox-sized suites was ebullient. "Urban Heaven at the Heart of It All!" it said, even though they were twenty-five miles from downtown. "Exclusive Living! Breathtaking Views! All the Amenities!"

Pussy reached into her bag to check that the rope was still there, and the knife. Then she grabbed the bear spray, quietly pulled it out, and held on to it for dear life.

The Food Chain

MONSIEUR DELACROIX AND I sat in a booth in a roadside dive somewhere between Ashtabula and Cleveland. We'd been on the road for hours and both we and the van needed refuelling. I had to give hats off to the visionary who'd come up with the franchise's retro decor of orange, yellow, and brown supergraphics, and white plastic tulip chairs along the counter. The visual caffeine perked me up. It was like a colour Xerox of the early '70s.

Monsieur was still picking at his food, but I'd chowed down like nobody's business. Limp-wristed jalapenos clung half-heartedly to a lava flow of microwaved Cheez Whiz hardening among the crevices of my few remaining nachos. The last of my curly fries gagged in the ketchup. My gut was filled with Pop Art repeating itself.

Monsieur sighed and sipped his antacid-pink shake. He took another bite of his patty melt. I swirled a finger around a cardboard plate to sponge up leftover salt, licked it, and stared at him.

"What?" he asked.

I pointed at the corner of his mouth.

"Oh."

He put down his sandwich and dabbed his mouth with a monogrammed handkerchief, removing the globule of melted cheese single that had nested there since his first bite and was driving me insane. I gulped the last of my cherry Coke and looked him in the eye.

"I don't see why it always has to be what you want," I said. Monsieur sneezed and blew his nose, allergic to air conditioning.

"They'll find out," I continued. "We've got too many for them not to. They'll sniff something at Customs. Why Detroit anyhow? Why not Buffalo? They're less suspicious in Buffalo."

"Oh please."

We were starting to get on each other's nerves. I was having second thoughts about our plan, which put Monsieur Delacroix a little too close to compromise for comfort. My best friend was a control freak, a tall, thin, walking-talking get-rich-quick scheme topped off by a mop of golden ringlets.

"We must be off soon, my dear. Time is money."

Monsieur looked at his Mickey Mao wristwatch. The face featured China's Great Helmsman wearing a Mickey Mouse beanie. When the watch moved, Mao winked. Monsieur had wrists that spun like propellers. Mao winked a lot.

"In a minute," I said. "I'm the one doing all the driving, remember."

Hazy light filtered through the window and illuminated his lineless skin. Monsieur looked remarkable thanks to a regimen of anti-aging personal care products. He flipped open his compact and checked to see how the Clairol was holding out. He caught me looking.

"It's my natural colour," he said. "It says so on the box."

Reassured, he unflipped, sat back, and gazed through the window at the freeway traffic, past the gas pumps and parking lot and, beyond the stream of cars and trucks, a factory. July's late-morning heat slithered, coiled, constricted, and slowly started to digest the scenery. Ventilation grates along the windowsill disgorged geysers of cold air. The silk ferns danced.

I reached across the table and began to feed from Monsieur's untouched, now cold plate of fries. We'd spent the last few weeks pinballing through the boondocks in the northeastern pocket of the Midwest, bouncing from small town to small town in Indiana, Illinois, Ohio, and even Pennsylvania. Monsieur had a name for every place we'd stopped: "Dupesville."

He'd spent his sweet time researching on the web, and the result was "a win/win sitch for the both of us — bottom-line-wise, my dear."

We'd suckered clueless geezers into selling old typewriters to us at a fraction of their true value to collectors. They thought we were doing them a favour. They thought these were junk. Typewriters from before World War II were worth a pretty penny. Anything after was made of plastic and worth shit. We were heading home to Toronto to set up a website and sell them to well-heeled typewriter fanatics competing with each other for the best ones. It just goes to show that there are too many loose screws out there with too much money and too much free time.

"Fuck this noise!" said the guy in the booth behind me, loud enough for everyone in the rest stop to hear.

"Ah, the immortal observation of Confucius," Monsieur chimed in.

He had a way of turning wherever we were into something you'd see on public television, even a fast-food joint, as though the burger grill sizzled with crinolines, bustles, whale-boned corsets, powdered wigs, and unbathed, perfumed flesh.

"Shhh!" I told him.

I half turned my head to try to see what was happening. I didn't want to miss anything. A girl sobbed. The guy, presumably her boyfriend, freaked. It all came out. Apparently, she was pregnant, and she wasn't going to have the baby. "It."

"Over my dead body," he told her.

There was a sucking noise, a straw interrogated ice, and I heard a swirl of ice cubes in a cup. She told him that no matter what he said he was wasting his breath, "Because it's not yours Kyle so let it fucking go."

Not his? Was she sure? She was sorry but yes.

"Fucking not mine. Wow. I mean. Wow."

Silence.

"I'm sorry."

Monsieur pouted because I wasn't paying attention to him. He pulled his plate away from me, put some salt on his fries, and then ignored them. Taking out a well-thumbed Stephen King novel, he posed thoughtfully, trying his best to make sure that everyone knew he was beneath his element. I didn't feel any obligation to tell him the book was upside down. Monsieur Delacroix was dyslexic, not just the way he read but the way he approached life. My friend hopscotched through existence like it was an M.C. Escher print, soaring upside down over the square that puts you out of the game.

Kyle said things like, "You're a no-good fucking cunt," and, "No way I'm sticking around with a fat slut."

He stood up and I got a good look at him. Kyle was cute, young, built, and obviously hung. He wore a checkered flannel shirt with the sleeves cut off, blue jeans, work boots, and a pirate-style bandanna.

He was out the door. He stormed across the parking lot and flung himself into a beaten-up white Ford Fairlane pitted with craters of rust. The mufflers were shot — and loud — but the kid's souped-up stereo was even louder, vibing over the angry rumble of ignition. Strains of Nirvana accompanied the helter-skelter screech of tires as he swung around and stopped in front of the window where we sat gaping at him. The dead lead singer screamed about the smell of teen spirit as Kyle mouthed "fuck you" at his girlfriend and took off down the feeder onto the freeway.

"My," said a well-fed woman of around fifty sitting in the booth behind Monsieur's ghoul-swelled noggin.

She helped herself to a forkful of a fajita salad with steak strips. She sat with two other women who liked their food. They looked like they worked together. I'd noticed a few mirrored office blocks nearby, plunked down by the freeway like big, glassy Rubik's Cubes. One of them rolled her eyes toward God or whatever it was making the tube-lighting above her flicker. The other shook her head and patted her lip with a brown paper serviette that had the round-and-round recycling arrows on it.

"What would you do if your Presley talked to Krystal that way?" the lip-patter asked the woman with the fajita salad.

"Well, you know, it's different. I mean, they're married."

"Oh Lord, Sara-Lynn, it's almost two thousand," ventured the woman with her eyes to God. "No man has the right."

"Well, to be honest," said Sara-Lynn, "I'd take him over my knees like when he was little and give him what for."

"I hear they like that. It's the thing now," the lip-patter said.

That broke them up.

"I may be a Christian, God save me," said Sara-Lynn, "but sometimes I think those lesbians have got one hell of a reason."

This sent all three into paroxysms.

The woman with her eyes to God stopped laughing and began to focus on polishing her glasses. "You know as well as I do, no man has the right to speak like that to a woman." She put her glasses on and leaned over the table. "Even a slut," she stage-whispered.

"People have lost their manners," said Sara-Lynn.

There was a silent mutual agreement and they ordered coffees. Their talk-show philosophy turned my heart into a question mark. I didn't say anything to Monsieur. He had two phobias: spiders and sentimentality. Still, I felt sorry for the girlfriend.

I turned around completely to see if I could catch a glimpse of her but all I could fathom was the back of a tangled mess of bleached hair showing roots. She got up from the booth and tried to hide her face as she shuffled toward the exit. There was a payphone just outside the door. She went to it, and I saw her burrow in her purse for change she obviously didn't have. I got up to help her out, dismissing with a shrug Monsieur's doozy of a look. He disapproved of people who used telephones. He preferred modes of communication that he said didn't rely on personality or emotional expression and were more accurate than the human voice, like text-based chat rooms and anonymous sex in public spaces. "Online or on your knees, dear," he had said.

I went outside and gave the girl some change.

"Thanks," she said. "You heard all that?"

I nodded. She was quite pretty.

"Oh. I heard what that old bag said. You must think I'm a slut too, huh?"

"No. I'd be a hypocrite," I said. "You're just young."

"Oh. Yeah. Well. Gee. Thanks and everything."

"He's just hurt," I said.

"You don't think he meant that stuff he said?"

"Yeah, he meant it. But that doesn't mean it's true."

"Oh. Right."

I turned around to see Monsieur inside at the cash register, paying. It was apparently time to go. He swivelled to inspect the girl as we headed across the parking lot toward the van. She was standing on the sidewalk waiting for whomever she'd called to pick her up.

"She's not that fat a slut," Monsieur commented.

I unlocked the door, got into the driver's side, slammed the door shut, and didn't let Monsieur in for a couple of minutes. When I did, he looked perplexed.

"I'm worried about you," he said, fanning himself with Stephen King and pretending to be breathless. "You've developed a temper."

"I think the word you're looking for is conscience."

Monsieur lit a cigarette. "My dear, it's not our fault if people are suckers."

"You don't get it, do you?"

"All of our transactions were above board. Can we help it if the hoi polloi don't know the value of an antique?"

"That's not what I'm talking about."

Monsieur tapped an impatient finger on the dashboard.

"Not everything's about us," I said.

He'd stopped listening. He was staring at our contraband. It filled our dented, rented budget van. There were dozens, all of them old and useless and worth their weight in gold. I turned on the ignition. To annoy him, I ground gears all the way onto the freeway. Monsieur feigned indifference.

"There's nothing more reassuring than the rattle of typewriters," he said. "Except, of course, the smell of money."

He opened the glove compartment and pulled out a stained *People* magazine. Princess Diana had a coffee ring halo. About a mile along the freeway, I careened onto the shoulder and came to a screeching halt. I glared at Monsieur.

"What?" he asked, looking up.

"I'm not going another inch until you stop humming *The Brady Bunch* theme song."

"Fine."

Monsieur huffed and continued to flip, but he kept his trap shut.

I was wrong about Detroit. I'd thought so many people being bumped off in that city on a regular basis might make them more vigilant at the border, if not paranoid as all get-out, but no. Then again, we weren't killers or even bona fide smugglers; we were quasi-smugglers or semi-smugglers or demi-smugglers, or whatever prefix meant we weren't professionals. We were just two-bit cons — artists, that is, not jailbirds.

The customs guard didn't know the value of our cargo either. My flirting with him didn't hurt. I was always a pushover for a guy in a uniform. It was the cover-up, me batting my baby blues, that got us through. Things might be different now if I'd realized that I was the one being outconned. I was starting to believe my own deception and was susceptible to someone else's hook, line, and sinker. My dishonesty was breaking down, and me with it.

Before we got to the border, we'd detoured for a quick eyeball at Cleveland and Detroit, cities we'd been through but never really seen. The business portion of our trip completed, Monsieur indulged one of his many hobbies, taking scrapings from highway, turnpike, and rest stop guardrails. "To see if America is rusting on schedule, my dear." He'd brought jars with him to store samples, which he planned to analyze when we got home.

In Cleveland, we paused in front of the Rock and Roll Hall of Fame. I wanted to go inside but Monsieur objected. We didn't.

"It's enough to be near fame, but not inside it," he said. "There you lose the ability to age gracefully."

Sitting at the steering wheel, I sipped my coffee, my peepers glued to the Hall of Fame. My brain bobby-soxed, boogied, did the Bump and Hustled; slam-danced, hip-hopped, and twitched in a mosh pit. When I flipped the dial on the radio and heard one golden oldies station after another, I wondered why people need sameness. I used to swallow the sound of the past too, like it was a sedative, becoming addicted to its comforting effects until I practically overdosed on familiarity. My life was charted in electric guitar chord progressions and everyone else knew the words. I hummed down the highway unwary of accidents.

The frequency was killing me and so was the pitch. I had to turn myself off. When the volume was up, I couldn't think and didn't really care to. Silence escalated the sound of my heartbeat drumming against tight, stretched skin. It was an odd sound, the tom-tom of mortality, but at least it was constant. Unlike Monsieur, who was draped in white noise like a crisp linen suit, my life was a Frankenstein of stitched-together pop songs, each one an echo of who I was fucking at the time — or wasn't.

We went down to the shore of Lake Erie and stopped by a chain-link fence outside a private airport called, imaginatively, Millionair. The tarmac was a charm bracelet of Cessnas and small jets glinting in the sun. That cheered him up. Monsieur heaved an optimistic sigh. "Money flies, my dear."

In Detroit we cruised downtown and wondered who drove the cars. They were parked everywhere but we didn't see any people. At one point Monsieur made me double-park in front of a store called Black Beauty. It had a window filled with wigs. Inside, more than a couple of jaws dropped. Monsieur purchased a supply of his favourite nail polish, Hard Candy, in the gunmetal grey shade of Ghetto Girl he insisted was flattering on him.

Dusk descending, we got back in the van and headed through the emptiness of lengthening shadows toward the border. We waited for the light to change at an intersection on a forlorn stretch of condemned brownstones boarded up with plywood planks. I noticed a gap gouged out of the granite in the foundation of a crumbling building. In it was a cat with her litter of kittens. Below them, among the weeds, sprouting through cracks in the sidewalk, someone had placed a plastic jug cut in half and filled it with water. Once more my heart curved and formed a dot, like it was answer on *Jeopardy!* and the question was "What is hope?"

"It's green, dear," Monsieur said impatiently.

We joined the stop-and-go rhumba of red tail lights on the Ambassador Bridge. After an hour's wait, we were finally interrogated by the cute-as-a-button border guard. I red-herringed him with my doe-eyed routine. I could practically hear the birds chirping and see the sparkles in his eyes like in an old movie as he did a half-assed flashlight deal on the back of the van.

"What's with the typewriters, fellas?"

"We picked them up for a museum in Toronto, sir," I said, trying to remember Monsieur's script. "For their industrial design archives or something. From a benefactor in Pennsylvania. They hired us."

"No kidding. You guys run a pickup operation?"

"Officer dear, you're positively clairvoyant," Monsieur piped in.

The guard ignored Monsieur and kept looking at me. There was something gentle about his expression that I liked.

"Everything's computer this computer that these days, eh? It's kind of hard to keep up," he said.

"You got it," I smiled, hating myself.

He grinned back at me. "Both Canadian?" he asked.

I nodded and handed our passports.

"You're a day older than me," he mentioned, passing them back.

"Small world," I said

He looked at me funny. "Where you headed?"

Monsieur leaned over and was in my face. "Toronto. But we're weekending in Windsor, officer darling. We're going to do the casino thing."

I demurely slammed my elbow into his ribs, and he backed off.

"Yeah? Where you staying?"

"Journey's End," Monsieur announced, giving me a look.

"Okey dokey then. Have a good time."

The guard lasered me with his impish green eyes, piercing me to the core. He was just my type: small, taut, and boyish for his age. It was almost a fever, this need I had to rip off his uniform and find out what he was hiding.

"Make sure you watch your wallet now," he said.

"Huh?"

"At the casino."

"Oh yeah. I will. Thank you, sir."

He waved us on. Monsieur rubbernecked to give the guard the once-over.

"He looks a bit like Brad Davis, my dear, don't you think?" he said and turned to me. *Midnight Express* was one of his favourite movies. A handsome young American caught with drugs at the Turkish border is sentenced to life in a hellish prison, where he is repeatedly raped, beaten, and humiliated. But he manages to make a dramatic escape against all odds. Sex, peril, and liberation — Monsieur's Holy Trinity.

"What?" he added when he saw my expression.

"'We're weekending in Windsor, officer darling?' You always butt in when someone's interested in me. You can't stand not being the centre of attention, can you? Can you?"

Monsieur yawned. "You've become so dull since you took up weightlifting," he soapboxed. "You need to do the nasty. A good fuck always does the trick. God knows your infatuations are hard to swallow but anything's better than the truth-and-beauty kick you've been on lately. I swear, the self-awareness movement is giving narcissism a bad name. Before you know it, you'll be reading self-help books. Then it'll be crystals, too much Celtic music, and one day you'll end up in a park wearing sandals with socks, doing something spiritual and bendy at an hour when decent people are at home sleeping off their martinis. Frankly, I wish someone would tell me why people are searching for their inner child when what they need to find is their inner daycare."

"Okay, okay, I get the picture," I said, taking the turnoff into downtown Windsor. Monsieur tapped into his internal customer years ago, and ever since, everything, it seemed, had a price, and I was the complaint department.

"We should celebrate our successful heist, my dear. I feel gamble-y all over."

We passed by the blaring neon of the Caesars Windsor casino and Monsieur clasped his hands together. "Oh Canada, it's good to be back. Well-mannered, well-behaved, polite, orderly, cold, no identity, lacking self-confidence. Hmm, I've just had a heart-warming thought."

"What?" I asked as I swerved into our hotel parking lot.

"We carry the passport of a psychopath."

I turned off the engine and pulled the safety brake. Monsieur went around to the back of the van to collect our bags. I sat for a minute while he fussed.

"My dear?"

Monsieur stood on the pavement and peered at me, holding his bags. I got out and helped him carry the luggage into the hotel, puffing and straining under the weight of Louis Vuitton.

IT WAS JUST before noon the next day. My heart and balls were blue. A lack of love and a lack of sleep had left me randy and off-kilter. I put on my five-and-dime sunglasses and took a pea-green look around. I couldn't believe my luck.

The next best thing to a man in uniform is a man in a union. The bistro's terrace was cheek-to-jowl with butt-smoking trade, free and rough, sexy, striking autoworkers from both sides of the border blowing off steam. They were beautiful and they were everywhere, sitting on plastic chairs at garden tables, some with girlfriends, some with family, some with buddies, some not with anyone and looking self-conscious about it.

I coveted a table with a patio umbrella. I had wanted to go inside, out of the heat, but Monsieur refused to put up with any more air conditioning. We stood like two beached whales in the direct sunlight at the front of the brunch lineup, sweating while we waited. There was a braided yellow wait-to-be-seated rope. I felt like I was being restrained from a homicide instead of an all-day breakfast.

Monsieur cruised two teenagers at a nearby table.

"Chickenhawk," I said.

He gave me the cold shoulder and continued to focus on his prey.

I was a little unsettled and confused by what had happened at the Happy Tap, a local watering hole, the night before, or rather what hadn't happened. I'd left Monsieur in the hotel room to sleep off the all-you-can-eat buffet, six hours of losing at the slots, and a cavalcade of martinis.

It'd been quite a shocker to find our border guard at the bar. I confess he seemed tickled to see me. I know I was tickled to see him. When he told me his name was Danny, an Irish ballad trickled like treacle across my cranium. The fuzzy bar lighting made him look a little like a leprechaun and boy did he have the gift of gab. Bewitched by his blarney, I suction-cupped his lips and we were at it non-stop for over half an hour.

I heard a crash and snapped out of my daydream. A nervous kid with a first-day-on-the-job look started scrounging around on the patio pavement, picking up pieces of broken glass. They were all over the place. The humidity siphoned my pores, and I was close to running on empty. There was a short, welcome breeze whenever one of the panicky summer student servers flew by with trays of eggs Benedict, huevos rancheros, white wine spritzers, sangrias, and beer. A quick swish of movement cockteased me with coolness. Then it dissipated into the dimness of the restaurant like a shameless deb, leaving me tortured by longing. The steaming soup of carbon monoxide and chlorofluorocarbons made me antsy. In weather like this all I wanted to do was drink, fuck, and sleep.

Monsieur Delacroix turned away from his quarry and eyed me from beneath the brim of his floppy sun hat. The armpits of his light beige safari-style outfit were stained with circles of sweat.

"They can't be more than sixteen," I said.

"And your point is ...?"

I told him he looked like Hannibal Lecter. He thought it was a compliment. "Come to think of it, a little Chianti would go down nicely. And I've always had a penchant for fava beans." Monsieur popped his eyes wide open, pressed his top teeth onto his bottom lip, and made a long sucking sound. People stared.

A shirtless bodybuilder walked along the sidewalk beside us. Monsieur's voice trailed away from me along with his eyes, as they followed the hunk to the end of the street. Monsieur sighed and he squinted at me, trying to look malevolent. "Tell me one of your secrets, Clarisse. And don't lie. I can tell."

"Oh, shut up," I said. "You're not normal."

"Normal is the biggest four-letter word in the world, my dear, which is why they had to add two extra letters."

The teenagers overheard us and were busting a gut. One of them smiled at me with tears of laughter in his eyes. A woman in a hostess uniform approached us.

"That young couple asked me to ask you two gentlemen if you'd like to join them," she said. She pointed at the teenagers. I started to offer my no thanks when Monsieur interceded.

"We'd love to," he said.

At least they had a patio umbrella. And an almost full pitcher of sangria. They asked the hostess for two more glasses, and she conferred with the nervous waiter who plunked them down in front of us lickety-split. They were still steaming, dishwasher fresh, and smelled vaguely salty with a hint of bleach. It was good to be in the shade.

"I'm Tate," said the boy as he poured sangria for us.

"Sharon," said the girl. She shook our hands vigorously.

I introduced the both of us. Monsieur sat down and showed a hint of talon.

The drinking age was nineteen. I was a bit surprised they'd been served. My curiosity obviously showed. Tate gave me a sheepish grin and mouthed "fake ID" to the syncopation of fruit slices and ice cubes plunking into a tumbler: one of the great sounds of summer. Then I saw the gold Amex card beside Tate's side plate. There was only one way a boy his age had plastic like that. I smelled gated community.

"To all the great slasher films ever made," said Tate, raising his glass. "Freddy, Mike, Jason, Leatherface, Hannibal" — he looked at Monsieur — "this is for you." We all reciprocated. I drank almost the entire tumbler and set it down with a satisfied gasp.

"You're an aficionado, I take it?" asked Monsieur, delighted.

Tate scrunched up his face. "Hunh?"

"He means fan," I said.

"Oh yeah, big time," said Tate. He squirmed in his chair and pulled a card out of the back pocket of his black jeans. He handed it to me.

"The Jeffrey Dahmer Fan Club," I told Monsieur. I handed it back. Monsieur nodded his head in approval.

"But he's dead," I mentioned.

Tate sat up straight. "He's a fucking martyr, man."

"No, he's a serial killer and he's dead."

"Whatever," said Tate.

The sun hit the top of his head, giving his dyed black hair a cherry-red aura. He boomeranged my glance and smiled. A cute set of choppers like his could cut through your average joe's misgivings, but not me.

Sharon looked uneasy. "We're not queers," she advised us. "We're Goths."

Monsieur smiled. "Everyone's got an angle," he said.

Monsieur was an expert on angles and appreciated good lines, so long as they slanted but didn't cross. He pretty much lived in a parallel universe, although parallel to what was the sixty-four-thousand-dollar question.

"And where, pray, did you two angels descend from?" Monsieur inquired.

"We're from Detroit," said Sharon. She made Detroit sound like a failed exam. "Grosse Point, if you're totally into factoids. It's a suburb."

I was right. An affluent bastion of privilege built on cars.

"Our friend told us this thing you guys say when you march," said Sharon. "How's that thing that Blake told us go, Tate?"

"We're here, we're queer, we're not just shopping," he said.

"Yeah, that's right. Fucking hilarious."

Monsieur contorted. "People who march should all be shot," he said. "Of course all we're doing is shopping."

I told them Monsieur wasn't very political and helped myself to more sangria. I was already feeling pleasantly buzzed but needed fortification for my date later.

"Oppression is no excuse for fascism," Monsieur added.

I kept my lips sealed. Sharon and Tate furrowed their brows and nodded. Tate's dog collar must have been uncomfortable in that heat, not to mention the black hooded robe Sharon wore. Her hair was dyed black like Tate's. They were both quite gaunt and could have used a little sunshine. Monsieur may have set out to rob the cradle but it looked like he was closer to robbing the grave. Not that it would have made any difference to him.

"And you?" Tate asked, beaming me with his pearly whites.

"What?"

"Are you political?"

I shrugged and looked down at my drink. "Groups give me the heebie-jeebies."

Tate stretched a leg under the table and tried to play footsie with me. It caught me off guard that Sharon didn't know he was a three-dollar bill. Whatever game he was playing, the rules were being written on the spot. I pulled away and tucked my feet under my chair.

I tapped a finger against my forehead. "This is political." I tapped the vicinity of my heart. "And this. Belief is action."

"Kumbaya," said Monsieur, waving his hand in the air to indicate another pitcher.

"Man, no kidding," Tate said. He yawned and I noticed his tongue was pierced.

"Tate, get serious," said Sharon. She held up a hand to shield her eyes from the sun. I detected a faint scar on her wrist. "You have a point, kind of."

I took off my sunglasses and rubbed my eyes. "I wasn't trying to make one."

I was preoccupied. I was thinking about last night, about Danny. I'd found myself even more drawn to him in civvies and itched to unravel the mystery of his jeans and T-shirt. "I'm not into one-night stands," he'd said when I made my move at last call. The lights went up full. There was a hickey on his neck, a little bruise of pleasure. The Happy Tap started to drain so we left. I was hurt; I hadn't said anything about one night. When I dropped him at his apartment, he gave me a peck on the cheek and said he wanted to see me again. What the hell was happening to me?

I was usually *comme çi, comme ça* about being turned down. I could hear the mosquito drone of that little devil Cupid. He was circling with his arrow, waiting to draw blood.

MONSIEUR KICKED MY shin and I came to. Our waiter anxiously deposited another pitcher, spilling some sangria on my lap.

"Thorry," he said.

"It's okay." I had a weak spot for braces, the poor guy.

By the time he was back with a cloth, I'd mopped up the stain on my pants as best I could, using a paper napkin decorated with a cartoon parrot sitting in a cabana chair and sipping a fruity drink. Monsieur and I ordered bacon and eggs over easy with toast, mine brown, his white. Then Monsieur topped up our drinks and proposed a toast to the younger generation. His accent had grown thicker, something he always pulled when he was trying to impress. It was a questionable dialect from one of Paris's murkier *arrondissements*. Honestly, if the Eiffel Tower had ever cast a shadow on Monsieur's curly bean, it was only in his imagination.

We clinked.

Tate downed his drink, wiped his mouth, and said, "It's the law of the jungle out there, man. The hunter and the hunted."

The kid had seen too many action hero flicks. Then again, so had I. He was sitting right next to Monsieur. From the corner of my eye, I noticed him grab Monsieur's knee and give it a squeeze.

"So, if you guys don't call yourselves queer, what do you call yourselves?" Sharon asked.

Monsieur leaned in, looking conspiratorial. "Thieves."

He was such a liar. We were just dime store swindlers with a truckload of old typewriters we planned to dump on a bunch of collector queens.

Monsieur swelled his chest and began to pontificate. "As Andy Warhol once said, good artists copy, great artists steal."

"That wasn't Warhol," I said. "That was Picasso."

"Details, my dear, details."

If God appeared in Monsieur's details, so did his stand-in, that hot-headed, horn-topped hoofer waiting in the wings, ready to stage a ruse and take over the lead.

Our breakfasts arrived. I sat back and troughed, staying silent while Monsieur held court with the kids. They showed him some CDs they'd bought. He faked interest until one piqued his fancy. Monsieur stopped eating and put down his knife and fork. His chin was shiny with bacon grease.

"That's Marilyn Manson," said Sharon. "He's awesome."

"That's our favourite CD of his," Tate added.

Monsieur peered at it so closely his nose touched the jewel box. Astigmatism prevented him from wearing contacts and he wouldn't be seen in public wearing glasses. I was trying to figure out how to tell him that his bronzer was getting dewy.

"*Smells Like Children*," he said, reading the CD's title aloud. "I agree entirely. It does."

"You should hear it," said Tate.

Monsieur put down the CD, picked up his knife and fork, and polished off a remaining rind smothered in congealing yolk. Sopping up guck with the last of his toast, he shook his head.

"I don't care about popular music, my dear," he said. "I care about popular packaging."

He popped the toast into his mouth, swallowed, put down his implements, shoved his plate to the side, napkinned his puss, and lit up a fresh smoke. The ghost of a lectern seemed to waver before him, or was it a pedestal?

"Let me tell you my Theory of Plastic," he announced.

I'd heard this theory before, but just in case he had any new insights I got out my pocket cassette recorder and set it on the table. Monsieur cleared his throat and was off to the races.

"Plastic as we know it had its start last century with the British Navy and the Industrial Revolution," he said. "The Brits conquered the world without a shred of remorse, the dears. You have to be careful about remorse, which is anathema to building an empire. Guilt quickly purges offensive action. It is the enema of the people.

"The Brits invented a new kind of human being. It was called the middle class and its purpose in life was to assume control through consumption. It forged mutations of what it did not have and advertised itself into believing that looking like the people in power was the same as being the people in power. The British Empire was viral with new cultures from starving places. They spread out and ate at the fabric of the status quo. To keep themselves safe from bad mojo, the middle class drew the drapes and stuffed their parlours with reproductions of what the outside world looked like.

"Then the twentieth century threw in a couple of world wars to help establish marketing guidelines and America was defiantly on top. Plastic took over. It was popular because it could be made into so many things and wear so many hats, and quickly. It made life easier, more convenient. More people could consume. Some people confused it with democracy. What happened next, we can attribute to male adolescents who weren't getting any sex."

Monsieur paused to ogle Tate and I thought I'd have to pass him a drool cup.

He continued. "They flirted with binary consequences instead of cock and pussy. These they set into sequence and boxed in plastic along with a network developed by the Pentagon, which — being Goths you'll no doubt appreciate this — has five sides echoing a pentagram, whose five-pointed star inside a circle is believed to ward off the devil. Fearing contamination, we drew the drapes, sat at home, and watched the plastic box's version of what the world looked like. But our homes were just as viral as the world outside, teeming with an infectious babble of voices pretending to be someone they weren't, most of them shopping."

At this point Tate put up his hand and asked what anathema meant so I handed him my pocket Oxford, always handy when Monsieur got going. Monsieur continued with a shudder.

"The spiders were trapped in their own web along with flies who'd followed their own buzz in, and no one could tell the predator from the prey. It was fabulous. Mind you, any housewife in India who doesn't even have tap water would roll her eyes if you told her the web is worldwide. But we don't live in India, so who cares?"

Tate and Sharon stared at him. I excused myself and went to the john. After I took a piss, I splashed some cold water over my face and put eye drops in my red-veined bulbs. I looked in the mirror and tweaked a grey hair. The lack of sleep showed, even more gruesome in the harsh lighting, like I was wearing vampire makeup. I hadn't had a chance to work out on the road, so I wasn't as cut as I'd been, but I didn't look too out of shape. The sangria stain had dried, forming a blood-red splotch around my groin. The automatic hand drier wasn't working, so I wiped my hands on my pants, bought some condoms from a dispenser, and went back outside.

The patio had thinned out. Monsieur's soliloquy was reaching its conclusion as I sat down in my chair. Our plates were gone, and the second pitcher of sangria was totaled. Tate was filling in a credit card slip.

"And so, you see, my dears, if you put Jeffrey Dahmer and Mahatma Gandhi naked into a locked room, their conversation would only be as good as the plastic that preserved it for future generations to hear and have a good laugh at."

Tate scrawled his signature and put away his gold-plated pen. "Who is Mahatma Gandhi?" he asked.

"He led India to independence. He was a pacifist," I told him.

"I think his biggest contribution was to fashion," said Monsieur. "He really knew how to work an off-the-shoulder moment."

"He was a martyr," I added. "He's dead."

Tate shrugged. "Whatever."

Sharon and Tate invited us to join them at a video arcade. Monsieur was bug-eyed at the prospect, but I declined. I skedaddled over to the hotel to bag a few beauty zs before my tryst, condoms shuffling optimistically in my pocket. I wondered why a guy like Danny would be toe-in-toe-out about going to home base. Most guys who liked me headed straight for the sack, don't pass Go, don't collect $200. Maybe he'd been hurt, but who hadn't? Besides, he seemed too sure of himself for that to be the case. Maybe that uniform of his really did hide something worth finding out. It gave me a hard-on just thinking about it.

I got to my room, set the alarm clock for an hour, and slipped between the sheets on one of the two twin beds, but I couldn't sleep. I lay there blinking at the ceiling fan. An out-of-whack spring gnawed into my back. Maybe Danny was just old-fashioned and wanted some kind of commitment. I guess if I was honest with myself, I had to admit that he'd tripwired my warning system. I didn't want to get into something I couldn't get out of without a ton of melodrama.

I suddenly remembered that I'd left my tape recorder on the patio table, so I got out of bed, had a shower, and went to retrieve it before I met Danny. The sky was starting to cloud over. As I walked at a quick clip to the bistro, my heart started to beat like a time bomb. It struck me that nothing in life was subtle anymore. People hunted for meaning the way they used to hunt for food, snaring diversions instead of sustenance.

"WHEN I WAS a kid, I'd get so bored I'd come down here to watch the people in Detroit kill each other," said Danny. He looked across the river and nodded his head at the city's skyline. "That was this group of us in Windsor's in-joke."

We sat on the grass by the edge of the water, having a late-afternoon picnic.

"Didn't you have a TV?" I asked.

"Sure. Cable. And before that we had a big honking antenna on our roof. Remember those?"

"Yeah."

The front end of a tattooed dragon mounted his biceps and peeked out from beneath the right sleeve of his T-shirt. The dragon's fire breathed his name. The sleeve was rolled up and I could tell he'd ironed it. Danny threw his bone into the bucket and got himself another drumstick.

"Scary, isn't it?"

"What?"

"Information, waves of it, penetrating our bodies without us seeing it, hearing it, or understanding it."

"Or tasting it," I said. I helped myself to a piece of chicken.

"Sperm counts are highly overrated," said Danny.

I glanced at the darkening sky. It looked like there could be lightning anytime. Danny belched and excused himself. His belch joined his uniform on my go-for-it checklist, even if it was kind of contradictory. The contradiction was sexy too. I don't know why I found bodily functions masculine. I was just as crass as the next guy on that count. A man was a man if he kept a cork in his heart but the more that flowed from other organs the better. Not caring was cathartic.

"Everything here was channelled in from somewhere else," said Danny. "Not just on TV, but the jobs and everything. It's so flat here no matter where you stand you see that rising above you." He pointed at the city. "Maybe that's why when I was growing up, I was always trying to be someone I wasn't."

The scenery evaporated as his voice reached out and wrapped around my heart like a snake. I wanted to be subdued, swallowed, to be inside him. Monsieur was wrong about voices. Dead wrong. I liked the gentle way Danny talked. It soothed me: part metronome, part poem, a stopgap in time. He was easy to be with. It was like having a brother.

He passed me the bottle. The brown grass crinkled as I rolled over onto my side, leaned on my elbow, and took it from him.

"Cheers," I said.

He finished chewing, swallowed, and tossed away another bone, wiping his mouth with the back of his arm. "My old man was basically in front of the TV all the time. He got disability when his back screwed up at the plant. Beer and TV, TV and" — he took back the Bud — "beer."

"The plant?"

"GM."

"Oh, right."

Danny sat quietly for a moment or two, then took a long pull from the bottle and wiped off his mouth again. I noticed for the first time how white and perfectly aligned his teeth were. I wondered if they were capped or even real.

"Why didn't you leave, if you thought it was so shitty here?" I asked.

"Home is home, I guess. Besides, everywhere is the same these days," he said and took a swig. "I did leave, once, a long time ago. I had to go to Toronto for a while."

"Had to? Why had to?"

He didn't say anything for a couple of minutes then got a thoughtful look on his face. He reached over and brushed the bangs out of my eyes. I hoped there weren't any grey hairs I'd missed.

"You're a good person," he said.

It was fine by me if he wanted to change the subject, but I thought it was weird that he'd suddenly become reticent after being so candid. I didn't believe in pressing people to dig up something they'd buried and left for dead. My closet had a skeleton or two, so I knew better.

"Not really," I said. "I'm just me."

"That's what I meant."

I wanted to get in his pants so badly I could taste it.

"Before it was called Windsor it was called South Detroit," he said. "Did you know that?"

"No."

"Yeah."

"No, I mean no I didn't know."

"Oh. Yeah. Well, it was. That was in the nineteenth century."

"Hmm."

I followed his gaze across the Detroit River to the Renaissance Center. Its chrome pistons towered high above the water's edge. The sun was completely gone. The prominent, sleek central tube of the complex rose like a fuck-you finger against a flat, surgical-tray sky. It was a last resort from the '70s, stuck among much older bowel-coloured buildings. I perceived a hint of heyday in their good deco bones, but they were tired and succumbing to osteoporosis. The vibrant beat of Motown had left long ago. Aretha Franklin's pink Cadillac had broken through the guardrails on the Freeway of Love and crashed. I thought about Monsieur's scrapings of rust.

The slate summer storm clouds hung low above the city and moved slowly toward us. A scent of ozone came in from off the water, tendrilled past us, and diffused through the resigned neighbourhoods of Windsor, whose once manicured streets had chipped a nail. They could have used a little of Monsieur's Ghetto Girl.

Danny passed me the bottle again and I finished it off, then tossed it into a trash can several yards away.

"Hey, good one," he said.

I shrugged and smiled. "Good hand and eye coordination. In high school I played basketball, baseball, and soccer," I lied.

He looked at me. My balls tingled and shrank. It was nice. I began to forget myself. Then he got shy. He scratched his head, folded his knees up to his chest, and rested his forearms on them. He said softly, "Y'know, you're all right."

"Thanks. I like you too."

"Can I trust you?"

"No," I said, and ruffled his hair. "Yeah."

Danny smiled, blushed, and buried his head between his knees. I felt a rush of blood and my skin prickled pleasantly. A sweet and sour ache throbbed against my breastplate. I hadn't felt that for a long time. We sat, not looking at each other, listening to the breeze rustle the leaves of a nearby poplar as our chemicals rubbed noses, giving birth to new DNA sequences, and committing multiple murders at the molecular level. I carried no condom to fit the air, no prophylactic for feeling. I was as vulnerable as I was volatile. For me it was like being a teenager all over again, without the music. That was okay. Our calm was the buildup to the 45 rpm hit single before the album came out. I heard it like an animal hears something in the silence beyond human earshot and in it finds the music of the future.

"You can touch me," I said.

"Here? In public?"

"No. Here." I drew his hand to my left pec and placed it there.

"No, keep it there," I said.

"Sorry. It's just that you don't seem like the nipple ring kind of guy."

I laughed. "I'm not that kind of guy. I just like to get my tits pulled every now and again."

"Like that ...?"

"Yeah."

He smiled. The delicate crow's feet around his eyes crinkled. Danny put his other hand on my chest and fell on top of me. I put my arms around him and kissed him, stroking his arms. His skin was unusually soft and smooth. We started to wrestle playfully, ignoring the stares of people who walked by as we rolled and tumbled over the ruined grass. Although he was smaller and lighter than me, Danny was strong. He managed to pin me down and straddled my hips. He held my arms against the ground. I couldn't struggle out of his grip.

"Surrender?" he said.

"No."

"Say Uncle."

"Unh-unh. No way."

I tried to break free, but the little guy was a tough son of a bitch.

"You don't give up easy, do you?" he said.

"Okay, all right, I give in. You win."

He relaxed on top of me. We started to neck. An elderly couple walking by us whispered and picked up their pace. I untucked the back of his T-shirt and slipped my hands underneath. He was muscular yet the skin on his back was as soft as his forearms, a child's skin.

"Nice," I said, looking in his green eyes, a forest I could get lost in and not care if I was ever found.

The entire sky lit up for a split second as lightning hit the top of the Renaissance Center. There was a crack of thunder. Then the rain started. We jumped up.

"Why don't we go over to the Happy and shoot a few?" Danny suggested.

"Sure." I was game to please him.

We ran all the way there, Danny a little bit ahead of me. He'd confirmed my second thoughts. I'd tell Monsieur he could do what he wanted with the typewriters. I was washing my hands of them. Danny was wrong, I did give up easy. I wanted to surrender badly. The best way to get control of my life was to let go of what little I had left and see what happened.

"THEY TOOK IT, my dear."

"What?"

"They took *it*, the typewriter."

I was standing in the doorway, silhouetted by the light shining from the hallway into our darkened room, casting a shadow. I'd been walking and walking and walking, trying to wrap my head around the truth about Danny. I was drenched.

Monsieur had drawn the curtains. I could make him out as a lump on the farthest bed. I walked in and turned on one of the bedside lamps, then went back and shut the door. I sat down on the bed beside Monsieur. He'd been covering his head with his arms. He put them down and stared up at the ceiling. He looked as hangdog as I felt and had a nasty bruise and cut on one side of his forehead. A bloodied hand towel was crumpled up beside his pillow. The pillow had some blood on it too, and bronzer.

"What happened?"

"My dear, you're getting everything wet."

He got up, pulled out some dry clothes, and started to change.

"So, tell me what happened."

"I'm so ashamed."

I wasn't in the mood for Monsieur's dying swan act. "Forget about that. Just tell me."

"Well, on our way to the video arcade, I started to tell Sharon and Tate about our, um, vocation."

"That was fucking brilliant."

"My dear, don't forget, I'm not attractive like you. I'm interesting."

"Yeah, well, sorry about that."

Monsieur propped himself on an elbow and lit a cigarette. "They said they wanted to see the typewriters."

"You showed them."

"Yes."

I didn't normally smoke but bummed one off Monsieur. He lit it for me.

"Oh," I said. "I get it now. The Sholes and Glidden."

"Yes."

"Your favourite."

"Yes. I was explaining to them that it was the first typewriter, as we know it. I told them that it looked like a sewing machine because Sholes and Glidden was in fact a sewing machine company. I said there was something poetic about the connection of type to clothing. They liked that."

"I bet they did. I bet they also liked the fact that it was worth thousands and thousands of dollars."

I fastened my belt and slipped on my cowboy boots. I went into the bathroom to comb my hair, keeping the door open so I could still hear Monsieur.

"I was in the middle of elucidating the QWERTY system, how it evolved so that the most commonly struck keys wouldn't jam," he said. "Suddenly I was hit on the head, and when I came to, the Sholes and Glidden was gone and so were they."

I tossed my cigarette into the toilet and flushed.

"Thousands of dollars down the crapper," said Monsieur. "Why are you smiling?" he asked when I peeked out of the bathroom.

"Crapper, I've never heard you use that word before."

"Well, my dear, after all this time together some of you has got to rub off. What do you think we should do?"

"Nothing."

"Nothing?"

"Nothing. They'll be long gone by now, safe at home in daddy's car. There's nothing we can do."

"But what about —"

"They're American. Our word's worth fuck this side of the border," I said. Being stripped of my expectations made me light-hearted.

"Can I use your umbrella?" I asked Monsieur.

"Yes, I'm certainly not going anywhere like this. It's over there on the chair by the desk."

I told him my plans. I told him about Danny.

"My dear, that's perverse," said Monsieur.

"Look who's talking."

I took the umbrella and headed for the door.

"Where are you going?"

"I saw a sign in an all-night store down the street. I could use a job if I'm going to stay."

"But here?"

"Yeah, here. I kind of like being on the border. The uncertainty gives me confidence."

"But my dear, Windsor?"

"They used to call it South Detroit," I said and walked out the door.

I WENT TO the all-night store and filled in an application. The Rasta guy at the cash told me there'd been fifty people in that day about the job but most of them were kids. He said I'd stand a better chance, I was mature. I'd probably get an interview.

"How much does it pay?" I asked.

"Minimum."

I got myself a cherry slushy and sat at a small counter by the window where a couple of losers from the casino sobered up on stale coffee. The store's decor was orange, brown, and yellow, like that place in Ohio. I guessed some retail pooh-bah somewhere must have ordained those colours. There was Muzak. I recognized a sanitized AM hit from my high school days. I looked out at the rain.

At the bar, after a game of pool, I propositioned Danny and he invited me home. There was a break in the rain, so we walked. And we talked. And he told me.

I always had a knack for looking at a person and decorating where they lived in my mind's eye and finding out that I was usually pretty accurate. Danny's place was no exception. His apartment was predictably decorated, neutral beiges and browns, decked out in the kind of furniture they advertise late at night on TV. It was carpeted wall-to-wall and scented with air freshener. There were knick-knacks on the sills, trophies from amateur league sports on the shelves, pictures of his family and of himself on the TV and stereo, some showing what he used to be like. I was in new territory, one without borders.

They had a good clinic in Toronto. He'd aced all the psychological tests and there'd been no post-op complications.

"Thanks," I said when he handed me a double rye and seven, "I need this."

I finished it in two gulps and set the glass on the coffee table.

"Use a coaster. Here."

"Oh. Sure. Thanks."

We were in the living room on a sofa, at separate ends.

"Why didn't you tell me before?" I asked.

"It wasn't any of your business until now. It's private."

"You led me on."

"No, I didn't. You wouldn't leave me alone."

"You knew how I felt."

"So? I didn't know how I felt. I don't make choices till I know. Do you? It seemed pointless to tell you until I knew if you were going to be a problem."

"That's a good one, me a problem. You're the one pretending to be someone you're not."

"Pretending? I'm not the one pretending. She was pretending." Danny pointed at one of the photos. He got up and walked across the room where he went through his CD rack and put one on. *Shadowland*, by k.d. lang. He sat back down on the sofa.

"Sorry, I didn't mean what I said," I said.

"Yeah, you meant it. But that doesn't mean it's true. Sometimes I get hit on by people who don't know their ass from a hole in the ground. If you want to meet a borderline case, transition."

I wanted to touch him but couldn't. Instead, I said, "Well, you know what they say, there but for the grace of God ..."

Danny gave me a thoughtful smile. "I'm more interested in the grace of men," he said.

I needed time to myself. I told Danny so when I left his place. I said I'd call him.

"When?"

"I don't know."

Just before he closed the door, he said, "There are some things in life so much like love you can't tell them apart."

I thought about it and said, "It's kind of like typing, isn't it?"

"What do you mean?"

"They used to make copies on carbon paper, replicas of what they thought and felt."

Danny smiled. "That's what happens to bodies," he said. "When we're gone, all we leave behind is carbon."

He leaned over and kissed me. It was the first time we'd touched since I'd found out who he was. It was scary but it was nice. I was turned inside out, my guts wrapped around my neck.

Earlier at the hotel, when I was in the bathroom combing my hair, Monsieur talked about things that didn't matter to me anymore, I gave myself a good look in the mirror. They say some people succeed because they trust their gut instincts, as though instincts are a secret well and trust a divining rod. From where I stood, instincts weren't that mystical, they were a squirming puzzle of pieces that somehow linked. It was a real art to put them in order. I needed to figure out how to rearrange my guts soon; they were tightening their grip on my throat. Maybe, I thought, it would be easier if I just let them choke me.

THE RAIN SUBSIDED outside the all-night store. The window was prismatic with the lights of passing traffic. I finished my slushy. One of the casino types got up to go and bumped into me on his way out, almost knocking me off my stool. He didn't even apologize.

It's like that these days. People have lost their manners.

Mister Makeup

ROSE STOOD OUTSIDE of a Judas Priest concert at the Pacific Coliseum wearing a dog costume, one arm over the shoulder of a teenage boy.

"Hug him closer!" yelled a girl holding a Polaroid camera, presumably his girlfriend.

Rose obliged and yanked his head closer to hers.

"Wait, just a sec," he said, sweeping back his mullet. Rose smelled weed.

The kid wore a Judas Priest T-shirt. The band's lead singer was a vision in black leather from head to toe, all of it studded. The sleeveless vest to show off his guns. The knee-high military boots. The gladiator cuffs on both his forearms. The police hat with a death's head instead of a badge. He looked like some of the men Rose had seen at a gay leather bar in Toronto that Trevor took her to when she visited last year, Cell Block. The lead singer and his bandmates had the same brooding, tough guy stance and come-hither glower. Rose smiled, thinking how much Trevor would appreciate the irony of the metalhead group's album title emblazoned on the boy's shirt: *Defenders of the Faith*.

Rose thought about Trevor all the time these days, ever since his diagnosis.

"Now smile!" the girlfriend shouted in a chirpy, pep rally voice, lurching Rose back to reality.

Rose held up a paw and waved in lieu of a smile. Pain shot up her arm. The product safety mascot's massive noggin was growing heavier the longer she had it on. She could swear it was digging permanent grooves into her shoulders. She thought she could feel her vertebrae collapsing and colliding as her spine compressed beneath its weight.

The Coliseum was on the grounds of the Pacific National Exhibition. It was the end of Labour Day weekend, the last day of the exposition. Rose was supposed to be strolling through the presentation halls, past the midway rides and along the game concourses, handing out product safety comic books to children and parents. But the heat had become so unbearable that she decided to settle on a stationary strategy and exploit the high traffic footfall outside the concert venue. Instead of passing them out one at a time as she'd been doing, she placed a towering pile of comics close by, which were rapidly disappearing. She could get back to the booth when they were all gone, shut it down for the night, and then grab some dinner with Sol.

An excruciating late-summer heat wave had been going on for weeks. Rose's burdensome costume enveloped her in heavy, unbreathing, synthetic fabric piquant with the dried perspiration of dozens of previous wearers. She accessed air though eyeholes covered in tight black latticework that masked her face. The tiny apertures allowed a limited, pinhole view of the world. From which, at this moment, she could discern more and more people crowding around her clutching their cameras. They were oblivious to the stifled lesbian sequestered inside, suffering in silence. Which, from Rose's experience, was pretty much par for the course.

"'Man is least himself when he talks in his own person. Give him a mask, and he will tell you the truth.' Oscar Wilde wrote that," Rose remembered her professor saying during a lecture in the gender studies course she took her last year of grad school, as an introduction to a slideshow on the day's topic, Sadomasochism and BDSM: Role-Playing in the Queer Community.

It was the university's first course in a new academic field. Intrigued, Rose had signed up on a whim. The professor was a middle-aged woman so earnest that she always seemed on the verge of panic. She had a perpetually astounded expression exacerbated by the long, severe ponytail she wore yanked back so tightly that her forehead never moved, and she always wore turtlenecks. Her appearance and manner seemed at odds with the slideshow she was presenting. Rose was familiar with the homoerotic illustrations by Tom of Finland — Trevor had a book — but most of the other students were not, gauging by the nervous giggles and a thumbs-down review from a back-of-the-room critic: "Give me a fucking break."

The professor began her lecture, clicking through cartoonish images of macho-man sailors, cowboys, cops, and leather daddies with skyscraper penises, Brobdingnagian bums, and chest to waist ratios so waspish they were Barbie-level ludicrous. The professor posited that gay men appropriated outmoded signifiers of masculinity to subvert biases about male identity. She said that leather play was an act of defiance and political transgression. "Thoughts?" she asked the class as everyone scrambled for their dictionaries.

"Oh please," was Trevor's clipped response that night at Cell Block. Finding herself surrounded by what looked like a live-action version of Tom of Finland, Rose had mentioned her professor's theory while they were grabbing a beer at the bar. "We dress like this to get fucked," Trevor continued, shouting above the dance music and adjusting his harness. "To get laid, not make a statement about gender norms. For pleasure. And girl, nothing is more subversive than pleasure."

"My professor said it, not me," Rose responded, smiling as Trevor handed her a beer. "Besides," she continued, looking around the bar, "I'm more interested in the female mystique than the male mistake."

"Good one!" Trevor replied, and they clinked bottles. "Oh, I love this song!" he added. The DJ was spinning "Sex Crime" by the Eurythmics. He grabbed Rose and yanked her onto a dance floor surrounded by bars meant to emulate a prison, a prison where all the inmates just got their Get Out of Jail Free card.

Rose always got a kick out of getting a rise out of Trevor, and vice versa. A mutual fondness for banter, puns, and repartee brought them together back in high school, where they wielded words as weapons to keep the bullies at bay. Or, more aptly, armour.

Incapacitated by cuteness, Rose squirmed, trying to get comfortable in her dog outfit. Oscar Wilde was only partly right. Her disguise hindered not hastened telling the truth. She was wearing it because she needed the money. Sometimes masks are transactional.

"Say cheese!" chirped the girl with the camera. There was a whirring sound, then a click, then out popped a picture.

"It'll take a couple of minutes to develop but I need to take another one," she said, giving her boyfriend a sour look. "Why'd you have to make the devil horns? You know my parents already think you're a bad influence. I want to be able to put this on my dresser mirror. If Mom comes into my room cleaning and sees you doing this" — she held up a hand with her two middle fingers and thumb pressed against the palm, her pinkie and index finger raised like horns — "she's going to go all Jesus on me. You know what she's like. Why do you think I have to hide my Madonna albums?"

"Okay, what-the-fuck-ever. How about a peace sign?"

"Sure, fine. Just don't look like an asshole."

Rose noticed a silver crucifix around the girl's neck. Rose

guessed it was meant to be ironic. Christ dangled at the epicentre of substantial cleavage further enhanced by a low-cut crop top. The big hair, the scrunchie, the stacked bangles, the crinoline miniskirt, the army boots — she was one of millions of Madonna clones mass-incubated by MTV.

"Okay, smile!" shouted the girl with the camera. This time her tone was demanding, not encouraging.

Rose half-heartedly raised her paw again. The kid made a peace sign.

"Perfect!" said the girl as her Polaroid regurgitated a snapshot. She waved the picture in the air to dry it, then brought it over to show them. "You're both SO cute!"

Rose nodded her head in agreement, then pointed at the pile of comic books.

"The comics are a little young for us," said the girl. "But I have two younger brothers. They'll like it."

The coupled drifted away into the crowd. Rose posed for more pictures, all the time keeping an eye on the quickly dwindling pile of comics. The last thing she wanted was another lecture from her supervisor, Ocean, about not meeting her quota. Team members were tasked with handing out a minimum of five hundred comic books every day of the three-week fair but somehow Rose almost always ended up with a substantial amount leftover. It wasn't Rose's fault that Ocean had overestimated how many they'd be able to distribute, got too many printed, and now had to justify the overrun to her manager.

The line for photographs was thinning. Weary families stumbled through the park's exit gates. Last-minute concertgoers rushed into the Coliseum before the doors closed. Things were still hopping at the other end of the fairground where the rides were, mostly high school and college students out for a final summer hurrah before classes started.

Rose looked around before removing her head to cool off. She didn't want a repeat performance of the other day when she'd taken it off and put it on the pavement to grab a quick drink from a water fountain, oblivious to a group of preschoolers lined up to ride the Teacups. Several broke out bawling when they saw the decapitated canine.

But before Rose had a chance to remove it, an older woman with two young children approached her.

"Do you think I could take a picture of you with my grandchildren?" she asked.

The woman reminded Rose of her own grandmother: the vestiges of an Old World accent, impeccable manners, intelligent grey-blue eyes. The physical resemblance was uncanny, and her clothes a little unsettling. She looked the way Rose's grandmother looked in photo albums, in pictures taken decades before. The vintage cream 1950s Chanel suit worn effortlessly. Coiffed hair, ropes of pearls with matching stud earrings, a pillbox hat topped with a hint of veil, and of course, white kid gloves. She wore a silver cross pendant, dutifully not ironically, sans the son of God. She radiated grace and confidence just like Grandma Esterhazy did. And, just like Grandma Esterhazy, Rose suspected you wouldn't want to get on her bad side.

Lily Esterhazy had been formidable in her day. She was the real brains behind the success of the flourishing seed company Rose's great-grandfather founded, and which his son — Rose's grandfather — had almost brought to ruin. Rose never met her grandfather. He died before she was born. He had quite the reputation for enjoying spending whatever the company earned, until Grandma Esterhazy reined him in.

He'd inherited the company from Rose's great-grandfather but didn't have a clue about how to handle money, according to Rose's father, who now ran the firm. Her grandfather was a "good-time Charlie" who would have ran the company into the ground. But Lily, Rose's paternal grandmother, could spin gold by pinching pennies. Lily and her grandfather fell in love after she was hired as a bookkeeper in the Winnipeg head office when the previous bookkeeper, Rose's Great-Aunt Daisy, retired. Lily could play the corporate purse strings like a virtuoso, and soon took over the company's financial management.

Rose recalled Trevor swooning when she showed him a photo album filled with pictures of her stylish grandmother in the 1940s, '50s, and '60s. How could she forget? From the moment they became friends when they were sixteen, Trevor had embraced Rose's indifference to fashion as a cause and made it his calling to educate her from his encyclopedic knowledge of who wore what when, and why. The comments came fast and furious as he flipped through the photo album pointing at pictures, and no exclamation mark was safe. "Oh my God! I can't believe she's wearing mix and match from Givenchy's first couture separates collection! Give me strength! Look, she's wearing an original Balenciaga barrel suit! And a Dior evening gown! This is beyond!"

Flying to Paris to see the shows was a rare diversion for Rose's workaholic grandmother. True, she was beautiful and fashionable, but behind the scenes, in business, Lily Esterhazy wielded an iron fist in an evening glove. She made the family rich.

Other than taking bookkeeping courses, her grandmother was self-taught. An avid reader, she amassed an immense library over her lifetime, which she bequeathed to Rose in her will, along with a considerable trust fund. Rose wouldn't have access to it until she turned thirty. Her grandmother's will had stipulated that Rose needed to get an education and to experience the world first. Rose and Trevor had planned a trip to Paris when the trust fund kicked in, in honour of her grandmother, but that seemed unlikely now.

There were no drugs for what Trevor had, and everyone who got it died.

"Grandma, why is the dog just standing there?"

Rose heard a child's voice and came to her senses. She saw that the woman they were with was wearing a blue tracksuit, not Chanel, and sensible walking shoes. Rose's heart sank. She was having visions again. She hadn't had any for a couple of days and was hopeful that maybe they'd finally stopped, once and for all. But no. Why wouldn't her grandmother leave her alone?

Rose waved the kids over. Each grabbed a paw. Their grandmother pulled an old camera from out of a leather case strapped to her shoulder, so old that it had a viewfinder and an accordion lens.

"Say cheese!" she said.

"Cheese!" her grandchildren shouted, grinning.

The kids hugged Rose, then scrambled back to their grandmother.

"Now who wants McDonald's?" she asked them as they walked away.

Rose wouldn't have minded some McDonald's right about now. She hadn't eaten all day and was ravenous despite the appetite-suppressing aroma of stale corndogs and rancid popcorn swirling around her, and the pungent history of body odour contained within her costume.

The flaming blue summer sky was starting to simmer down with the approach of twilight, suffused with an orange glow from wildfire smoke seeping over the mountains and into the city. Early evening brought little relief. The haze formed a dome that trapped the heat like a pressure cooker. The air hung heavy, and impatiently still. Even the birds were listless. Normally, seagulls and crows would be circling in a feeding frenzy, ready to swoop and snatch fairground treats. Now they perched silently on power cables, railings, and rooftops.

Rose noticed a solemn row of ravens lining the gutter along the Coliseum's roof, black beaks pointed in the same direction, westward to the ocean, as though collectively sensing a storm on the way, or some kind of truth hidden to humans, perilous, hopeful, and indifferent. Then something set them off. They launched en masse from their various perches, screeching and squawking as they spiralled upward, swarming over the top of the Coliseum, then off into the distance.

Rose felt herself rising into the air as though lifted in the wake of their wings, uncoupled from her body, and no longer fettered by her cumbersome costume. Suddenly there was a poof of smoke from which emerged a disembodied hand. Rose recognized the white glove right away. It reached out and caressed her cheek.

"Rise up, Rose, rise up!"

"Grandma?"

"Rise! Show your power. Dance toward the sun!

"What the fuck?" Rose muttered under her breath.

"It's time to celebrate, Rose. Spirit time has come!"

Why was her grandmother reciting the lyrics to "Rise Up"? The song by Parachute Club was one of Rose's favourites. It was her coming out song, and her coming out album.

"Those who are easily shocked should be shocked more often," her grandmother's voice reverberated in a series of gradually diminishing echoes.

It was a Mae West quote, one of Trevor's favourites. Why was her grandmother quoting Mae West?

But before she could think anymore about it, loud shouting brought Rose crashing back to Earth. She arrived in her body with a jolt and looked around. A couple of teens with a boom box were walking by playing Parachute Club. Then, from around the corner of a closed candy cotton kiosk, appeared Ocean, flapping the product safety comic book in one hand, and looking fit to kill. Sol was following closely behind, lifting her arms in a shrug as if to say sorry. Rose sighed and removed her head. Ocean was in her face ranting before she had a chance to enjoy the rush of comparatively cooler air.

The comic book had been written for ages four through seven, but the insert Rose and Sol had put inside it was for adults and teenagers. It would raise eyebrows, no doubt. There would be outcries of moral outrage, for sure. That was the point. Rose was having last-minute doubts that morning when they were stuffing the comic books, worried they'd be cornered and assaulted by an angry mob. But Sol calmed her down, assuring her that no one was going to see it until they got home.

She was probably right. No one ever opened and read the comic book right after they were handed it. Some just took it out of politeness, then tossed it in the nearest trash can. Others glanced at the cover with mild curiosity, or in some cases chuckled over the cute artwork, then stuffed it away to look at later. Parents grabbed it from their kids, citing sticky fingers and saying they could read it later when they got home.

Rose and Sol had waited for the PNE's last day to distribute what Sol liked to call their "message in a bottle," for two reasons: their contract ended at midnight so they couldn't be fired, and, if they were lucky, the media would pick it up the same week college students were flocking back into town. The chapter on guerilla media tactics in Sol's ancient, dog-eared copy of Abbie Hoffman's *Steal This Book* had proved invaluable. They'd also mailed copies to local papers, and TV and radio stations.

Now, apparently, the cat was out of the bag.

"What were you two thinking?" yelled Ocean. "I'm going to get fired for this! Is that what you wanted? I'm going to get fucking fired!"

That was the last thing Rose heard before she passed out.

"THE MOST IMPORTANT thing is to stick to the script," Ocean announced on the first day of training three months earlier, as she inserted her right hand into one of the puppets. She held it up to show everyone the proper way to manipulate its arms and head. "The second most important thing is to respect your puppet. Think of it not as an extension of yourself, but as your avatar."

Rose looked around the room. There were eight of them besides Ocean, a motley crew of arty university students hired to be puppeteers for a federal summer program to teach children about product safety. At twenty-seven, Rose was older than the rest, whom she deduced were all undergrads. There was a lot of black: clothes, hair, makeup, attitude. Except for Rose, who wore a peasant blouse and heavily adorned jeans, her usual colourful mash-up of patterns and prints.

They sat around a long wooden table in a boardroom in a government building downtown, one of those rooms that take beige to a whole new level, with fibreboard ceiling tiles and jaundiced lighting. A long floor-to-ceiling window faced the reflective glass facade of a skyscraper across the alley. Rose could make out a sliver of the North Shore Mountains through a space between it and an adjoining building.

Ocean stood at one end of the table beside an AV cart set up with a VCR and TV, on which they had just witnessed the puppet show they were training to perform for the edification and disaster-avoidance of preschoolers and early grade schoolers across metropolitan Vancouver and the rest of the province. Posters along the wall opposite the window promoted *The Adventures of Kronk and Bongo*. Someone had done a haphazard job thumbtacking them. They were unevenly spaced, and crooked.

Tall and lean, with long, straight blond hair, Ocean seemed as fresh as laundry dried outside on a breezy, sunny day, then taken inside to be starched and treated with stain guard. She looked like she did lots of yoga, or maybe dance. A physique like hers could only have come from years of training and sacrifice. Her movements were fluid. Her eyes sparkled like tidal pools. Yet not far beneath the surface there seemed to churn a flow and eddy of competing currents. Something tensile lurked in the shallows. Her carefully manicured demeanor of well-being seemed forced and fragile, as though menaced by an undertow threatening to pull her under.

Rose adjusted the batik scarf tying back her curly, red-hennaed hair, then reached into a backpack and pulled out a steno pad and a pen in case she needed to make notes. The backpack had seen better days — certainly more exciting ones based on the mosaic of buttons, badges, and patches from faraway places that conjured up vistas of swaying palms and ancient temples, rice paddies and crystal lagoons, wind chimes and incense, land mines and Agent Orange. It smelled of cinnamon bark and cloves, and was quite pungent apparently, based on the side-eye Rose was getting from a girl with big hair sitting next to her.

Rose countered with a smile. "I like your scrunchy," she said. She clocked the girl's stick-on name tag. "Tamara." She pulled a pack of herbal cigarettes from her pack with a flourish, waving it at Tamara as an explanation. Tamara shifted uncomfortably and looked away.

Rose had picked up the habit while travelling through southeast Asia on a gap year between earning a graduate degree in playwriting at UBC and her upcoming pursuit of a doctorate in theatre studies at the University of Victoria. She was planning a dissertation on the history and use of puppetry as a political tool. Part of the reason she'd been in southeast Asia was to spend some time studying shadow puppet theatre with puppet masters in Thailand and Indonesia. Rose's parents cut her off when she came out, and her grandmother's trust fund didn't kick in for another three years, so Rose relied on loans, grants, and whatever work she could get. When this gig came up, she happily gave notice to the restaurant where she'd been dreading a summer of waiting tables. It was a good wage, you got a car for work, and they gave you a per diem for out-of-town trips.

"What the fuck is an avatar?" asked someone seated down the table from Rose, in a tone laced with a subtle incredulity suggesting that they were all being fed a bunch of baloney.

It was 1985. Computer avatars weren't a thing yet. Rose knew what an avatar was but didn't want to come across as a know-it-all. As the brightest student in her high school graduating class, she'd learned her lesson. Always being the first person to raise your hand in class and correcting other students — or worse, your teachers — banishes you to solitude in the Siberian corner of the lunchroom, cold shoulders and sneers in the halls, and the perpetual taunting of self-appointed apparatchiks who dictate social norms from atop their pedestals of populism and self-aggrandizement. She'd hang out there with her equally disdained best friend, Trevor. He was gay, didn't try to hide it, and had it worse than she did. She hadn't come out yet.

Over lunch they'd discuss schemes — pipe dreams, really — for toppling the status quo, searching for succour in the annals of socialism, temporarily uplifted by the early Lenin-era Soviet acceptance of homosexuality, only to be let down by Stalin making it a crime again. China was no better. Che Guevara was a homophobe. And Castro jailed queers. This made them wary about becoming puppets of Communist ideology. Capitalism too was out of the question. No way would they support the West's military-industrial complex. They decided to settle on being anarchists. This seemed the most flexible option, and appropriate considering that they were too young to vote anyway.

"That's why babies are so happy," Trevor had reasoned one day over lunch, as he and Rose surveyed the adjoining tables with seating arrangements that reflected who was at the top of the athletic, art room, and lab geek hierarchies, and who was at the bottom. "Because they're anarchists."

Living in a capitalist democracy meant you had the right to exercise free speech, as currently evidenced by a popular headline scrawled on washroom walls and transit stalls, "AIDS kills fags dead!" This was a popular sentiment, albeit lacking journalistic jurisprudence: the disease was killing everyone who got it, not just fags. The slogan, a take on an ad campaign for a well-known brand of insect repellent, was popping up everywhere, especially in toilets, churches, and other places where shit went down. Missing the memo about loving the sinner but hating the sin, religious zealots trumpeted that AIDS was God's way of punishing homosexuals. They were mum on the fact that somehow the Lord had overlooked lesbians.

Trevor had been diagnosed a few months back. Although he lived in Toronto now, Rose kept in close touch with him. They talked on the phone almost every week. Every month she received in the mail a copy of his own exercise in self-expression, a photocopied, hand-stapled zine called *Roach Clip*. As explained in his introduction to the first issue, he'd started the zine as "a voice for people with AIDS like me. People treat us like cockroaches because they're ignorant, so why not give them some clips of what life is really like for us? I mean, it's not like I have anything left to lose." Trevor desktop published the zine using a new Mac that had been donated to an organization of PWAs he belonged to. Rose had the most recent issue of *Roach Clip* in her backpack. It included his most hard-hitting article so far, "My Life as a Monster." There was a picture of Trevor looking thin and gaunt, his face spotted with lesions.

"That's a good question, Solange, but let's keep our use of language respectful," Ocean said. "What's an avatar? Maybe Kronk can tell us."

She was referring to the puppet draped over her right arm, which was supposed to be an alien from outer space. It had a large, bulbous, green head with pointy ears, tufts of orange hair, stocky antennae, and yellow eyes, and wore a sparkly, azure kaftan trimmed in gold. It was bald; its head had a seam at the back that made it look like a bum. According to the puppet show script, Kronk and his friend Bongo — who looked identical except that Bongo's glitter kaftan was periwinkle, not azure, and his tufts of hair were yellow, not orange — visit their friend on Earth, a goofy-looking dog called Buddy who wants everyone to get along. And not kill themselves using everyday household products.

"Kronk is always happy to help," Ocean continued in a voice Rose guessed was supposed to sound extraterrestrial but instead sounded suspiciously like Santa Claus — a C-list department store Santa in a big box mall in a distant suburb far from talent or verisimilitude.

"Um, you can call me Sol like you used to at home, Ocean. And yeah, sure, let's hear what the puppet has to say. Bring it on!"

Rose turned to get a better look at Sol, drawn by the dripping honey of disdain in her voice, not to mention her revelation. This seemed to get everyone else excited too. "Like you used to at home ..." What did that mean? Shoulders unhunched and swivel chairs squeaked as everyone twisted in the direction of Sol's voice. Nothing motivates a group better than gossip. Or wakes up a roomful of world-weary liberal arts students, now all staring at Sol.

Slender and boyish, Sol sat slumped back in her chair, idly doodling in a scribbler, her legs stretched out, feet crossed on the table. She wore ripped black jeans, topsiders, and a *Like a Virgin* T-shirt from Madonna's Virgin Tour. Ironically, no doubt. Her thick black hair was shaved at the sides and back. Long at the front, it tumbled down over her forehead and eyes.

"Everyone, meet my sister Solange," said Ocean, staring at her with a cautionary look. Rose marvelled at their lack of family resemblance. "Solange Sparrow. Sorry, I mean Sol."

"Give us what you got, Kronk," said Sol, putting down her pen. She looked at Ocean with a big albeit disingenuous smile. "Tell us what avatar means."

Ocean sighed as she held up Kronk. "An avatar," she said, making Kronk's mouth move and using the Santa Claus voice again, "is something that is a visual representation of what you are supposed to be. In other words, Ocean has become me!"

"Really, Ocean, that's what an avatar is?" Sol asked. "I thought it was a Hindu-Sanskrit word that meant the earthly materialization of a religious deity. Are Kronk and Bongo Hindu?"

Ocean sighed and let Kronk fall to her side. She slumped slightly and her eyes briefly clouded over but she quickly rallied herself, widening her toothy grin to full beam mode. "It also just means when someone becomes the embodiment of something else. Now everyone come and get a script."

Ocean heaved a cardboard box off the floor and onto the table, opened it, and pulled out a stack of coil-bound manuscripts. *The Adventures of Kronk and Bongo* entailed Buddy's efforts to stop his interstellar guests from inadvertently committing suicide, killing each other, or maiming themselves for life by drinking, ingesting, touching, and/or breathing in the fumes of toxic household products, and to teach them the universal hazard symbols. These were displayed prominently on large black spray cans positioned on the board table in front of Ocean, emblazoned with graphics in Day-Glo colours: a bony hand, the skull and crossbones, Earth exploding, and a flame that looked like a racing car decal. Ocean had already regaled them with a lurid recitation of household horrors, factual events from police reports across Canada.

"Remember everyone, the third most important thing is to have fun!" said Ocean as she handed out the scripts.

Bongo and Buddy dangled on hangers on a rolling rack next to Ocean. Some costumes also hung on the rack. There was an outfit for a character called Patches the Clown that included a long colourful patchwork vest, striped balloon pants, a synthetic orange wig, and a big red nose. Apparently one of the two puppeteers on each team would take turns playing Patches, whose job was to introduce the show and engage in some lively banter with children in the audience. It would end up that no one wanted to be Patches because it meant having to put on whiteface, clown makeup, and a big red nose, not fun outside during the peak of summer, resulting in inter-partner bribing, deal-making, and in the case of the Victoria regional team, blackmail.

There were also life-sized Kronk, Bongo and Buddy costumes. Ocean had mentioned that the two most successful puppet teams would be chosen to staff a product safety booth at the Pacific National Exhibition for three weeks near the end of summer, and that they would wear the getups to walk around the fairground, greet children, and hand out *The Adventures of Kronk and Bongo* comic books.

"I've put you all in teams. Team Prince George and Northern BC: Daphne Goretski and Tom Eagle. Team Kelowna and Southern Interior: Elizabeth Orenstein and Tamara Glebe. Team Victoria and Vancouver Island: Albert Choy and Marina Balaskas. Team Vancouver and Lower Mainland: Solange Sparrow and Rose Esterhazy. Everyone, find your partner!"

"Now I want you all to do a line reading," Ocean continued once everyone was seated with their partners. "Play, experiment. Try different voices. You need to give your characters personalities. Maybe even backstories. The more subtext, the more depth you can give them, the more entertained the kids will be, and they'll recall the messages better."

"This is going to be like putting lipstick on a pig," Rose stage-whispered.

"No kidding," said Sol. She flipped the hair out of her eyes and pondered. "Hmmm ... a backstory. What do you think?"

"I think that the script doesn't give us anything to work with."

"But the puppets do," Sol responded. "I mean, look at them."

Rose and Sol regarded the puppets hanging lifelessly across the table.

"Look at what they're wearing," Sol continued. "They look like drag queens. Maybe they're lovers on their home planet and do drag shows there."

"Sorry, I didn't hear you properly," said Rose, cupping an ear. The room had erupted into a cacophony of silly voices as the teams read through their scripts, trying things out.

"Maybe they're lovers on their home planet and do drag shows," Sol said, so loudly this time that a hush fell over the room.

Ocean overheard the comment. "What part of sticking to the script do you not understand, Sol. This is a government program. We can't change anything. Especially, we can't make the puppets gay. It's not appropriate for kids."

"So what you're saying is that drag queens are inappropriate for kids but horrific death by exposure to poison, fire, explosives, and skin-melting acid is?" asked Sol.

"No, I'm saying that teaching kids how to avoid a" — here she inserted air quotes — "horrific death by exposure to poison, fire, explosives, and skin-melting acid is appropriate. Not everything has to be a Gay Pride parade, Sol. Safety doesn't have anything to do with politics."

"I guess it depends on whose safety you're talking about," Sol whispered under her breath as Ocean walked away.

Rose was starting to warm to her new partner. Plus Sol was kind of hot.

"I'm going outside for a smoke," said Rose, holding up her pack of green tea cigarettes. "I need a break. Want to join me?"

"Sure."

Rose wanted to get Sol alone so she could get the lowdown about her family connection with Ocean. They stood outside the building's main entrance, huddled beneath an overhang next to some planters to escape a deluge of late-May rain. Sol clutched her notebook close to her chest.

"No thanks," said Sol when Rose offered her a green tea cigarette. "My father used to smoke them. When we lived in, you know, Saigon." She gave Rose a sly glance. "That's what you want to know, right? Everyone's curious when they find out Ocean's my sister — well, sort of sister. I get it. I'm used to explaining." She smirked. "Sometimes I think I should print up a cheat sheet and hand it out. It would save a lot of time."

Sol was from Vietnam. She was eleven when her family managed to get out of Saigon, just before the Viet Cong entered the city. Her father had worked with the Americans, who abandoned him. They hid out in a village until they could secure passage on a refugee boat. Her parents didn't survive the sea voyage. Sol barely did. She had a younger brother, but they got separated in the refugee camps in Hong Kong. She never saw or heard from him again. A church group in Vancouver sponsored her and several other Vietnamese orphans, most of whom were adopted.

"The Sparrows took me in."

"So that's how you and Ocean are sisters."

Sol smiled. "No, not really. More like stepsisters, kind of. Her parents were hippies and moved the family to a commune in the Gulf Islands when she was, like, seven or eight. Her two younger brothers were born there. That finally ran its course and they moved back to Vancouver. Her parents met my adopted parents at a Gestalt Therapy centre. You know, mindfulness and all that stuff. Living in the here and now. Getting in touch with your true self. Exorcising the would haves, should haves, and could haves. And in their cases, fucking each other's spouses.

"Ocean's dad started sleeping with my mom, my dad started sleeping with her mom, and then they thought it would be great if we all moved in together. So we did. None of us four kids wanted to. It was okay for a while, I guess, until it wasn't. The jealousies and resentments started to mount. There were fights, bad fights. Then Ocean slept with my father and things got nasty, so I got out and found a place of my own. Next, my mom left and moved to Victoria. Then my dad and Ocean's mom moved in together. My stepbrothers went with them."

"Now Ocean and my dad have that big house all to themselves. But not for long. Ocean recently let us all know that they're trying to get pregnant. That's part of the reason I got this puppet gig. Ocean did it last year and the year before, then got bumped up to supervisor. She knew I needed a summer job, and feels guilty, so put in a good word for me. But if she thinks it makes anything better, she's wrong. Free love sounds like a good idea but sometimes polyamory is just a fancy word for clusterfuck."

"Wow," said Rose. "That sure is a lot of information. Don't get me wrong, I appreciate people who can be as candid as you are. But you know that cheat sheet you mentioned earlier? You might want to think about it for real."

"Yeah, I know," said Sol. "I'm a talker. There are some things I keep close to my chest."

Rose eyed Sol's notebook, took a last drag of her cigarette, and tossed the butt into a nearby trash can. She slowly exhaled, but the smoke didn't have its usual grassy green tea aroma. This was a sweeter fragrance, a floral scent. She sensed notes of rose and jasmine, citrus and vanilla. Then it hit her. It smelled like the Chanel No. 5 her grandmother always wore. As the smoke dissipated, Rose noticed a shadowy figure emerging from a thicket of rhododendron bushes in one of the planters leading to the office tower's revolving doors. The apparition started to walk toward Rose, and quickly came into focus. It was her grandmother. She was wearing the Schiaparelli evening gown she'd asked to be buried in, and her face was painted with mortuary makeup.

She stopped abruptly in her tracks and pointed at Rose.

"Ask about the notebook, Rose." It sounded as though she was whispering in Rose's ear even though she was standing some distance away. "Ask about the notebook."

Then she vanished back into the bushes, disappearing as quickly as she'd appeared.

"Rose? Rose?"

Rose heard Sol's voice. It sounded like it was coming from the end of a long tunnel. Rose came to with a jolt. Sol was staring at her with concern.

"Rose, are you okay? You stopped talking and were just standing there staring into the distance, like you were in a trance."

"I'm fine," Rose said with an unconvincing smile. "Can I see your notebook?"

"What? My scribbler? Why?"

"You were doodling in it upstairs."

"I wasn't doodling. I was drawing."

"I'd like to see."

"I don't usually show anyone my art," said Sol. "But what the hell, okay."

She passed Rose the notebook. Rose opened it up and flipped through the pages.

"These are amazing," she said quietly, passing the book back. "I think you should see this."

Rose yanked Trevor's zine from out of her backpack and handed it to Sol to read later. It was time to head back upstairs to training. Rose cast a cautionary glance over her shoulder before entering the revolving door. The rain was falling harder now. A bus passed, splashing pedestrians. There was a big ad on its side for New Coke. "Change for the Better!" read the slogan beneath a picture of a beautiful young woman holding up a can of soda and smiling. A prankster had blackened some of her teeth. The devil horns were a nice touch.

"I LOOK LIKE Bette Davis in *Whatever Happened to Baby Jane?*," said Rose. The clown nose made her sound congested. She was inside the puppet tent putting on her Patches the Clown makeup. She stared at her face in a small mirror. Her makeup had started to run. Her big red lips were bleeding out. So was the black makeup around her eyes. Small streams of red and black trickled down her whiteface, which was starting to decompose.

It was mid-August, a week before the PNE, and the hottest day of the heat wave so far. The tent was made of polyethylene. There wasn't a proper air vent, so it could be stuffy even on cooler days, but today it was intolerable. They were doing a series of shows on a searing concrete plaza outside the Vancouver Art Gallery downtown. They normally performed three shows a day, usually driving from one location to another. This time, they were doing three shows all in the same place. Sometimes they were lucky and performed inside in air conditioning, like in a mall or a school gymnasium. They could usually find a shady spot to set up when they were outside at a park or playground. But here, there was no relief from the sun. The puppet tent was like a pressure cooker. Rose couldn't stop her makeup from melting.

"Like who in what?" asked Sol, busy prepping the puppets for the next show.

"Bette Davis. She was a big star in the 1930s and '40s. She did this movie in the early 1960s to revive her flagging career, *Whatever Happened to Baby Jane?* They were making 'hagsploitation' movies back then with movie stars that used to be beautiful but had aged. People went to gawk at how far they'd faded, like watching a car accident you can't look away from. Bette Davis plays a batshit-crazy, over-the-hill alcoholic who's trying to revive her career as a child vaudeville star, even wearing the same kind of clothes. She ends up looking like a horror movie clown." Rose sighed. "Like I do now. It's actually a great movie. It's one of Trevor's favourites. Joan Crawford's in it too. She was —"

"I know who Joan Crawford is. You made me sit through all of fucking *Mommie Dearest*."

"I didn't make you," Rose remarked. She was powdering her face to try and stop the makeup situation from getting any worse. "You wanted to rent *Alien* but lost the coin toss. Oh God, now I look like a horror clown in a fog bank."

"What is it with gay men and famous old female movie stars?"

"I don't know," said Rose. "What is it with lesbians and U-Hauls?"

"No more wire hangers!" said Sol, laughing as she strung up Buddy on a hook made from a bent clothes hanger. "You know, while we're on stereotypes and clichés."

Rose and Sol had devised a system for putting up and organizing the puppet tent. It came in a huge duffel bag, an assemblage of tarps, tent poles, pegs, clips, and guy lines that took about half an hour to assemble. First, they had to lay out the tarps and slide the tent poles into their pole sleeves. Then they had to connect them with snaps and the clips and secure them with the guy wires. Next came the puppets. There were three puppets but only two sets of hands — sometimes only one, when Patches was out in front of the crowd. While whoever was doing Patches got ready, the other would string up Kronk, Bongo, and Buddy on a wire in such a way that all the puppets were easily accessible.

They had to be careful to check they were sliding the right puppet onto their arms. No way did Rose and Sol want a repeat performance of the West Point Grey Daycare debacle, when Sol mixed up Buddy and Bongo to the consternation of a dozen three-, four-, and five-year-olds. "That's not Buddy!" "That's not even a dog!" "That's Bongo not Buddy!" "I have to pee!" "Where's Patches?" "Can Buddy live with me?" "I have to pee too!" "Can we have ice cream now?"

Rose, at the ready with Kronk on her arm, kept telling Sol to vamp. "Vamp! Just vamp!"

"What? What do you mean?" Sol hissed back. "What the fuck is a vamp?"

"It means improvise. Just make something up."

"Then why didn't you say that?"

Unfortunately, by this time Sol had completely forgotten about Bongo. The puppet was flailing back and forth like it was having a seizure.

"What's wrong with the spaceman?" shouted a child.

"I think he's dancing!" shouted another.

A few kids began copying Bongo, swaying side to side, thrashing their arms, and jerking their heads up and down. Then a couple of them began to cry. Rose and Sol couldn't get back on track after that. Kronk made a quick appearance to announce that the show wasn't going to proceed because Bongo and Buddy were sick. Stand-up comedians say that there's nothing tougher than a comedy club audience, that if you lose them once, you've lost them for good. They should try cutting their teeth on the daycare circuit.

THE FIRST SHOW of the day on the plaza at the Art Gallery was coming up. Sol peeked through a side of the puppet curtain to suss up the audience. There were lots of tourists and the place was packed.

"There's at least a hundred kids out there," she told Rose.

"How do I look?"

"Like hell but I still love you," said Sol.

"Yeah, well, thanks."

"Now get out there!"

The Adventures of Kronk and Bongo started with Patches the Clown running around from behind the puppet tent honking a clown horn and yelling, "Hello everybody!" To which, most times, a couple of kids would yell hello back. This time was no different, until Rose got to the part where Patches asks the children to guess his name.

"Can anyone guess what my name is?"

There was a stony silence. A couple of kids shrugged.

"Can anyone tell me what I'm covered in?"

Normally, at this point a few would yell out "patches," to which Patches was supposed to say, "That's right! I'm Patches the Clown!" Next, Patches would introduce Buddy the Dog, they'd banter, then Buddy would tell Patches that his friends from outer space were going to arrive for lunch soon and that he had to get ready. Then the puppet show would start. This time, however, things didn't go according to plan. For some reason, this was the moment that Sol decided that she wanted to vamp.

"Can anyone tell me what I'm covered in?" Rose asked the crowd.

"Makeup!" came a voice from behind her. Rose turned around to see Buddy the Dog staring at her.

"You're covered in makeup! You're Makeup the Clown!" Buddy shouted, turning to the audience. "Hi, everyone! I'm Buddy!"

"Hi Buddy!" responded a little girl in a cornflower dress sitting on the ground in the front row.

"And this is my friend, Makeup the Clown! I want everyone to say a great big hello to Makeup!"

"Hello Makeup!" yelled the same girl.

"Hello Makeup!" followed the rest of the children.

Rose managed to muster a horrifying smile. The red greasepaint spreading from her lips made her lips look like a crime scene. She turned to wave at the little girl, only to see her grandmother Lily sitting there instead, shaking her head disappointedly. She was wearing a green, checkered Guy LaRoche coat, if the fashion liner notes Trevor had emblazoned on Rose's brain all those years ago were accurate.

"You look terrible, Rose," she said. "Are you getting enough sleep?"

"It's makeup, Grandma. Clown makeup."

"Not a circus I'd care to see," said her grandmother.

She chuckled, stood up, and walked toward Rose. "Oh, well, now it makes sense. You never were one for makeup, at least not to make yourself pretty. Which is fine because you're as pretty as can be without it, to me. Though when you were young, you liked to get into my makeup bag while I wasn't looking. And then you'd put on a little show. You had a flare for the theatrical back then, before you turned shy and bookish. Here, let me clean this up for you."

She pulled a handkerchief from the sleeve of her coat, wet it with her tongue, and began wiping off Rose's makeup.

"What the fuck, Grandma!"

Her grandmother pulled back with a startled expression. "I don't recall you having a salty tongue."

"I picked it up after you died. Life goes on."

"Speak for yourself. And hold still!"

Rose's grandmother sighed and lowered her handkerchief.

"I'm sorry, being dead doesn't always bring out the best in

me. Take it from me, Rose, resting in peace has its drawbacks. It's not as easy to keep up with things. And it's not like anyone drops by to visit and fill you in on what's been going on. Oh sure, they show up once a year with flowers. But they don't stick around. They say, 'We miss you,' talk about you like you're not even there, then rush away to get on with their lives. And before you know it you've got a granddaughter with a mouth on her like a sailor."

"What are you doing here, Grandma?"

"I know where you got it from," her grandmother continued, ignoring Rose. "You got it from me. I never swore around family, especially you grandkids. But at the office, well, there were times when a few colourful bon mots — strategically placed, mind you — was the only way to get through to some of the men who thought they knew better.

"No one saw me coming. Everyone saw a nice, well-dressed, well-behaved Christian lady in pearls. I know that you young women today, with your blue jeans and Gloria Steinem, think lipstick is the enemy, but fashion gave me the element of surprise. I mean, at the end of the day, fashion is just a calling card that gets you into the right places — or gets you kicked out. Clothes, makeup, keeping a trim figure — that was my Trojan horse. It got me through the door. Then I showed them my brains. And, when stronger measures were called for, some lip."

"How Helen Gurley Brown-ish of her," Rose heard Trevor whispering in her ear. Brown's *Sex and the Single Girl* had been on the reading list in Rose's gender studies course. Rose applauded Brown's early feminist celebration of female sexual empowerment. But her advice to women to exploit that power and get ahead using sexy clothes, makeup, and other feminine wiles belonged in a museum, under plexiglass with the other fossils. Brown went on to run *Cosmopolitan*. Rose imagined that the road to hell was paved with *Cosmo* articles about how to satisfy your man. She gave Trevor an informal book report one night after they'd smoked a joint. He wanted to read the Gurley Brown book, so she loaned him her copy.

"Well that explains Madonna. And Mae West too," he told her after he'd read it. "And Coco Chanel and Marilyn Monroe, come to think of it. They were different times, Rose. Your grandmother has a point."

"Of course, I have a point," interjected her grandmother, snapping her fingers to get Rose's attention. "Focus, Rose!"

"You heard what I was thinking?"

Her grandmother nodded, holding a compact and powdering her face to conceal the necrosis.

"How?"

Her grandmother sighed and put down the compact.

"Waves."

"What?"

"Electromagnetic waves, Rose: radio waves, microwaves, light spectrum waves. I'm a projection bobbing like flotsam on a million frequencies travelling through you and around you everywhere all the time. I know everything you're thinking."

"Why are you here, Grandma? Why do you keep showing up?"

"But I'm not here, dear. Weren't you listening? I'm dead." Rose's grandmother sniffled and began to softly cry. "I am six feet under. I have shuffled off this mortal coil, gone the way of all flesh, and given up the ghost. I have passed beyond the veil, Rose, and paid the ferryman. I have ceased to be."

She paused to dab the tears under her eyes to macabre effect, casting a quick glance to see if Rose was commiserating. She seemed unaware that while dabbing her face she'd rubbed off some of the mortuary makeup, revealing a cadaverous pall beneath.

"Are you in heaven, Grandma?" Rose asked.

"Clearly not," her grandmother said, looking around with a bemused smile and tucking away her handkerchief. "Unless heaven is a public plaza leading to an art gallery. Which, come to think of it, might not be such a bad thing. Besides, you don't believe in heaven so don't patronize me."

"Sorry. But what are you doing here?"

Her grandmother sighed. "You tell me. You manifested me, after all."

"I didn't manifest anything," Rose protested.

"Yes, Rose, you did. You won't let go. Of me or your friend Trevor. Except you're burying him before he's gone. You're turning him into a memory while he's still alive. I deserve to be a memory. Not him. Not yet."

Rose felt something tug at her clown vest and looked down. It was the little girl in the cornflower dress. "Don't cry, Mister Makeup."

Rose realized that she was sobbing uncontrollably. Panicked preschool faces looked up at her with pained expressions. Some parents exchanged concerned whispers. Then a few of the kids started to howl. Rose looked around and saw why. Sol had emerged from the puppet tent with Buddy dangling off her arm, realizing too late that the optics weren't great.

"Buddy's dead!" yelled a toddler at the back. "That man killed him!"

"Are you okay?" Sol whispered into Rose's ear.

Rose nodded.

"Good," said Sol. "Then let's vamp."

"Don't worry kids!" said Rose. The smile she forced to buoy their spirits appeared more crazed than comforting thanks to her *Grand Guignol* visage. The only reassurance it offered was a promise of nightmares come bedtime. "This is my assistant,

Solange. She's not a man. Tell everyone that Buddy isn't dead, Solange."

"That's right, Rose," Sol said nervously. Rose gave her a look. "I mean Patches. I mean Makeup."

"Then why don't you tell everyone what *is* wrong with Buddy."

"Sure, Makeup. Buddy's suffering from heat prostration. That's when someone overheats and faints. Because it's too hot. Like it is now. But we can help him."

"How?" Rose remarked, the sweat trickling uncomfortably down her back and legs.

"Let me show you."

Sol stood behind Rose and gingerly slipped the puppet back onto her arm. She crouched, laid Buddy on the ground, and pretended to give the puppet mouth-to-mouth resuscitation. She jerked her arm to make it seem as though the puppet was coming to.

"See everyone, Buddy's just fine," announced Rose while Sol stood up.

Sol made it look like Buddy was whispering something to her, then she whispered into Rose's ear.

"Buddy says thank you for caring so much about him," Rose announced. "He's still not feeling very well. He needs to rest. We're going to postpone the show, but you can come back in an hour for the next one. In the meantime, why doesn't everyone help themselves to an *Adventures of Kronk and Bongo* comic book!"

THE NEXT MORNING, Rose and Sol received a summons to come into the office. Ocean was livid. Several parents had filed complaints with the Federal Department of Consumer and Corporate Affairs, which sponsored the program.

"You can't keep cancelling scheduled shows," Ocean said. She was trying to be officious but seemed more weary than managerial. Rose sat with her arms crossed, staring out of the window behind Ocean's head as she spoke. Sol doodled in her notebook. "I can't fire you because it's too late in the season to find and train someone else. And stop doodling, Sol. It's inconsiderate."

"Oh, gee, sorry," Sol replied sarcastically. She put her Sharpie away and looked at Ocean with a fed-up expression. "It's not doodling, Ocean. It's drawing. I do it when I'm bored because I have an artistic temperament, not an attention deficit disorder."

Ocean's eyes darkened like the sea before a storm. "I'm sorry I'm boring you, but the both of you need to get your acts together. And you, Rose, these 'fits' you keep having are a problem. Maybe you need to see a doctor. Whatever, they need to stop."

"They're not fits," said Rose. "They're visions. They're, I don't know, numinous."

"She means spiritual, divine," Sol weighed in.

"I know what numinous means," Ocean responded tersely. She turned to Rose. "Are you on drugs?"

"No," said Rose. "But they sound like a good idea right about now."

Sol snickered.

"It's not funny, Sol," Ocean fumed. "This is a program paid for by taxpayers and I'm accountable. We represent the Canadian government. 'Makeup the Clown' is not an appropriate ambassador. Which brings me to another issue: the kissing. There've been reports."

"The kissing?" Rose queried.

"Reports?" added Sol.

"On three different occasions, children reported seeing the two of you kissing behind the puppet tent. Their parents contacted us. They weren't happy about, in one parent's words, 'my kid being exposed to homosexuals.'"

Sol rolled her eyes. "Then maybe we should add a fifth hazard symbol to the puppet show. We could add Lesbian to Poison,

Flammable, Explosive, and Corrosive, with the symbol of combusting labia."

"There's no need to be so graphic," said Ocean.

"Yeah, there is," Sol responded, heatedly. She held up her notebook. "I'm a graphic novelist, Ocean. Being 'graphic' is who I am. Not that you care or would even notice. You're too busy fucking my father."

"That's enough," Rose said gently, worried about how things were escalating. She reached over and placed a hand on Sol's leg.

"Listen, I don't care but other people do. And my job's on the line," said Ocean. "It's bad optics."

"You're one to talk," Sol countered in a deadpan voice.

"Okay, we'll be more careful. It won't happen again," Rose said. Never comfortable with confrontation, she was eager to ease the tension.

"All right," Ocean replied. "But if I get another complaint, there will be consequences."

Sol was sullen and quiet on their way out. She turned to Rose as they were taking the elevator down to underground parking.

"She's pregnant," said Sol.

"What?"

"Ocean. She's pregnant."

"Oh."

"I was thinking about the plan. Should we go ahead? Trevor said he'd be into it if we did."

"I don't know. I guess so. Yes, let's do it," Rose replied, feigning conviction.

Rose had been having doubts about their plan all along but hadn't said anything because Sol was so enthusiastic about it. Now the doubts were creeping back. Rose never thought that they'd really implement it. She figured that their plotting was capricious, for fun. She was also conflicted about Sol's reasons, worried that Sol was treading the fine line between altruism and vengeance. Did she want to make a political statement or get back at Ocean?

ROSE HAD GUESSED correctly; Ocean had been trained as a dancer. She stood over a credenza littered with framed photographs of Ocean at different ages: a six-year-old girl at the barre in ballet class, leg extended; a teenager in a black body stocking entangled in a cluster of other teenagers in black body stockings at a modern dance recital; performing in a cruise ship production of *Cats*. Rose had spent years quietly observing dancers as she studied and earned experience behind the scenes in theatre. She could always tell which ones would be successful. Their eyes had a certain quality. They, well, danced. She didn't see that quality in Ocean's eyes, at least not in any of the photographs. They churned with the same contained conflict Rose had noticed her first day of training, The spotlight captured her focus and determination, and her ambition, but her gaze lacked the joy, revelation, or sense of freedom Rose was used to seeing in people born to be onstage. Instead, her eyes brimmed with defiance, and secrets. They didn't let you in; they kept you out.

Above her head, Rose heard the repetitive whoosh of a printer spitting out pages. They couldn't use the office to make copies of the insert or go to a library; they'd be found out. Sol still had a key so they'd snuck into her family's house to use her father's photocopier. He was away on a business trip and Ocean was at work. Rose was keeping watch just in case someone showed up.

"Are you nearly done?" Rose shouted.

"Yeah, almost!" Sol answered from upstairs.

There was a photograph of Ocean with Sol's father. She smiled at the camera, sitting on his lap while they shared an intimate moment. The age difference didn't bother Rose the way it might bother other people. The first woman she had an affair with had been almost thirty years older too. Rose realized it was the only photograph in which Ocean's smile seemed genuine. And her eyes were dancing. She looked genuinely happy, and safe. But safe from what?

To some, the lens might suggest a potpourri of underlying complexes at play — Oedipus, Electra, Madonna/Whore, and other so-called neuroses dreamed up by straight, long-dead men. Rose commiserated with Sol's distress about her family's internecine sexual dramas, but she was reluctant to judge, let alone diagnose. It took a lot to rile Rose. When she was eight, the first time she took communion, the priest had delivered a fire and brimstone sermon about the evils of homosexuality. It was 1969. Canada had just decriminalized sodomy and its awkward side bit gross indecency.

After the service, outside the church, Rose's grandmother had taken her aside to tell her that she disagreed with the priest. "Father McNamara is wrong, Rose. I don't know what he's thinking. An open heart starts with an open mind. Jesus couldn't have made it any clearer. Everyone deserves love, even homosexuals. Oh, and please don't tell your parents what I said."

Rose ran straight home right after, went to the bookshelf where they kept the Encyclopedia Britannica, and looked up homosexuality and sodomy. It was way more interesting than Father McNamara's sermon, and much more informative.

Looking closer at the photograph, Rose could understand the attraction, sort of. Sol's father looked good for his age. He had curly, shoulder-length, salt and pepper hair, a well-groomed beard, and a trim physique from doing outdoorsy things. There were pictures on the wall above the credenza of him kayaking, rock climbing, and running a marathon. There were also photographs showing various stages of the house's construction.

Sol's dad was an architect. He'd designed the house. It was situated on mountainside property in North Vancouver, surrounded by rainforest and straddling a creek. The weekend Homes section of *The Vancouver Sun* had featured it several years earlier with the headline "West Coast Postmodernism." Rose remembered because she'd come downstairs one Sunday morning to find her mother reading the article at the breakfast table. She'd asked her mother what postmodernism meant but her mother didn't know either. Once again, the Encyclopedia Britannica came to the rescue.

The house was made using mismatched, reclaimed wood, with doors retrieved from residential teardowns. One of the walls featured flagstone salvaged from a demolished hotel. The house had vaulted ceilings and floor-to-ceiling windows and was meant to "respect the local ecology" and "integrate the natural and man-made environments," according to the newspaper. Rose stood in the main living space, an open area concept that eradicated barriers between rooms and "motivated flow from living space to living space."

She looked out the window at a primordial landscape of ancient firs, pines, and redwoods soaring skyward and casting shade. Far below, life tussled for space in the light, needy and chaotic: massive ferns, alien-looking plants with thick stalks and elephantine leaves, mammoth mushrooms jutting out from stumps and tree trunks, colossal boulders glistening with wetness, carpeted with squelching moss. Mosses and lichens of myriad textures and shades clung to every surface: dark green, thick and velvety; olive green, bulbous and clustered; sage green and wispy, dripping from boughs and swaying in the breeze.

By contrast, Rose thought that the house's neat and tidy interior was self-conscious and overly organized, compulsively so. Furniture was spare, arranged for visual effect. The word "staged" came to mind. Tones were muted to highlight paintings and photographs strategically mounted and spaced as in a gallery, meticulously lit. Constricted by curation, its lifeblood drained, the art inside contradicted the anarchy outdoors. The immense windows were supposed to create a connection with the natural elements outside and impart a sense of openness. Instead, the airtight space seemed hermetically sealed. Rose felt like she was in a biosphere, not a home. Or maybe a mausoleum.

Oddly, there were no other family photos. Two families used to live here but now it was just Ocean and Sol's father. The rest were long gone, their photos removed, walls and tabletops wiped clean of their memories. Now Rose started to understand Sol's rage. Abandonment and betrayal aren't so easy to forgive.

Suddenly, from out of nowhere, Rose heard the sound of a splash coming from the other side of the room, the sound someone makes when they dive into water. She turned in the sound's direction. It seemed to be coming from a framed picture on the far wall. She walked over for a closer look. It was a print of a painting, a hyperrealist image in bright colours that suggested someplace warm. There was a signature: David Hockney. Rose had never heard of him. A woman and a man stood at the edge of a pool watching a young man swimming underwater wearing a white bathing suit, or maybe tighty-whities. The three figures seemed detached, isolated from one another. The woman faced away, her back to the viewer. Until, that is, she turned her head and stared at Rose.

"Grandma?"

"Hello, dear. We've been waiting."

"Waiting? Waiting for what?"

Her grandmother smiled like a young mother patiently putting up with her toddler's antics. "You know."

"No, I don't," said Rose. "I really don't."

Now the man who was standing at the edge of the pool looked at Rose.

"Trevor?"

He pointed at the swimmer. "Let me drown, Rose. Let me drown beautifully. Save me when I'm dead."

"Huh?"

"All done," said Sol, interrupting Rose's reverie. "Now all we have to do is fold, staple, and stuff them into the comic books." She stood in the doorway at the bottom of the stairs, holding a large box weighed down with reams of paper. "What's wrong?"

"Nothing," said Rose, trying to sound chipper.

"You had another vision, didn't you?" asked Sol. She carefully lowered the heavy box onto the floor, stretched, and kneaded the small of her back.

Rose nodded.

"Are you still nervous about doing this?"

"Yes. But you're right, it's important. I think I'd regret it now if we didn't."

They each took one side of the box and lumbered out of the house.

"IT'S ABOUT DAMN time!" Trevor had said over the phone from Toronto two years earlier when Rose told him that she'd slept with her gender studies professor. "And don't worry that you're coming out later in life. You're lucky there's a market for older lesbians. Not like us fags. One crow's foot or grey hair and we're ready to slip into a faded wedding dress and wander a ruined mansion like Miss Havisham, pining for a love that never was and will never be. Or pay for a hustler."

"I'm only twenty-five, just like you, you drama queen," Rose replied. This was before Trevor's diagnosis. Now aging was the least of his worries.

Rose had had a complicated relationship with men. Not that they weren't attracted to her. Plenty were drawn to her curves, porcelain skin, and thick ginger hair. Several had called her an

"Irish beauty" over the years, when they first met her. Hungarian, she would correct them. Inevitably they all hightailed it for the hills, threatened by Rose's brains, opinions, and tongue. In the beginning, they said that being smart made her even hotter. But the smart men she fucked wanted her to be a little less smart than they were, and eventually broke things off. Those less cerebral vamoosed post-coitus the minute they spied her bookshelves, never to be seen again.

Rose didn't really mind. She finally admitted to herself that she liked sex with men but didn't want them hanging around. It was time to plunge into the lady pool. The realization — or admission, rather — proved timely. It coincided with a female ejaculation workshop she found out about at an end-of-term Womyn's Potluck at the university.

She was surprised to encounter her gender studies professor there, who always seemed so uptight. Rose was more surprised by what her professor was wearing: a black leather, body-hugging catsuit with matching ankle boots and gloves. It reminded Rose of the pictures of Emma Peel her professor had shown during a lecture called Women Warriors. The term "warrior" was suggestive, not strictly literal. As well as the iconic crime fighter played by Diana Rigg in the 1960s cult classic TV show *The Avengers*, the professor's roster included paintings of Joan of Arc, armoured and ready for battle; Moving Robe Woman, a formidable Sioux warrior; writer and critic Gertrude Stein, whom Rose thought looked like a tough-guy union boss; iconic 1930s movie star Marlene Dietrich, being seductive in men's clothes; Ripley, the ass-kicking astronaut in *Alien*, wearing a military jumpsuit and carrying an assault rifle; statuesque pop singer Grace Jones, looking severe in an angular brush cut and sharply tailored suits; and so on.

Later that night, they snuggled, listening to the Parachute Club tape her professor wanted her to hear. Her professor drifted off, but Rose couldn't. Sex had been a real eye-opener. She'd never used a strap-on before. Their brief affair was strictly sexual, no strings attached. Rose was indifferent when her professor was offered a tenured position at a college in the UK and moved away.

"You need to go through your slut phase and get it out of your system," Trevor had said on the phone, and Rose agreed. She didn't want anything to interfere with her studies and travels. She took Trevor's advice and embarked on a series of flings. Meeting Sol complicated things, especially when Rose saw the illustrations in Sol's notebook, and all the other notebooks piled in her closet.

Rose was familiar with manga due to her travels through Asia. They were a modern style of comics that incorporated elements of traditional Japanese art, elements that were also evident in the art of shadow puppetry Rose was studying. But she'd never seen lesbian manga before. Sol had appropriated, reengineered, and repurposed the sexist style of heavy metal comics, making a mockery of misogyny. Sol's women were warriors. Armed, armoured, pulchritudinous, and pneumatic, they were edgy, erotic, and ready to rumble.

One of Rose's favourite storylines was Sol's retelling of the Helen of Troy myth. In Sol's version, a group of sapphic fighters commandeer the Trojan horse, kill and replace the Greek soldiers, enter Troy undetected, then liberate Helen and whisk her away to Lesbos. Rose wasn't sure she was comfortable with the parts about raping and pillaging but came around when Sol pointed out that "they're conquerors, Rose, not candy stripers."

"I love it!" Trevor exclaimed when Rose called him about their idea. "Let me check with Ian," he added. Rose heard the receiver thud, some footsteps fading into another room, the barely audible rise and fall of Trevor's muffled conversation with his boyfriend, and then footsteps returning. "Ian thinks it's insane, which is a good thing, but we both wonder if it's legal."

"Just a sec," said Rose, handing the phone to Sol, who was sitting next to her leaning in and listening. "They want to know if it's legal," she asked Sol.

"We could be charged with attempting to promote civil unrest, maybe, or perhaps for piggybacking on a government publication without the government's knowledge or permission," said Sol. "But the Department of Consumer and Corporate Affairs will weigh the pros and cons of damage control. We're criticizing the government's lackadaisical response to AIDS, which is a consumer protection issue. A day in federal court wouldn't look good for them in the court of public opinion, and there'll be lots of opinions, for sure. The homophobes will be out in full force. Let's not fool ourselves. We're doing this to incite civil unrest. It's guerilla theatre."

Trevor wrote it. Sol illustrated it. Rose imagined it: a graphic novel of Trevor's zine article "My Life as a Monster," a visual Odyssean hero's quest through a nightmare world of bigots, bullies, misinformation, disinformation, malignant physical decay, dying horribly, then the denouement; he rises like a Phoenix, transformed into a superhero fighting ignorance from his fabulous throne in a gay club at the end of the rainbow. At first, Trevor liked the way that Sol's superhero costume made him look hot. He was a little worried when his boyfriend Ian expressed concern that the storyline was a bit much.

"Some people might think that two hungry aliens from outer space who visit a talking dog and try to eat and drink dangerous chemicals until he teaches them what the hazardous symbols mean is pretty out there," Rose reassured them both over the phone. "If Buddy really cared about keeping Kronk and Bongo safe, why is he storing poisonous products in his kitchen? He knows they're coming for lunch. He knows — you'd think, because they're friends — that they can't keep out of trouble. If that isn't a plot contrivance, I don't know what is. Don't get me started on the songs."

The script for *The Adventures of Kronk and Bongo* included songs for each of the hazardous symbols. Each time after Buddy saved them from a hazard, Kronk and Bongo would break into a song and dance number, teaching the kids the chorus and trying to get them to sing along. "Flim-Flam-Flammable" for the flammable symbol. "Look Mom, No Hands" for the corrosive symbol. "Mister Skull and Crossbones" for the poison symbol. And "Everyone Go Boom" for the explosive symbol. The playschool tunes and cutesy, upbeat lyrics cast a cheerful spin on grisly mutilation and lingering death. Rose and Sol had attempted to up the cool factor by rewriting the song lyrics and applying them to the tune of popular songs on the radio that kids would know, like Madonna's "Burning Up" for flammable, but were shot down by Ocean. She showed up to do spot checks every two or three days to make sure they didn't deviate from the script, which was why and how the idea for the comic book insert came about. That, and Rock Hudson.

"ROCK HUDSON'S GOT AIDS," Sol said, handing the front page of *The Vancouver Sun* and a cup of coffee to Rose, who was still in bed. "It's on the radio, too. Everyone's talking about it. He's in France getting some kind of fancy treatment."

The he-man movie star and sex symbol had been hiding behind the Hollywood publicity machine's facade of heterosexuality for decades but now the jig was up. Somehow his illness got shoved aside as the media focused on the "shocking" revelation that he was gay, once more making AIDS homosexuality's plus one, brooding off-camera away from the red carpet. They even called it "the gay plague." *LIFE* magazine came out at the same time with a cover that said, "Now No One Is Safe from AIDS," but most people preferred the "gay plague" version and stuck with it.

Rose and Sol realized that they had to leverage the news cycle and distribute the insert while the topic was hot. The final morning of the PNE found them stuffing it into the product safety comic books. They were in the booth in the Canada Pavilion, a fake spaceship with amphitheatre seating and a large monitor that looped a video of the puppet show. One of them would staff the booth while the other paraded around outside handing out the comic book. Sol took the morning shift as Buddy, Rose the afternoon.

Just before she donned Buddy's head, Rose reached over to kiss Sol. "I love you," she said, but Sol pulled away. She seemed distracted, and a little impatient.

"Sorry, just a lot going on," she mumbled, and went to freshen a pile of comic books on a table by the booth's entrance. She didn't wish Rose good luck as she usually did.

Rose turned around in the doorway before she left the booth, but Sol ignored her. Rose knew that instant that she'd fallen for a version of Sol that Sol wanted her to see. Not the real thing.

Rose donned Buddy's head and stepped out into the fairground.

ROSE WOKE UP on a cot in a medical tent near the Coliseum, attached to an intravenous drip for dehydration. Ocean was sitting next to her, patting her forehead with a cool, wet sponge. Sol was nowhere to be seen. Rose scoured the room for signs of her apparitional grandmother, but she was nowhere to be seen either. The nurse made her stay for about an hour, then she started feeling better. Ocean offered her a ride home.

"What happened to Sol?" Rose asked.

"Who's Sol?" Ocean gave Rose a worried look.

"Your sister. Well, not really your sister. You know, she was with the family that moved in with your family. And now you're sleeping with her father."

Ocean pulled into a parking space in front of Rose's apartment building. "I don't know what you're talking about. Why would I sleep with someone's father?"

"Sol, my puppet partner!" Rose said in earnest.

"I don't know what's gotten into you," said Ocean. "That heat really did a number on you. I'm your puppet partner. And a lot more," she added as she got out of the car with Rose, much to Rose's surprise.

"What are you doing?" asked Rose.

"Um, going up to our apartment," answered Ocean. She opened the car's trunk and pulled out a box. "Do you want to help me? There's another box of comic books. I'm actually really proud of us that we've only got these many left."

Rose went round to the back of the car and eyed the box suspiciously. She pulled out one of the comic books and flipped it open. Out slipped the insert, a graphic novel, *My Life as a Monster*.

"You did it, Rose. You and Trevor, that is. I'm really proud of you. You're such a talented artist. Now everyone will know, after all the years you spent hiding it. There'll be fallout tomorrow when the media gets wind, but that's what we wanted, right?"

"Right," Rose replied, disoriented and unconvinced.

Upstairs in the apartment, after they'd put the boxes away in the utility room, Rose and Ocean sat down on the living room sofa and had a glass of wine. They lit some candles. The night air was warm, the window open. The soft light of street lamps bathed the room in an amber glow. Photographs jostled for space on a table across the room; pictures of Rose and Ocean, Ocean dancing, Ocean sitting with her father in the cool house he designed and built in Lynn Valley, Rose and Trevor clinking glasses in a leather bar, Rose in Ho Chi Minh City.

During her travels in southeast Asia to study shadow puppetry, Rose had spent some time in Vietnam learning about water puppetry. In the photograph, she was standing in front of a water puppet stage fringed with water lilies, a local Buddhist symbol for rising from the physical to the spiritual world. It was a set for a puppet play based on an epic Vietnamese poem, *The Tale of Kieu*, about a young woman who overcomes adversity and suffering in her quest for love and redemption. It was Rose's favourite puppet play.

Rose's hair was long, thick, red, and curly in the photograph, unlike now. She'd had it straightened, dyed black, and drastically cut as soon as she got back to Vancouver from Vietnam, further estranging her parents. Trevor called her the minute he received the photograph she'd mailed him in Toronto.

"I love it! You look like a whole new person!"

Once, when Rose's grandmother was still alive but nearing the end, Rose visited her in the hospital. Something her grandmother said had stuck with her ever since.

"You have to kill the woman you were born to be to become the woman you want to be."

Forgetting Pauline Kael

NOT TOO LONG ago I found out how Hollywood helps the homeless. I was almost home from the Y one evening to shower and change before I went to Kalpesh and Dmitri's for dinner when I suddenly remembered that I was out of cash, so I made a quick detour to the ATM. The season's first snow fell softly. It conspired with the early darkness, cocooning the crowds and cars, muffling the chaos of rush hour. It was cold but exuberant and vital, not the deadly, savage slap-in-the-face of mid-winter. Crisp, butch, flirtatious snowflakes tingled my cheeks. The bar, restaurant, and store windows along Church Street were awash in a yule tidal wave of festive lights and decorations. The street was incandescent with panic. Flushed, shop-till-you-drop faces slipped by me soundlessly on the cushioned sidewalk. Panhandlers stood in doorways, shuffling from side to side. The traffic seemed to float.

A United Way Santa Claus clanked his bell outside the Body Shop.

"Hey girl!" said Santa. "It's me."

I stopped and stared. He pulled the beard away from his face. It was a demi-beard, actually; the top half was real. I'd've recognized that handlebar moustache anywhere.

"I don't believe it," I said. We air-kissed.

He snapped his beard back in place and shrugged. "A girl's gotta have a hobby."

Hart ran accounts payable in the very first ad agency I worked at. He was the only person I knew who still called his male friends "girl" or said things like "smell her" without irony. His vernacular was furnished with doilies and throw pillows. Joey used to joke that Hart was like Jurassic Park, that somebody found a chunk of petrified amyl nitrate containing a mosquito from which they extracted the DNA of a '60s cliché and cloned him. Somewhere, Joey proposed, on a faraway tropical island, enormous homosexuals lumbered through the rainforest tossing out quips like, "Oh Mary it takes a fairy to make something pretty," scaring small mammals half to death with elaborate table settings.

An attractive man walked by. "And what would you like for Christmas?" said Hart. "Why don't you sit on Santa's lap and tell him your secret?" The fellow turned around and gave Hart a filthy look.

"Well. Smell her."

"You're too much," I remarked, in a hurry to get going.

"Merry Mary," he said.

I went on my way, walking through the city's gay village, past the 501, Woody's, Sailor, Crews, the Black Eagle, and the signs: Hairy Butt Contest, Bad Boys Nite Out, The Drag Kings at Tallulah's. A cute guy from the gym was walking his pit bull. I'd seen him in the showers. He was full of attitude when he worked out, indifferent to the world, but now he gave me the eye and smiled. His Eddie Bauer parka was open to reveal a clinging, synthetic zip-up top popular in the clubs. His hair was short and frosted, combed forward Caesar-style. The dog had a studded S/M collar and a rhinestone tag.

"Hi."

"Hi."

The dog sniffed my pant leg.

"Morrissey likes you."

I didn't say anything, and I didn't pet the dog. Tempting as it was, I didn't want to encourage Morrissey's owner. I felt funny because I knew he'd been with Joey several times and even though it was a long time ago, and even though Joey was dead, it bothered me. I kept walking and he evaporated into the crowd, pooch in tow, accompanied by the Christmassy jingle-jangle of a chain-link dog leash.

"Hockey tickets! Who's got hockey tickets? Tickets for tonight! Who's got hockey tickets?" a scalper shouted at fans swarming Maple Leaf Gardens. "Hey chief."

"Sorry," I said. "Not tonight."

I crossed the street to my bank. The lock on the bank machine door had been broken for months. I swung it open and walked in. The enclosure smelled of ammonia.

"Hi Roscoe."

He stirred and sat up on his cardboard mat, blinking at me with bloodshot eyes. I handed him a couple of my emergency cigarettes. I'd given up chain-smoking but kept them around for special occasions. If I gave up too much, what would be left? Beatitude, sure, and its half-wit twin, Boredom, drooling upstairs in its chair in the attic, playing with a hat pin.

"Thanks," said Roscoe. "You're a saint. Not like most of these buggers."

Taking a deep breath, I lit one for him, then stepped away to the furthest machine so I wouldn't suffocate. I didn't know how old Roscoe was. He looked about seventy but was probably around fifty, from the sound of his voice. I knew his name because my mother had drummed good etiquette into me. "When you meet someone new, always introduce yourself, ask their name, and remember it the second time around. First impressions rarely count. Second ones stick. Remember their name the second time and they'll always remember you."

Her white glove philosophy used to drive me crazy, but she was right. The first time I encountered Roscoe, back in my drinking days, he was happily playing his harmonica, an old tune I recognized from down east. I was with some guy I'd picked up and was getting out money to take him to an after-hours club. To impress my new companion, I gave Roscoe a fistful of bar quarters weighing down my jacket pocket from all the change the bartenders gave me, hoping for tips. He shook my hand.

"Luc," I said. "Luc Robichaud."

"Roscoe," he replied. "Just Roscoe," he added, suspiciously. "Fag?"

"Sure. Here."

I gave him a Players Light. Next time I made certain to remember his name and sure enough Mom was right. I was a comrade from then on. I read my dismal bank balance, weathered by the relentless recession. My savings had dwindled. I was jobless. Thank God the condo was bought and paid for. Roscoe unscrewed and drained the last of his Chinese cooking wine.

"Jesus loves you."

"Jesus loves everyone," I said. "He's too promiscuous for me. I need something stable."

"It's not a choice."

"Roscoe, don't yell."

"He helps those who help themselves."

"Hey, easy now."

"He died for your sins."

"Roscoe, relax."

"You'll love Him despite yourself."

"It wouldn't work. We're both tops," I said as I escaped out the door. I looked back through the glass. Roscoe seemed to think that his right hand had become a pair of scissors and was snipping at the air with complete concentration.

I stood at the crosswalk waiting for the light to turn. Across the street the crowd around the Gardens had thinned. As I waited, I thought about why some Christians and romantics anthropomorphized eternity. How could someone put all their bets on one guy? Having worked in advertising for years, I was suspicious of the power of rhetoric. It was a very small step from repetition to reputation. From the Pentateuch to *Playboy*, Love had a great team of copywriters. They made it look simple, said it was inevitable, then kept it just out of reach. For me, the best way to forget the future used to be to drink myself stupid and quite possibly get laid in the process, until Joey.

When Joey was still (but barely) alive and pretty much a permanent satellite orbiting Planet Morphine, I fell off the wagon. I'd have liberating, daylong, tectonic hangovers that clashed like continental shelves, freeing ideas so clear and deep, I could float in them for hours without touching bottom. On one such day it struck me that sacred is an anagram for scared. I managed to traverse the mists of time to tell Joey and he briefly defogged to give me his who's-going-to-take-care-of-you-when-I'm-gone look.

"Maybe you should stop anesthetizing yourself and face your fear," he Twelve-Stepped.

I opened my mouth to say something snide, but he read my mind.

"Pain and fear are not the same thing," he said.

Joey had a point. Who was I to talk? What I really needed to do was grapple my terror to the ground and screw it senseless. Sober. But I couldn't. Not then.

The lights changed and I made my way across the street, turning up my collar in the wake of an icy gust of wind.

"Hey chief."

"Sorry guy," I said. "I already told you. I don't want any tickets."

"Fuck you too."

Several safe yards up the block, I turned around and gave him the finger, then popped into a convenience store and bought some ginger ale.

MY PLACE REEKED. You could have spread the air on a cracker and served it with a pinot noir. I thought about doing the dishes but when I turned on the kitchen light, they looked too beautiful to disturb. The counter, the table, the sink, and the stovetop were alive with colour: seashore blues, sunset purples, and lichen greens. From the remains of my appetite and aversion to order had evolved a flourishing polypary of stunted brains, furfuraceous tumours, and blanketing webs, a bonsai coral reef settling over the shipwrecks of pots and pans.

I dimmed the light on my ecosystem, tripped over books and lecture notes on my way through the living room, and flung open the balcony door. A fresh metallic chill fumigated the room. I navigated through my bad housekeeping into the bedroom and opened the window there as well. After Joey died, before I made the decision to quit my well-paying job and go back to school, Muscles Maid Service came in once a week. Now I couldn't afford them. Without Muscles, my lifestyle had atrophied.

I took my soggy shorts and tank top out of my gym bag, tossed them in the direction of the laundry hamper, and unclothed in the pearly paper glow of my fake Noguchi floor lamp. I always get horny after a good workout. The combination of the soft warm light and a cool cross draft tickling the hair on my legs aroused me even more. I still had some time to kill so I popped a porno into the VCR, jerked off with toe-curling abandon, then showered, splashed myself with cologne, put on a clean T-shirt, sweater, and pair of jeans. Feeling refreshed, I left.

TIME ...

Time to kill. Dividing your time. Finding time. Buying time.

One night Joey and I were watching a prime-time soap opera because Joey thought a blond guy on it was cute when he turned to me and said, "We're all nuts, thinking we can commodify time or separate it into bits. Time doesn't have a beginning or end, or even a here and now. It has a top, a bottom, and curving sides. Time is a round aquarium we circle like goldfish with gaping jaws and astonished eyes as we try to figure out that murky unbreathable light show happening beyond our vision and ability to survive. Outside its walls is where the real stuff starts, and we can't even get beyond the fucking goldfish bowl. We float to the top of time when we die, decompose, then drop back down to the bottom. Maybe the Internet is the answer, taking us past our limitations. Maybe one day we'll evolve into thingies with Pentium chips instead of livers. Memory-intensive crap processors. Maybe time is just a snake biting its tail."

"Do you think Valerie's going to snag Brandon away from Kelly?" I asked.

He gave me one of his looks, took some of his pills, redistributed his duvet, and lit another cigarette.

Now I see what he was getting at. I mean, the moment of his death is inside me every second, whether I'm conscious of it or not. These days time is the only thing I can count on to replenish itself. I've got all the time in the world inside me. This very moment is repeating itself. And I am always inside Joey like the very first time, holding him, licking his neck, and I'm pushing and I'm pushing and I'm pushing and ...

Everyone automatically assumes I'm positive but I'm not. I'm guilty. Why did I blame myself? Why did I blame everyone else for letting me? Blame. All you've got to do is take away the *b* and it's lame.

CELEBRITY PLACE WAS a six-block walk. That was the name of Kalpesh and Dmitri's condo complex, two twenty-storey cylinders of red brick that towered above the sex workers on the corner of Maitland and Jarvis, across the street from a neoclassical building that housed a high school. The lobby was decked out in old movie posters and potted palms. Six different suite styles were named after legendary movie stars. Their one-bedroom pie slice of luxury living was called the Jean Harlow Suite. I'd tricked once with a waiter/model leather fetishist who lived in a Greta Garbo Suite.

"Dante was a bad boy. He pissed on the Thinker," Kalpesh said as he ushered me in.

"That's not something you hear every day," I replied.

The teensy Chihuahua usually yapped and clawed when someone came to the door. He was nowhere in sight.

"He's in the doghouse," said Kalpesh. "We're teaching him a lesson. We're not letting him watch television and he doesn't get to see his Uncle Luc." He smiled at me. "Let me take your wrap and put it in the closet."

"Thanks," I said, and gave him my biker jacket.

"Let me get you a ginger ale," he said. He headed into the kitchen, where I heard someone chopping food.

"Hey babe, long time no see," Dmitri yelled from beyond the kitchen door.

I smelled marijuana. There was also a piquant waft of curry. A fridge door opened and there was a clank of bottles. I went into the living room and sat down on their couch. As always, the heat was up too high, and the TV was on with the sound off.

The pissed-upon Thinker posed in the corner. It was a replica of Rodin's sculpture that looked quite real but was fabricated from Styrofoam and fibreglass. The Thinker was as light as a feather. Kalpesh had swiped it from a movie set where he worked as a set decorator. That was how Kalpesh and I became friends, through work. I used to hire him as a stylist for shoots back in my agency days.

Their place was filled with ersatz antiquities and faux masterpieces: prints of famous Renaissance paintings and Medieval-looking triptychs, Greco-Roman statuary, and gilded frames, all balanced by the spare lines of Modernist fixtures and contemporary Italian furniture. It was too kitsch for me. I needed to put on a pair of mental sunglasses to sit in it for more than a few minutes. I adjusted my shades.

"You take it in. I'll finish off here," I heard Kalpesh say.

Dmitri entered the room carrying my ginger ale and a beer for himself, a large spliff dangling from his mouth. He wore a pair of faded cut-offs and nothing else. He put our drinks down on the glass and chrome coffee table, sat beside me, inhaled deeply, took the joint out of his mouth, and pulled me close so that our lips met. He shotgunned me, staring into my eyes until my lungs were about to burst. I started to cough.

"It's been a while," I said.

He gently thumped my back. Dmitri was about as good-looking as it gets. We'd slept together once but Kalpesh didn't know. It was the summer before last, the night before Pride Day, a few weeks after Joey died when I was drinking the life of the party at a party I couldn't remember. Somehow, I connected with Dmitri in a bar. We ended up in his room at the Executive Motor Hotel on King Street. He was up from Buffalo for the parade. Over breakfast I could tell he was trouble, a nineteen-year-old cling-on looking for a daddy. Not my scene. I played it cool for the rest of the day and at a post-Parade warehouse party I pretended we'd just met and pawned him off on Kalpesh.

"I think he likes me," Kalpesh whispered as they were washed away by a wave of euphoria whitecapped with Ecstasy. They'd been attached at the hip since.

Dmitri was an illegal alien, an American. "Land of the free, homo of the brave," he liked to say. He worked under-the-table on top of the table at a strip bar on Yonge Street. Kalpesh dragged me there to watch him once, never having caught on to the fact that I'd already enjoyed a personal appearance. Dmitri was introduced by the disembodied voice of a used-car salesman who informed us that there was a special on tequila shooters at the bar until the end of the performance. Gyrating to a funk song, he took off his clothes on a stainless steel stage, backed by a floor-to-ceiling mirror that gave the all-male audience a complete view of his chassis.

I scoped the denizens. Dancers worked the room in G-strings and jockstraps. Occasionally, one of them would usher a patron beyond the backroom's darkened doorway for a private table dance. Dmitri hopped down after his set and briefly joined us. He showed me how the dancers used an elastic band to keep themselves hard.

"S'interesting," I said. My tenth gin and tonic had kicked in.

Later, I patched together the rest of the evening based on what Kalpesh told me. A tall, broad-shouldered muscle puppy in a shredded leather loincloth, with shoulder-length curls and bangs that made him look like a Greek god, approached me. He put a hand on my crotch.

"M'I sposed'a cough now?" I asked him.

He didn't laugh. "I could do a guy like you for a discount," he said, twitching his head at the backroom. He discreetly guided my hand into his bulging jock where there was a small, strategically placed bottle of poppers. I paused to consider. Kalpesh pinched my elbow and gave me a dirty look.

"Ooooooo!" I said to my assailant in the sissiest voice I could muster, "Momma told me good things come in small packages. Zat true?"

In a flash he was out of my face and halfway back to Mount Olympus.

"You're shameless," Kalpesh admonished me.

"I juswanned t'elp him with his PhD," I said. "Or his pH balance. D'you see 'at fuckin' hair. Fuckin' dancer. Get a haircut!"

Apparently, I had my shirt and socks off and my pants wrapped around my knees by the time they managed to get me off the stage and into a cab that night. Nobody had mentioned it since.

There are a lot of things people don't mention because they can't. I know because I used to try to talk about what it was like when Joey died but I couldn't find the words. Really, there were none. When love became synonymous with death, I got Tourette's syndrome of the heart and found myself barking, in silence, at strangers.

Dmitri's arm was resting on the back of the couch, brushing against my neck. He passed me the joint and I finished it off. Kalpesh, looking half-crazed, rolled in with plates, cutlery, and napkins, got fussy, then rewound himself back into the kitchen. We tried to stifle our giggles.

"We're not eating in the dining room?" I asked.

"Kalpesh got a video. Didn't he tell you?"

"No. What?"

Kalpesh made a triumphant return, carrying in a huge tray loaded with lamb korma, papadums, potato rotis, and a cucumber salad with yogurt and dill.

"What?" he said. "What's so funny?"

He placed it on the coffee table in front of us and wedged himself between me and Dmitri. He'd poured himself a glass of red wine.

"It's the restored version of *Citizen Kane*," said Dmitri. He read from the video box. "Director's cut."

"Oh, come on. Director's cut? Isn't Orson Welles dead?" I laughed.

"Good point," said Dmitri, trying to compose himself. "It says 'Director's Cut' right here."

I took a deep breath. "Then it must be true."

"They can do anything they want in Hollywood now with computers," said Kalpesh. "Isn't it fabulous how everything old is new again?"

"You're right, Kalpesh," I sputtered. "It's pretty fabulous."

"What's with you two?" said Kalpesh. "I.G.Y.H.T.B.T. I guess you had to be there."

We subdued ourselves and ate dutifully. It was a good copy of the film. No matter how many times I've seen it, I'm always completely sucked into the story of the megalomaniac newspaper magnate Kane.

"Man, I'd kill to live in a place like Xanadu," said Dmitri, passing me another joint.

"Isn't that the film's theme?" I offered, taking it. "Killing to be in Xanadu?"

Kalpesh sighed dramatically. "We keep forgetting you're Pauline Kael."

"Who's Pauline Kael?" Dmitri asked.

"I can't believe you don't know who Pauline Kael is!" said Kalpesh.

"She was an important film critic," I told Dmitri. "She used to write for *The New Yorker*."

"And Pauline Kael's been to Xanadu," Kalpesh interjected, looking at me with a twinkle in his eye.

It was true, I had been. Back in my waitering days I saved up a bunch of money and went on a pilgrimage to San Francisco. I was going through an activist phase and wanted to soak up a sense of gay history, or something like that. But the Castro was a faded Mecca. It was the mid-1980s. The Village People were dropping like flies. Try as I might, I couldn't get laid even if my life depended on it. I found the city so depressing that I rented a car and went down the coast. At San Simeon I found what I'd been looking for in San Francisco, a fantasy made real. I took the tour of William Randolph Hearst's fairy-tale castle. It was proof that you could make anything out of life you wanted to, no matter how bizarre, and no matter what the cost. San Simeon was a potpourri of unrelated *objets d'art* and historical styles. It was like Kalpesh and Dmitri's apartment, except bigger and not fake.

When *Citizen Kane* was over, we sat around talking about our favourite old films, reliving our favourite scenes, reciting our favourite lines. *Chinatown, Rebel Without a Cause, The Women, Born Yesterday, Taxi Driver*, and others were brilliantly exhumed and reanimated.

Then Kalpesh and Dmitri got into a contretemps. They couldn't agree about who it was.

"It was Kim Novak," said Dmitri.

"No, it wasn't," said Kalpesh. "It was Jayne Mansfield."

"No. It was Kim Novak."

"Jayne Mansfield."

I kept my lips sealed because I knew who it really was.

"How could it be Jayne Mansfield when it was Kim Novak?"

"Because you're wrong, that's why."

"How can I be wrong if you're wrong?"

"Everyone in the world knows it's Jayne Mansfield. What planet have you been on?"

"The planet where everyone knows it's Kim Novak. The planet where everyone's right."

"Read my lips, Dmitri. Jayne Mansfield."

"Read mine. Kim Novak."

"God, I hate it when you think you know something you don't," said Kalpesh. "I'll bet you twenty bucks it was Jayne Mansfield."

"I'll bet you twenty it was Kim Novak."

"I'll go get *Halliwell's Film Guide*," Kalpesh announced.

I sat there, mum. Kalpesh went into the bedroom to retrieve their film guide. There was a spasm of yelps.

"Shut up Dante, I'm not in the mood."

Kalpesh came back into the living room and sat down with the tome in his lap. He flipped through it, looking for the movie in question.

"You're both wrong," I said. "Twenty bucks says it was Lana Turner."

"You're on," said Dmitri.

Kalpesh found the page. He checked, then looked at me.

"I hate you. You're right."

"He's your friend," Dmitri mentioned as they fetched their wallets.

"You keep forgetting I'm Pauline Kael," I said.

They each handed me a bill.

"Did you know that Jayne Mansfield was the original choice to play Ginger on *Gilligan's Island*?" I said smugly, sitting there with a couple of twenties in my paw.

THEY SAY THAT hindsight is always twenty-twenty, but it isn't always so. I'd stared too closely too long at the past and almost blinded myself.

"Prop me up," Joey said. "And close the door. That woman's moans are driving me crazy."

"I can only do one thing at a time," I replied.

"And open the blinds. I want to see the sunshine."

"Window?"

"No. Okay."

I quietly followed his instructions, then sat back down beside him. He removed his oxygen mask and took my hand.

"When it comes time, this is what I want you to do," he said.

"What?"

"I want you to take the *e* out of my name and bury it with my ashes."

"All right."

"That way you can tell people I was Joy." He looked at me angrily. "Put it down, you'll forget. Joy!"

He lay back against the mounded pillows and stared at the opposite wall.

"You have, haven't you?"

"What?" I asked.

"Slept with someone."

I gazed around at the bedpan, the paper bag for sputum, a stack of magazines, the pale green walls.

"No."

He looked at me sideways. "I thought so."

It was the last conversation we had.

I LEFT KALPESH and Dmitri's that night forty dollars richer and feeling quite full of myself. The route I took home went by a hotel that was part of a chain. As I approached it, I got an idea.

"Do you have any single rooms available?" I asked the front desk clerk, an older gentleman in a toupee.

"Lots," he said. "It's off season."

"How much?"

"$39.95 with taxes."

"I'd like to take a room then, please," I said. "The name's Roscoe."

"Last name?"

"Just Roscoe," I said.

The clerk started to hand me the room key.

"Hold on to it. It's not for me," I said. "It's for a friend. I'll be right back with him."

The front desk clerk didn't want to let Roscoe have the room, but I put up such a fuss that he finally caved. Roscoe was quite confused until he got into the room. He thanked me over and over, then suddenly shrank into a corner. "What do you want from me!" he cried. "I ain't no faggot." He crossed his hands in front of his crotch. I finally convinced him he had nothing to fear and settled him into a chair to watch television.

"It's the Antichrist," he said, scowling.

"Then change the channel," I replied, and closed the door behind me.

The clouds had cleared. The snow had stopped falling. It lay three or four inches thick, covering Jarvis Street, blushing in the glow of the street lamps. I walked past some working gals shivering in a bus shelter. A salt truck went by. There was very little traffic.

I heard a soft scuffle behind me and turned around to see one of the women from the bus shelter, furrowing snow with her go-go boots as she hurried up to me.

"Hey hon, you wouldn't happen to have a spare cigarette, would you?"

"Sure. Here."

"Oh thanks."

I lit it for her. After she'd exhaled, she picked something out of a tooth and looked at me. "I guess it's too much to ask if you've got an extra condom."

"Um. I guess I'm not using it tonight so you might as well have it."

I gave her the spare in my wallet.

"Are you sure?"

"Go on. Take it."

She put it into the pocket of her fake fur bomber jacket and scurried back to her friends in the shelter. She paused to turn around and shout, "Hon, you are one fucking lifesaver."

That made me feel good.

At Church and Wellesley, I noticed something lying on the sidewalk outside the Body Shop and went to check it out. It was Hart's Santa toque. I picked it up, shook it out, and put it on my head. As I was crossing the street a couple of young guys who were a bit drunk sashayed arm in arm up to me and walked by my side.

"Hey Santa, you got a nice butt," one of them said.

"Thanks."

"Hey Santa?" said the other one.

"Yeah?"

"Okay. Now, like, you go around asking everyone what they want for Christmas, right?"

"A girl's gotta have a hobby," I said.

"That's just so he can get those little boys on his lap," his friend cut in, laughing and slapping me on the back.

"Shut up," the other one said, and hiccupped. He smiled at me.

"No really, I was wondering ... like, what is it that Santa wants for Christmas? I mean, you're Santa. You can have anything you want."

"What do I want?" I asked.

"Yeah, what do you, Santa Claus, want more than anything in the world?"

I stopped walking and looked at them. It was very cold. Their cheeks were flushed bright red, and their eyes danced with booze.

One of them rubbed his hands together to keep them warm.

"I want to go home," I said, and walked away.

My mind was as clear as the new night sky, obsidian now, and deep with stars. I could think. I watched a pinprick of light disappear beyond the high-rise horizon as a plane descended into the airport far away. For a moment I was convinced I could survive anything, even joy.

Heart Deco

"HIPPITY-DOO-DAH!" IAN EXCLAIMED when Doreen walked into the room. He was emptying small bottles of perfume out of a box onto the boardroom table.

"Shut up," she responded.

"That's quite the maternity frock. I've never seen so much paisley. I didn't know the Mod look was back in."

"I'm not talking to you."

"You remind me of this guy Billy in high school. He tacked an Indian bedspread to his ceiling to make his room look like an Arabian tent. I thought he was the coolest guy in Corner Brook."

"Don't get me started," said Doreen.

She dumped her purse onto the floor and eased her swollen belly into a chair at one end of the long table, which was half covered in filled and semi-filled navy blue velveteen bags, giveaways for the fundraiser.

"He was so cute," Ian continued. "But royally fucked up. He used to play *Dark Side of the Moon* over and over and over and over and over and over and over and over and —"

"I said shut up. I'm still mad at you."

"In grade three Billy made me sniff model airplane glue. Once we showed each other our bums. Gosh we learn young."

Doreen ignored him and looked at the unfinished work spread out in front of her on the table. "So, what exactly happened to Randy and François?"

"One of Randy's drugs did a number on him. He's in Emergency. François is on the warpath at Social Services trying to find out what happened to his disability cheque. You know, the usual. Sorry I had to drag you from work."

Doreen shrugged. "You had to leave work too."

"So why are you mad at me?"

"You know why."

Ian stared at her. "You're mad because of that? Really? Honey, buy a wrench and get a grip."

"It's all so simple for you, isn't it?" said Doreen.

"What's not simple about sex?" Ian asked, perplexed.

Doreen didn't answer. She took up a pair of scissors and began cutting lengths from a spool of gold ribbon, to tie around the tops of the gift bags.

"There's one more box of perfume samples in storage. I'll be back," said Ian as he left the room.

Doreen dabbed her neck with a tissue and undid the top button of her dress. A summer heat wave saturated the building. The air conditioning was on the fritz. A large rotating fan rattled in a corner, bringing little relief to the stuffy, windowless boardroom. Squares of fluorescent lighting on the checkered fibreboard ceiling cast a lunar glow over the beige walls and brown carpet. At one end of the room, on an easel, was a felt pen drawing of how HIV attacks cells, left over from a volunteer orientation. Homoerotic posters of attractive same-sex couples in a variety of suggestive poses festooned the walls. Community group circulars crammed a carousel rack. Next to a shelf displaying dildos and dental dams, a TV and VCR sat on an AV trolley stacked with a half-dozen copies of TAO's new safer sex video for sadomasochists, *Slap Happy*.

It was a Monday afternoon. The offices of Toronto AIDS Outreach were electric with tension. Hotline phones rang. In the reception area an earnest crew licked, sealed, and postage-machined envelopes. Overworked counsellors and their drug-cocktailed clients clattered up and down the corridors, closing and unclosing doors. The air was heavy with more than humidity and the stench of stale coffee. Everyone seemed to be on edge, burnt out, about to snap.

Doreen heard the murmurings of a support group behind closed doors in one of the rooms down the hall. A voice raised in protest was followed by overlapping comments, some spotty laughter, a silence, then the monotone hum of someone calm. She popped a CD into a portable player and turned it on low. Gershwin gently swirled around her. She kicked off her shoes and stretched her toes. When was it, she wondered, that people started to compare sadnesses?

She stiffened when Ian muscled back into the room, his gym-defined arms straining to contain a heavy box of perfume samples.

"This is it," he said, scuffling across the carpet in brand new Doc Martens. He reached the table, dropped the box with a thud, and wiped the sweat from his brow. He ran his hands through his hair. Resting a haunch on the board table, he took a small vial of perfume out of the box, removed the cap, and sniffed it. He wrinkled his nose, put the cap back on, and read the label.

"Eau d'Or, eh," he said. "More like Eau Dear if you ask me. The blue-rinsers'll like it."

He smiled his boyish grin. He looked much younger than thirty-five: not a single grey hair, a toned physique from years of professional skating, trendy Queen Street West clothes, an ease of self that distinguishes Newfoundlanders from other English Canadians. He was at home in his own skin. From the moment she met him, Doreen saw why her brother had adored Ian. Everyone did.

Nonetheless, she wasn't going to let him off the hook that easily. She ignored him and fussed with her ribbons, curling them for a decorative touch.

Ian sat down, nervously fiddled with a crystal talisman hanging on a leather thong round his neck, then folded his arms and looked at her. "Dor, you're supposed to be sealing them gift bags, not giving 'em frigging hairdos."

She tightened her lips. Humming softly to the music — a few years earlier Ian had toured with Gershwin on Ice — he scooped up some condoms and lubricants from a basket of free samples, got up, and deposited them into his gym bag. Doreen gave him a frosty glance.

"I swear," he said, sitting down again, "you're behaving just like your brother. I thought he owned the copyright on cold shoulders. Now I can see it was a patent on the franchise. I'm immune to it, Doreen. I don't know why you're so ticked off, or what you think it will accomplish."

"It's going to take me a while to get used to the idea, that's all."

"It's not an idea," said Ian. "It's a boyfriend."

"It's just a bit soon."

"It's been seven months."

She snipped a piece of ribbon and slammed down the scissors.

"I need some fresh air."

Doreen slipped on her sandals, struggled out of the chair, and grabbed her bag. Her maternity dress flowed all the way to the floor, billowing with each step. She felt like a Haight Ashbury Love-in. She wouldn't have been surprised if at any moment a Volkswagen van covered in flower power decals pulled up and unloaded a coven of pupil-dilated hippies who congregated around her lighting candles for Grace Slick.

"I only told you because I thought you'd be happy for me,"

Ian hollered nonchalantly after her as Doreen left the room, oozing fecundity and feeling like shit.

There was no one else on the fire escape landing. Two folding chairs and a tin ashtray filled with cigarette butts languished in the heat. Clinical white August sunshine bleached the brick apartment building across the alley. The torpor siphoned in traffic and footfall from the nearby street. Doreen removed a frayed magazine from one of the chairs and sat, glad the landing was in shade and that there was at least a bit of a breeze.

She took the phone out of her purse and rang the warehouse. Doreen ran her own business, brokering set decor for movies and television shows. She should have been there. The co-chair of the fundraising committee didn't normally do assembly line work, but as Ian, the other co-chair, so often said, "Shit happens." Reassured by her assistant that there had been no major catastrophes, and that at the last minute he'd been able to secure six Wassily knock-offs as well as a new Eames lounge for a movie about a corporate scandal, Doreen hung up and put away the phone. It was an American movie, set in New York but shot in Toronto where Manhattan is 25 percent cheaper to recreate. Half the time you watched a movie set in America, you were watching Canada in drag.

Doreen looked down at the alley. An elderly woman came out of a doorway and stood on a stoop scattering breadcrumbs. Pigeons swooped down and started to peck. There was a momentary commotion of ruffled feathers as a territorial seagull kamikazed the crumbs, fighting off pigeons. The old lady came back with a broom and shooed it away. Cooing, the pigeons returned to their feast. There was a shrill squeak of wheels as a man with a wild mane of white hair rattled his shopping cart of worldly belongings down the alley and around a corner.

Doreen heard the flick of a cigarette lighter and turned her head. Ian stood in the doorway lighting himself a smoke. His pale blue eyes twinkled with atrocities. Together, they'd watched her brother die. Doreen never ceased to be filled with wonder at the endurance of gentleness in a world quickly becoming medieval. She was dismayed with herself for being so angry at Ian but couldn't excommunicate the deep sense of betrayal she felt. But whose betrayal?

She put a hand on her belly.

"How are the kids? Are they as pissed at me as their mom?" asked Ian.

"They're fine. They're independent thinkers, like their mom. They think I'm being too hard on you."

Screening had revealed twins, two healthy girls. Yukio, her husband, was thrilled. She, less so. After two years of discussion, she had been prepared to settle for one, preferably a boy to name after her brother. Now they were arguing about names. This had been the only setback. Yukio was being surprisingly supportive, all things considered.

"They've got their dad's flair for diplomacy," Ian said as he sat down in the other folding chair. "Their mother needs to be reminded that Trevor and I didn't have sex for the last year. I mean, I'm only human."

"I know."

Ian gave her a bemused look. "Is there a manual you've been reading that I don't know about?"

Doreen rubbed her temples to ease an encroaching headache. "What are you talking about?"

"You know, that tells you how long you have to be an AIDS widow before you can lift the veil of celibacy?"

"Stop being facetious."

"Stop being sanctimonious. Eight years together and I never slept around."

"I know."

"They give fags a Purple Heart for that."

"How do you expect me to feel?"

"You could be fair to me," Ian said calmly. "All of a sudden Trevor's a saint, you're a martyr, and I'm prancing around on cloven hooves. Oh please."

"Sex isn't the issue," said Doreen, making a point of waving away his smoke. "It wouldn't bother me if it was just anonymous casual sex. This is different. This is, you know."

"What? Love?" Ian chuckled. "It's a bit premature for that."

He bent over, stubbed his cigarette in the crowded ashtray, and sat up again. "It was supposed to be casual. I wanted it to be casual. He wanted it to be casual. We stumbled across each other in a chatroom, talked dirty, found out we were into the same things, he zapped me a JPEG, I zapped him a JPEG, we emailed a bit, and before you know it, he showed up at my apartment in a slave boy ensemble. I don't know if it's love, but it's chemistry."

They were interrupted by a hyperactive, skeletal young man from Community Development. He wore a long-sleeved turtleneck despite the heat. It hid his lesions. "I thought you'd like to see this," he said, a bundle of nervous energy. He handed Ian a copy of *The Toronto Star* folded open to the entertainment section and went back inside.

Ian looked at it and passed it to Doreen. "It's the ad. Looks good."

She inspected the half-page advertisement.

BREAKFAST AT TIFFANY'S

A Champagne Buffet Brunch

Tiffany & Co., Bloor Street West

All proceeds in support of the Toronto Aids Outreach

Hosted by drag sensation

TAWDRY HEPBURN

(There was an Avedon-style photo of the celebrity in cat's eye sunglasses, a scarf wrapped around her hair, posing with a long cigarette holder.)

Featuring surprise guests and a fashion show by
The Truman Capote Memorial Bowling League

Sunday, August 16, Noon
Tickets $150 (charitable receipts will be issued)

Original items from the classic movie will be on display!

"They've done it again," said Doreen. "How many times do we have to tell these people that AIDS is all uppercase!"

Ian shrugged and yawned. "Chill, Doreen. Everything doesn't have to be a big deal. Everything won't fall apart if you're not around to make sure it doesn't. The world has a funny way of continuing to turn on its own." He sat back in his chair and closed his eyes. "We've sold 75 percent of the tickets. We should sell out."

Doreen took a compact and lipstick out of her bag. "I have to be at Tiffany's later, at four, for a meeting with Chantal," she said as she touched up her face. "Can you finish off the gift bags on your own if we're not done by then?"

"Sure. Still mad at me?"

"Not mad. Disappointed."

Ian opened his eyes and looked at her. "Disappointed? In me? No-no-no-no-no-no, I don't think so. Take a closer look in the mirror, darlin'. You're coming in for a crash landing if you don't cool them jets of yours. You've got two others to think of now. You better start taking it easy."

"There's too much to do." Doreen closed her compact, loudly.

In the alley below, their feeding finished, a flutter of wings announced the dispersal of pigeons. They soared upward and perched on windowsills and wires. Even though it was a kilometre away, Doreen could smell the lake's toxins brewing beyond the downtown bank towers, the black Toronto-Dominion van der Rohe cluster and its taller, illegitimate glass and steel offspring, which stymied a view of the lakeshore. Vertical and horizontal, it was a huge city of grids, spreading out into a patchwork of suburbs, making it easy to map out where and how people worked, and where and how they lived, and contain them. Doreen had grown up in Vancouver by the mountains and the sea. From her perspective this city's terrain was flat, exposed, vulnerable, unsurprising, except for ravines incising the earth's flesh, creating an arterial tangle of parks and nature areas.

"They've built on the bones of a Presbyterian banker," Ian had commented once. He said that life here was lived undetected in the cracks. He called it the folded city. Its notable features thrust outward and upward and were completely man-made: simple, functional, declarative, but unemotional. Doreen recalled someone saying it was New York run by the Swiss.

An unrestrained piano lesson escaped through Venetian blinds across the street, in a hodgepodge of sour notes.

"I was lying about the slave boy part," said Ian.

"I know."

A siren melted into the urban cacophony. Come back here, Doreen thought. Save me.

"But he is a bit of a leather queen," Ian added.

"YOU'RE JOKING, AREN'T you? Exactly how progressive are we supposed to be? Even we have our limits," her mother had said over the phone from Vancouver when they told her. "Are you sure you want to do this?"

"We've already done it, Emily. Obviously," said Doreen, sitting in Trevor and Ian's living room.

"Ian's got good healthy sperm, and plenty of it," Trevor piped in on the bedroom extension.

"That's a little more information than Mom needs," said Doreen. "Sorry, Emily, Trevor just took his morphine pill."

It was about a month before Trevor died. Ian was at work at the multimedia studio where he was a project manager, his new vocation since hanging up the skates.

"Jack's going to be a harder sell than me, let me tell you," Emily said.

"You're the one who always overreacts before thinking about things, not Jack," said Doreen.

"What the hell's going on?" her father said in the background in his professorial, amused way.

Through Emily's ineptly cupped hand over the receiver, Doreen heard her mother say casually, "Oh nothing. Your happily married daughter is pregnant with our terminally ill son's gay lover's child, that's all. You know our kids, always on the cutting edge. They used a syringe apparently. In a clinic."

"Go ahead. Talk like I'm not here," Trevor mumbled. "I don't mind."

There was a banging sound as their father picked up the extension in his study. Doreen pictured him sitting back in his plush chair in front of his desk, swiveled around to stare out the window at the cedars and Douglas firs across the street, on the edge of the forested park surrounding the university where both her parents had taught before retiring.

"I realize it's supposed to take a village, Dor, but hell, some village," said Jack. "How's Yukio about all this?"

"He's ecstatic," announced Trevor.

"Is that you son?"

"Hi Dad, I love you."

"Some people with fertility problems adopt," Emily interrupted. "Some make do."

“I know son. I love you too,” said Jack.

“And some people choose to do what I chose to do, mother,” Doreen said, raising her voice. “You were the first person to teach me that a woman has the right to choose what to do with her body. Remember? So, I damn well chose.”

“He’s on his morphine, Jack,” said Emily.

“Yukio wants kids. It was either Ian as a donor or a stranger,” said Doreen.

“I love you too. Mom,” Trevor interrupted.

“I know sweetheart, and I love you.”

“And Doreen loves both of you too so don’t get mad at her.”

“We’re not mad, Trevor. We’re just getting used to the idea,” said Emily.

“It’s not an idea, it’s a child,” said Trevor. “Isn’t it fantastic?”

“Fantastic is probably the word that best sums it up.”

“We’d like to talk to Doreen in private, Trevor, all right?” Jack interjected.

“’Kay.”

After Trevor replaced the receiver, Emily jumped down Doreen’s throat with, “Have you gone insane? Has Yukio? Has Ian?”

“No one’s gone insane except you from the sounds of it,” Doreen remarked coolly.

“Ladies, please,” refereed Jack.

“I thought you’d be happy for me,” said Doreen. “For us.”

“I hope you know what you’re doing, Doreen,” said Jack. “You’ve always been determined and strong-willed.”

Trevor — frail, cadaverous, wearing a green bathrobe — entered the living room. He sat down on the couch beside Doreen, picked up the television remote, and turned on the set. She put an arm around him, and he rested his head against her shoulder. She could have snapped a bone by pinching him.

"Please just be honest with yourself and make sure this isn't a gesture to compensate for Trevor when he's gone," her father continued.

Starved, petulant models were frowning down a runway to the frenetic beat of electro jungle. Doreen took the remote from Trevor and turned down the volume on Fashion Television.

"Children aren't meant to replace the dead," said Jack.

A TRANSGENDER BUSKER had set herself up outside TAO's entrance, beside the bottom of the wheelchair ramp. Rather plain, frumpily attired in Sally Ann, she warbled Tin Pan Alley love songs, accompanying herself on a portable keyboard. There was a home-made cassette tape for sale. Doreen deposited some change into a bucket with a sign that said "Hi Sweeties" as she rushed by to reclaim her car from the parking lot.

Gunning it up Church Street, she steered with one hand as she guzzled from a bottle of mineral water. There was a snag at Carlton. A streetcar had stalled in the middle of the intersection, its trolley snapped from the wire. The cars ahead fought with the oncoming traffic to squeeze through. No one paid attention to the lights. Pedestrians did a Highland fling, heads turning this way and that, feet down from the curb then up from the curb then down from the curb again. The streetcar's metal pole wandered anarchically in the air, sparking when it accidentally hit the cable, defying the driver's attempts to reel it back in. One by one the horns began. Doreen was no exception. She bared down on hers with manic fury. A man in the next lane signalled her to shush, then gave her the finger.

"Asshole," she said loudly, slumping onto the steering wheel in a surge of tears.

The streetcar cleared the intersection. The traffic moved again.

The car behind her honked and Doreen regained her composure. She continued up Church, this time at a crawl.

She slowly drove down the narrow streets of toney Yorkville, on safari for a parking spot. The patios were brimming with *bon ami*; their well-heeled, well-dressed patrons giddy with summertime. Doreen would have given anything to join them, to sit unfettered at a table beneath an awning, with a spritzer and a good magazine. She finally found an unclaimed wedge of curb in front of a designer boutique. She fed the meter and waddled down to Bloor.

A beautiful young man with multicoloured dreadlocks was crouched on the pavement adjacent to Tiffany's, building a silhouette of the Toronto skyline out of pennies for a crowd of appreciative tourists who snapped his photo. Some dropped coins and bills into an overturned cap. Doreen stopped and caught her breath. She recognized him: ten years ago, her twenty-sixth birthday, her leather miniskirt phase, not too long before she moved to New York. She was celebrating at the Cameron on Queen West, where a friend was playing in a rockabilly band, the Fabulous Steve McQueens. That was back in the days when she was still attracted to artists, especially if they were dry and witty. She'd picked the sidewalk guy up in a fog of pint draft and whisked him to her place for a delirious night of unbridled skank. In the morning he went home to his parents in Burlington. He was only seventeen.

He briefly glanced up from the sidewalk and smiled at Doreen, clearly not recalling her.

"That one on the left edge of the observation deck's a Centennial penny," she said, flipping him a fiver.

She heaved her stomach into Tiffany's. The blast of air conditioning was a welcome relief and brought her back to her senses.

She felt old.

An orderly calm ordained the aisles and display cases of the legendary jewellers. The joint rocked with feng shui. Honey-toned wood and ambient lighting imparted the serenity of an Eastern shrine. Shoppers spoke in reverential tones. Tanned attendants presided with respect and reserve. There were no saffron robes, but the amber hue of skin beneath the suits and skirts of customer service sufficed, thanks no doubt to beta-keratin supplements and evenings at the electric beach. How else, Doreen conjectured, could a clerk get a tan like that?

She was ushered upstairs by an older gentleman wearing an impeccably tailored three-piece suit. He had the fastidious wrists of a sissy in a 1930s movie. A thin-haired comb-over swirled around his scalp like a Japanese sand garden. He deposited her in reception where she reclined in a Barcelona lounge and waited for her conference with Tiffany's head honcho, Chantal Roan-Kenting, whose office door was closed.

Chantal came from old Toronto wealth. She and her brother-in-law, an estate agent, were on the outreach's board, the connection to the money wads in affluent Rosedale and Forest Hill. Doreen had first met her in New York when she was studying design at Parsons, where Chantal gave a series of lectures on the business of design. Their paths had crossed numerous times since then and they had become good friends. Chantal was going to be the children's godmother.

An androgynous young woman in a black suit, with dark hair in a severe, angular bob, appeared carrying a Styrofoam container and plastic utensils. She smiled professionally at Doreen, briefly disappeared within her boss's office, then came back and took her place at the reception desk. She put on a headset and tackled the array of technology, ensconced in the custom-crafted, mahogany-veneered reception cubicle featuring modernist chrome lighting fixtures with halogen bulbs, and carved into the wainscotting, little deco hearts made of maple.

There was a buzz.

"Ms. Roan-Kenting will see you now."

"Thank you."

Chantal sat behind her desk, smoking. She was a trim, handsome woman in her mid-fifties, with thick salt and pepper hair in a short, no-nonsense cut. She wore a pearl grey Donna Karan skirt suit and matching shoes.

"Oh, damn. I'm sorry Dor, I wasn't thinking. Sit down. I've got an air filter here. I'll put it on."

Doreen made herself comfortable. Chantal's office was white, white, white, and sparsely but strongly decorated. Tube-metal Bauhaus furniture, a black glass coffee table, and a zebra rug in one corner; in another a huge terracotta urn overflowing with a tendrilling, sub-tropical succulent. There was some African statuary, an original Josephine Baker poster (framed), and a large Jackson Pollock. Its brilliant splatters spilled into the room with jazzy anarchy.

Chantal smiled at her flirtatiously. "How's Yukio?"

"How's Kate?" Doreen answered, looking at her partner's photo on the desk, in a brushed aluminum frame from Urban Mode. Half-finished Greek salad floundered in an open Styrofoam container.

"Late lunch," said Chantal. She shoved the container toward Doreen. "Do you like Kalamata olives? Here, take them. Can't stand them."

"No thanks," said Doreen. "Yukio's got me on a complete health kick. He watches everything I eat. Low sodium, high fibre, lots of fruits and vegetables, no wine, no coffee, no sushi, no prepacked prepared foods, red meat at a minimum, a ton of vitamin and mineral supplements."

"How dull."

Doreen shifted in her chair to get more comfortable. "I feel like a petri dish, things being carefully added to me so that I don't pop out a mutant strain."

"I'm sure it will all seem worth it when the time comes. How much longer?"

"About five weeks. Sometimes I think we're all too careful. Why can't we just let nature take its course? My mother's generation threw cocktail parties up until the water broke."

"That's how they got through it," said Chantal. "God knows the first contraction would have had me screaming for a martini. Of course, it was never an issue for me and now I haven't the option. Nonetheless, people are right to be careful. Nature can't be trusted these days. It's on the warpath."

"You say that as though people aren't a part of nature."

"Western religion's been trying to make that point for several centuries, just in case you hadn't noticed," said Chantal. "So now nature's fighting back with the big guns and it's got truth on its side. Truth is more potent than God, even if he is backed up by a nuclear defence strategy. The truth is built with devious armour, like a cockroach. It'll tough it out through anything, even corrupted atoms."

"My relatives would call that immoral," Doreen remarked.

"Amoral. Nature isn't conscious. That's its purity. Truth doesn't have morals. That's its survival."

"But people are a part of nature. We're animals," said Doreen.

"The problem with the world is that most people don't want to believe it. That's what's immoral."

Chantal opened a file on her computer screen, scrolled, and clicked Print. A laser printer hummed softly as it spewed sheets of data. She stood up and went to the window, opened the lowered blinds, and peered out onto the congested traffic of Bloor Street.

"I've been reading how in the future people will be fighting wars on the Internet," she said. "What a joke. Biology will be the death of us, not technology."

"You can take the gal out of the lecture circuit, but you can't take the lecture circuit out of the gal," said Doreen.

Chantal smiled. "Sorry." She removed a stack of paper from the printer tray and collated them into two piles, one which she placed into a folder and handed to Doreen. "Shall we?"

They spent some time discussing the protocol for Sunday's gala, after which Doreen pored over a publicity report from Tiffany's PR team. The press had picked up the story and wanted passes like crazy, thanks to a glittering guest list. It was to die for. The event promised to be a cavalcade of Who's Who, Who Was, Who Would Be, and Who's That? The A-list included an internationally acclaimed lesbian vegetarian torch singer (who everyone wanted to talk to); a Québécois disco sensation (who no one wanted to talk to); the only local player on the two-time World Series–winning team (who everyone had already talked to); a world famous horror movie director (who refused to talk); the bestselling Canadian woman writer in the world (who everyone was afraid to talk to); and the only out gay male comedian on North American television (who wouldn't stop talking).

"By the way, Miz-know-it-all, I disagree with you about technology," said Doreen, putting the folder into her briefcase. "Biology obliterates but technology deceives. It's the perfect theatre for war. Good warfare isn't based on death, it's based on deception. The person who wins a war without a single loss of life, that's who we should be afraid of."

Doreen folded her hands over her children. Chantal sat back in her award-winning ergonomic Herman Miller chair with robotic adjustments and swiveled to look out the window, her profile to Doreen.

"Sun Tzu," she mentioned softly. "*The Art of War.*"

"But then again," said Doreen as she got up from her chair, "who's fighting?"

DOREEN DROVE HOME. She hadn't been joking when she said she felt like a petri dish. The image had stuck ever since the doctor at the clinic inserted the syringe, and later made the unsettling pronouncement: "It took." Not "You're pregnant," but "It took." Yukio suffered from a congenital abnormality that produced antibodies to his own sperm, crippling them, forging them head to tail. They'd tried all sorts of treatments on him. But none "took."

AIDS — Artificial Insemination Donors.

ART — Artificial Reproduction Technology.

Doreen didn't fail to appreciate the irony of the acronyms on the literature the clinic handed out. Despite her doubts, she was developing a strong attachment to the little monkeys inside her, turning her into a globe, an attachment so strong it sometimes overwhelmed her. Soon they would emerge into the world and slowly, steadily move apart from her. She just hoped she didn't fuck them up. It seemed to her that there were two kinds of people in the world: the kind who run in circles chasing their tails, and the kind who sit still and enjoy the comedy swirling around them. Right now, Doreen felt as though she was sitting in the centre of her own circle, watching the amazing farce she had created of herself turn into a vortex.

The black widows stared as Doreen parked in front of her renovated Edwardian row house. Mediterranean and husbandless, old women in funereal garb spent the steamy summer evenings congregated on their porches gossiping, yelling at their grandchildren playing road hockey beneath the enormous, spreading chestnut trees, and minding everyone else's business. She smiled and waved at them. They smiled and waved back.

Doreen and Yukio lived on a street in a neighbourhood people once called working class, west of the downtown core. The block was made up mostly of Italian and Portuguese families, who faced attrition as young professionals moved in and sandblasted. When Doreen and Yukio first moved into the neighbourhood, they had aroused a certain amount of suspicion, exacerbated by Trevor's frequent wheelchair visits in the TAO van. Unlike Doreen's cleanly revealed brick, her neighbours' homes were painted bright colours: yellow, red, an astonishing green. The yards were fantastical. One featured Virgin Mary as the centrepiece of a birdbath on a foundation of plaster seahorses. In another, a psychedelic pieta was framed by immense sunflowers and rainbow whirligigs. Who knew what the landscapers were thinking in the yard with Snow White's Seven Dwarves and a flotilla of ceramic swan flowerpots, arranged in a tableau around the Crucifixion and a Dutch windmill, the entire scene accessorized by Christmas twinkle lights that went on at dusk year-round.

The ice didn't really break until Doreen's pregnancy was evident. Then there was a common thread stretching between Doreen and the porch elders like a tightrope, both sides maneuvering with caution, meeting somewhere in the wobbly middle. It would doubtless snap when the children appeared without Asian features, and questions formed.

"Good evening, Doreen. You work too hard," said her next-door neighbour Paulo, flirting with her as Doreen stood at the front door fumbling with keys. "It's no good for a woman having a baby, let alone two! You should be at home."

Retired, house-proud, he sat on the stoop looking aristocratic, flanked by two enormous porcelain hounds. He held disdain for his fellow Portuguese on the block. "I'm a baker. They're just fishermen," he'd informed her once.

He meant back home. Here, his compatriots were longshoremen. No one ate fish from Lake Ontario. The water was too polluted. Doreen appreciated Paulo's flair for dramatic omission and gift for poetic licence. Through lace curtains, she could see the large screen TV in his living room. It had been on ever since he got the satellite dish.

"Keeps me out of trouble," said Doreen, smiling at Paulo before she went inside.

She disabled the alarm system and carried her briefcase into the kitchen where she found a note from Yukio on the table and, in the fridge, a Thai chicken salad he'd prepared for her. He'd gone to work. Yukio was an entertainment reporter at a local TV station. He wouldn't be home till after midnight. She put the salad on a coral-coloured plate from their Fiesta collection, poured herself some juice, and took her meal out onto the deck overlooking the backyard.

The heat had subsided, but it was still bathwater warm. The sun slanted through the treetops, burnishing the leaves, dappling the lawn and Yukio's vegetable garden in a filigree of honey. The air was still. Cicadas electrified the early evening, tiny hums rising and falling like miniature buzz saws. The concentration of light, dense humidity, and smell of earth mingled with freshly mowed grass enveloped Doreen in a serene hysteria. Midsummer's intensity made nature seem almost sentient, watchful, slightly menacing.

The soft staccato rhythm of studio audience laughter droned through Paulo's screen door. Doreen recognized a recycled sitcom from the 1970s, Trevor's all-time favourite. Several years earlier, before Yukio, near the end of Ian and Trevor's first year together, they had invited Doreen to a Halloween party in a huge warehouse. There were costume prizes. Trevor had come up with the idea of going as graduates of the Betty Ford rehab centre. Naturally, he was Mary Tyler Moore. Ian was Liz Taylor. And

Doreen was Liza Minnelli. Two "burly gym queens," as Trevor referred to his friends, completed the scenario as attendant nurses. A professional makeup artist they knew did their makeup. Ian and Trevor even went as far as renting a wheelchair for Liz. Upon their entrance they circled the dance floor handing out copies of *The National Enquirer*.

They were a big hit. They won the contest. The prize was an all-expenses-paid trip for two to Detroit for a weekend of festivities called White Heat. A party circuit had recently evolved within the Toronto-Montréal-New York triangle, whose central focus was, according to Trevor, "Dancing semi-clad in the semi-darkness, semi-detached." They gave the prize to the two nurses, who were thrilled.

Later that night, Ian apprehended Doreen and took her outside to smoke a joint. "We need to have a sister-in-law talk."

They huddled in a doorway, which buffered them somewhat from the chill late-October wind. They were in an old industrial neighbourhood on the periphery of downtown. Above them, perched on the building's roof, a huge billboard flogging designer jeans was strategically tilted toward traffic streaming along the expressway by the lake. Doreen, dismayed, could smell winter fast approaching. She'd never adjusted to the barren months that shrouded the vast city in brown and grey, and missed the rainy, green balminess of the west coast.

They toked in silence, then Ian tossed away the roach and said, "Trevor's inherited your family's neurotic tendency not to want to cause anyone worry. He won't tell you so I'm going to. We both got tested. I was fine."

There was an icy gust of wind. A whirlpool of dead leaves careened down the middle of the road. A garbage can lid fell with a resounding crash. Dance music pulsed behind the warehouse door. A car drove by. Another drove by in the opposite direction.

The door swung open. A group from the party slipped onto the cracked sidewalk and dissipated down the street. The clatter of heels diminished beneath the jaundiced glow of the street lamps. Doreen found herself counting to the rhythm of the red airplane warning blips on the tip of the faraway CN Tower.

DOREEN TOOK HER dishes inside and put them in the dishwasher. She emptied water from the pan beneath the dehumidifier, then went upstairs to the office to check her website. She turned on the ceiling fan, put a CD into the wall unit, and sat down in front of the computer. There was a crackle of static as it started up. The screen erupted into blue sky. Doreen relaxed, finding comfort in mechanics. "Strange Fruit," sang Billie Holiday in a cleaned-up recording. The veils of heroin and digitized sound mastering couldn't conceal the deep furrows of her pain as her blues wreathed like perfume round the small room and snaked through the window, spreading a hint of gardenia into the summer evening.

There was an email from Ian, yet another list of things to do before Sunday. Her site had seventy-two hits that day, one requesting a proposal submission. An American network was getting comparative quotes from Vancouver and Toronto facilities, in preparation for a new cop show set in Boston. She began to put together a quote, but soon found herself growing dopey with fatigue, tranquilized by a tropical dusk turning the lawn outside to rust.

She shut down the computer, turned off the CD player, and barely made it to the bedroom where she passed out as if drugged. She awakened to darkness; through parted curtains a silhouette of treetops was carved into the starlit sky. A cricket wove in and out of the white noise of city. Yukio, warm, spooned against her back beneath the sheet, his arms around her, his breath soft on her neck, his cock hard on the small of her back. She turned around and trailed her fingers through his long blue-black hair. He smiled when she stroked his cock.

"Hey."

"Hey."

His hand traced its way slowly down her body. His fingertips brushed her breasts gently, circling slowly. Then fully on her belly, stroking downward. His hand inside her, cool and warm at the same time, searching for her and knowing how to find her. Her hand playing with him, tickling. His sighs. Hers. A mouth on the skin, gliding down to her, gliding inside her, and completion. Then he knelt on the bed before her. A mouth on the skin, the taste of his flesh, warm, smooth, and hard. His hardness in her mouth. A mouth on the skin, a hand, he came.

They lay together sleepily. The cricket was gone. The hum of the city was now no more than a backdrop to the soothing swoosh of a breeze through the trees in the backyard.

"Ian's got a boyfriend," said Doreen, staring at the ceiling.

Yukio yawned. "Yeah? It's about time, a good-looking guy like him. I'm surprised it took so long."

"It's called bereavement," Doreen said angrily.

"It's been seven months."

"That's what Ian said."

"And they didn't do much for a long time before Trevor died."

Doreen rolled her head to the side and stared at him. "Ian said that too. How'd you know?"

"Ian told me at the wake. You know how drunk he was. He told me not to tell anyone."

"That's Ian all over, pissed or not. He just wanted to tell everyone himself. He likes to get a lot of mileage out of his self-sacrifice."

"So? Good for him. He should. He went through hell. I like Ian. I'd do him if I was queer. But I like you a whole lot better,"

Yukio announced, stretching and turning on his side to snuggle with her. "Besides, he's my sister. I never thought I'd see the day I'd call a guy my sister but Ian's got a way, doesn't he?"

"Yeah," she said softly.

"What's this new guy like?"

She traced a finger up and down Yukio's muscular forearm.

"Doreen?" Yukio leaned over her. "Shhh."

He brushed back her hair and gently wiped away the tears. She drew in tightly against him and nuzzled his chest. His arms held her tight, the only person in the world who could contain her. Doreen, for the moment, felt safe.

"HE DOES NOT look like Freddy Mercury," Ian said defensively.

They were standing by the Lalique display. Doreen snuck another peek at Ian's boyfriend, who was at the buffet arranging cutlery.

"Yes, he does," she said. "Totally."

A conglomeration of slender young things had agreed to staff the event, all dressed like Audrey Hepburn, in chic '60s getups. For two months, two dozen ambi-drogynous waistlines with matching egos had complained — as the talent often does — about accessories that didn't look right and impossible fitting schedules. There was also quite a bit of chafing over colour schemes; what matched, what didn't, and which colour made so-and-so look fat and couldn't possibly be worn, no, never. The largest costume house in the city had donated all the outfits, alterations, and repairs. The hyperactive young man responsible for nipping and tucking the twenty-four Audreys was in a complete state and had practically resigned but discovered that Valium was a more pragmatic solution to dealing with nervous collapse than quitting, and more fun too.

Doreen delegated various responsibilities to the Audreys, then turned her attention to the vice president of the TAO board, the owner of a big Bay Street communications firm. The woman was over at men's watches tampering with one of the flower arrangements. The arrangements had been created by some of Toronto's top florists, all of whom had donated their services. The florists, who were all friends, watched with horror from behind a nearby column.

Floored, they dashed like mad for a table where mimosas were being poured into champagne flutes. Doreen intercepted the woman and navigated her away from the flowers. Several flutes later the florists were florid and resigned. The dragon lady's reputation was charmingly eviscerated.

A few guests had arrived early, including the bestselling writer. "To make sure I get some grub," she announced sardonically to a buzz of amused approval. She wore a floppy hat, a practical pantsuit, and shoes that breathed. She waylaid a white chocolate croissant, then made her way to the mimosas and the florists. Much to their delight, she joined the conversation and added a little spice to the mincemeat they'd made of the dragon lady. The first flank of paparazzi formed a circle around them. A barrage of automatic flashes exploded.

"Is this how you weed out the epileptics?" asked the writer.

Everyone laughed.

The store was soon packed with Toronto's elite, all of them wearing red ribbons. Silver trays of drinks and hors d'oeuvres floated above the crowd. A jazz trio played.

"It has a curse," Chantal explained to the writer. They were by a display case featuring the African Heart Stone ring, an enormous emerald with a large heart-shaped ruby centre, set in platinum and surrounded by a cluster of tiny sapphires. Doreen was next to them, trying to look interested. Yukio stood back with a videocam, chronicling their exchange for that night's news.

"It was discovered in Zaire when it was still the Congo," Chantal continued. "The chief of the tribe it was purchased from warned that it would 'visit great horrors on whomever tried to keep it.'"

"Good story. I'm always looking for something to plagiarize," said the writer.

"It's just superstition," chuckled Chantal. "That kind of mumbo-jumbo wouldn't be helpful to a writer like you."

"A writer like me uses all the mumbo-jumbo she can get," she remarked, peering closely at the jewel. "It certainly is beautiful."

Doreen felt a wave of nausea. Yukio turned off the videocam and sidestepped over. "You okay?"

"I just need some fresh air," she said.

"Need some company?"

"No. I'll be okay."

She made her way out the back exit.

Ian and his boyfriend were perched on the edge of the loading dock, having a smoke and holding hands. She awkwardly sat down beside them. They sat in silence. The air was fresh from a recent rainfall. Pigeons pecked among the trash cans. The alley was rainbowed with oily puddles. A large white cat, mottled in orange splotches, leapt from out of nowhere and dispersed the birds. It landed on the asphalt and padded self-confidently over to Doreen.

"Hello, Cat," said Ian. "You big old slob."

It jumped onto Doreen's lap, purring. Doreen scratched the soggy cat behind its ears. She discovered a collar, black velvet studded with pale blue rhinestones.

"Someone's taking real good care of you, aren't they?" she said.

The cat closed its eyes and purred.

It was nice and peaceful. Quiet, except for the gentle patter of dripping water and the cat's soft rumble. A snaggle-toothed row of telephone poles trailed into the distance. Phallic, sleek, tough, and soundless, they sagged with cables. Sheathed and unnatural, the cables hid something human inside. If I were to cut open only one cable, thought Doreen, I'd break the silence and unleash the symphony of a thousand trapped conversations.

The Prayers of Miss Atomic Blast

"WHERE TO?"

The cabby checked us out in the rear-view mirror.

"Elysium," I replied.

Our taxi swerved out of the hotel driveway. Manoeuvering thick traffic, we sped up a feeder onto the freeway, heading away from downtown. Monsieur Delacroix and I craned our heads to look out the back at a Celine Dionysian skyline of casinos outshining the stars in the desert night sky. It was real *purdy*.

"What's going on?" asked our driver.

His manner had a been-there-done-it delivery. Taxi drivers are like spies. They see and hear what you and I can only imagine. They keep their cards close to the chest. Play yours right and they might disclose something. I turned around in my seat and tilted back my black Stetson. I didn't want the hat to hide my face. Leaning forward with a flirtatious three-cocktails-under-the-belt grin, I produced a flush.

"Pardon me?" I asked.

"What's going on at Elysium tonight?"

He seemed to think that it was strange we were heading away from the Strip. Maybe he thought that two guys who were light in their loafers, and well-heeled to boot, would be more inclined to *partay* in a ritzier dive. I'd grown weary of mega-spectacles and refried celebrities. The new Las Vegas, with its amusement park rides, fake international landmarks, and theme hotels — like New York–New York, where we were staying — had unending tee-hee-hee appeal but we could have been anywhere. Just once I wanted to experience the real Vegas. My friend had taken a bit of persuading.

"We're going to see a country and western drag show, taxi driver darling," said Monsieur Delacroix, sounding bored. He looked out the tinted window, munching on his bag of nacho chips.

"A drag show at Elysium? That's new," said our taxi driver. "A drag show? Really? You sure?"

"Yup," I answered. "It's called *Honky Tonk Angels*."

The cabby glanced at us in the rear-view mirror like we were chumps. Assuming a poker face, he kept quiet. I sat back, drew the brim of my Stetson over my eyes, put on my black Ray-Bans, and tried to look smouldering. I'd made my choice and cast my die, rolling snake eyes. There was no turning back now. Or rather, no running away. I felt myself falling into a burning ring of fire.

"YOU AND YOUR egalitarian flights of fancy will be the death of me," Monsieur had said earlier in our hotel room, trimming his toenails and sipping champagne. "There's no such thing as the real Las Vegas, and no point in digging for depth. Scratch the surface and you won't find anything except more surface. Unless, of course, you're on a run and hit pay dirt. We should thank our lucky stars that some gorgeous criminals had a *carpe diem* moment all those years ago and envisioned what this place could be."

"You mean a place where hard-working people come to lose their money?" I asked as Monsieur headed into the bathroom to discard his toenail clippings. I was standing in front of a mirror checking out my new chaps and cowboy boots.

"Listen to you, Miss Voice of the People," said Monsieur as he came back into the room. He sat down on one of the two double beds, put on his black velvet opera pumps, adjusted his pink silk cravat, and looked at me. "Don't assume that they're all hard-working. That's an insult to decent, honest layabouts. So, keep your lazy-phobic microaggressions to yourself. We're unfairly targeted as it is."

"Sorry," I said drily. I sat down on an armchair and rolled up the sleeves of my T-shirt to show off my guns. "You're right. I should be more sensitive. I know how the rise in hate crimes against the indolent and slothful keeps you up at night."

"Well exactly," said Monsieur, pouting. "And by the way, we prefer work-challenged."

Monsieur stood up and walked over to the dresser beside our hotel window. He opened a top drawer and took out the family size bag of nacho chips he'd gotten from a vending machine earlier, thinking it was a slot machine. He ripped open the bag and shoved a mittful of chips into his mouth.

"People come here to win money, not lose it," he said, "They come here because it's possible, not because it's probable — and certainly not because they think it's realistic, the darlings. Stock markets, banks, the tooth fairy, prayer — speculative money makes the world go round, my dear. At least the casinos don't pretend otherwise. They're the only ethical financial institutions left."

Monsieur drew back the curtains and raised the blinds. They'd been shuttered for our beauty nap earlier.

"Come here, my dear," he said, waving an arm to usher me over.

I got up from my armchair and joined him, bringing my champagne. It was my third glass. I couldn't face my fear of heights on an empty liver.

The hotel looked like the Manhattan skyline. Our penthouse suite in the Empire State Building had a sweeping view. The room overlooked a roller coaster next to a replica of the Statue of Liberty. Beyond, the city spread out before us, incandescent and hungry. It was early evening. By day, Vegas retreats to the shadows like a B-movie vampire. Drained of colour, lacking a pulse, compromised by daylight's scrutiny, it lies in wait for the dark, one eye open. After sunset, it comes alive to glamour us, baroque, bamboozling and smelling blood.

"Just look at it, my dear," said Monsieur, letting out a self-satisfied sigh. "The American Dream, built by mobsters."

He offered me some chips, but I declined. I didn't want to get chip dust all over me. Monsieur seemed oblivious to the dayglo orange powder settling on his white dinner jacket, glistening like glitter on its contrasting black lapel.

"Las Vegas is a work of fiction. A glorious forgery. A wondrous fake. Smoke and mirrors, darling," said Monsieur. "Take away the razzle dazzle and the 'real' Las Vegas is nothing but sand, rock, scrub, and service workers as far as the eye can see. And really, my dear, who wants that?"

"You forgot snakes, spiders, UFOs, and nuclear fallout," I said, watching a nervous group of tourists loading onto the roller coaster far below.

"Leave it to you to always see the glass half full," Monsieur replied, his face lighting up. He clapped his hands together with glee, oblivious to the chemical residue coating his white lambskin gloves. "Fortunately for us, progress prevailed over nature. Where else can you see the Eiffel Tower, an Egyptian pyramid, and the canals of Venice all in one place?"

"Or the world's largest Coca-Cola bottle," I added. My sarcasm sailed right over his head, no mean feat considering how high Monsieur's stylist had piled his platinum, back-combed bouffant.

"The humble tipple of the working people," said Monsieur, nodding thoughtfully. "Well, there's your reality, my dear. Which you'd see more clearly if you stopped rolling your eyes. If you ask me, it's a much more appropriate symbol of American virtues than Miss Liberty. At the end of the day, there's no getting around the fact that she's from France, with its spoon-fed socialists running around beheading everyday people just because they have a little extra pocket money. That poor, sweet Marie Antoinette. What did she ever do to anyone other than set trends? The French Revolution wasn't a fight for liberty. It was a crime against fashion. There's a website that proves it. That's why I left, you know."

"You're from Canada just like me," I corrected him. "You've never even been to France, and definitely not in the eighteenth century."

Monsieur paused for a moment and shuddered as though struck by a sudden chill. "Ugh, Canada. Even worse. Socialism with an American accent. Except in Québec of course, where speaking American is outlawed. That's why I left there too. And I have been to France. Loads of times. In my other lifetimes."

Although he was normally wary of organized belief systems that weren't conspiracy theories, Monsieur was steadfast in his devotion to three guiding principles that he lived his life by: reincarnation, revisionist history, and resisting arrest.

He stepped away from the window to refresh his champagne flute and brought back the bottle to top me up. We were interrupted by the hotel phone. Our taxi had arrived. We heard a sudden flurry of screams from the roller coaster outside while we were leaving.

"Ah, the birdsong of survival," Monsieur mused sentimentally as I closed the door on their shrieks of elated panic.

I'D NEVER PAID much attention to country music until Monsieur gave me a Johnny Cash greatest hits CD for my birthday. It was part of his ploy to get me to change my image. We used to be partners in crime. But the balance shifted when Monsieur struck gold investing early in the digital gay porn boom. A few years back, he'd lobbed all his lucre from our most successful scam to date at a Vancouver-based site called Hosers.

"People in government, the military, and education around the world need something constructive to do with themselves while they're twiddling their thumbs in between telling everyone how to think and behave," he'd told me.

Monsieur didn't have a head for business or a mind for numbers. Those things don't make you rich. But he had a heart for risk. Hosers became the world's busiest gay porn site. And he was right. The three largest groups of unique visitors had government, military, or education URL extensions and IP addresses. Monsieur, the site's second-biggest shareholder, sold half his stock while Hosers was still on top, before competitors wedged themselves a piece of the pornography pie. He made a killing. Then, when the site diversified into day trading, Russian brides, and self-help, he made more millions.

But his windfall changed our relationship. I wasn't his partner anymore. I was his entourage. That's why I was dolled up like I'd just hopped off an Appaloosa at the OK Corral, serving *Man in Black* realness. Monsieur was going through a Wild West phase. After bingeing on Westerns, or movies that he thought were Westerns — *Midnight Cowboy, Rhinestone, Butch Cassidy and the Sundance Kid* — he'd roped and steered me into my new gunslinger getup: a little bit midnight, a little bit rhinestone, a little bit butch. I admit I was relieved to kiss the motorcycle cop phase goodbye. And I liked the way the spurs on my boots jingled when I walked. It was kind of sexy. But underneath I was chafing, and it wasn't the chaps. Playing second fiddle was starting to rub me the wrong way. I think that's why Monsieur agreed to Elysium.

I had a soft spot for talented cross-dressers and so was excited to come across the casino's ad in the Las Vegas show guide. There was a picture of three over-the-top queens in scare-dos and tarantula eyelashes, ostensibly doing country greats like Patsy Cline, Loretta Lynn, and Tammy Wynette. Yay-hoo! Talk about standing by your man. At $9.99, a little lip-synch about a lot of heartache was just the ticket. For $14.99, you got prime rib too.

Las Vegas was obsessed with red meat. Monsieur and I couldn't take two steps without someone dangling a slab of beef in our faces. It reminded me that one of my grandfathers died of a heart attack right after eating a steak. He was big on drinking and gambling. My other grandfather ran away with another woman. Several of my aunts married abusive alcoholics. Add a simple chord progression and a pickup truck, and my genealogy could be a country hit.

Maybe my disinterest in country music was denial. If so, I was in the right town. People should give their denial a holiday at least once a year and this was the place for it.

"Do you fellas gamble?" asked our cabby as we swerved onto an exit ramp.

"Not me," I replied.

"And a good thing too," Monsieur jumped in, causing motes of nacho dust to dance in the glow of the dashboard. "He wears his heart on his sleeve."

Life would be easier if that were the case, but Monsieur was wrong. I wore my heart deeper down, on my skin. He'd branded it there years ago. It made me incapable of deceit and — Monsieur was dead to rights on this count — it made me a terrible gambler.

Nothing I did could cover up the scar. It wouldn't heal. I kept exposing it and getting burned again, which nonplussed Monsieur. If there was one thing that peeved him more than a hopeless romantic, it was a hopeful one. Monsieur locked his heart away years ago for safekeeping and had forgotten the combination to the safety deposit box, let alone what city it was in. Being heartless made him a formidable if unlikely foe at the card tables.

"On the other hand, driver dear, I am apparently a whale," said Monsieur as he scrunched up his nacho bag into a ball. "That's what they call a high roller."

"I know what it means," said our driver, sounding unconvinced.

"I can't say I'm too thrilled about the term, not with this girlish figure. I've been lobbying for barracuda, but so far no takers. I considered dolphin then quickly came to my senses. Everyone knows that dolphins are the Marxists of the open ocean. All that community organizing. Even worse, some are Trotskyists. I read it in a chatroom. Texas Hold'em has standards. No one wants a slippery socialist with superior intelligence and telepathic capabilities to pull up a seat at the table, especially one from another species. I think I may be warming up to the idea of orca. If I must be a whale, I might as well be the most photogenic one."

I kept mum while Monsieur anthropomorphized predatory marine fauna and made unsubstantiated claims about the politics of sea mammals. I'd long ago given up trying to make sense out of his rambling trains of thought — unscheduled trains, mostly, hurtling toward each other on the same track and, inevitably, crashing. Or, sometimes, chugging laboriously along a track leading nowhere. I listened to him grasp at maritime metaphors, waiting for the most obvious one to drop. In a city of card sharks, Monsieur was a Great White.

I thought that Monsieur's success was a fluke the first time it happened. But then it happened again. And it kept happening. His reputation spread through the casinos like wildfire, ever since he won a million bucks at the World Series of Poker a year earlier. On a dare.

I had invited Monsieur to try out a casual poker game a few nights after he liquidated his porn shares, in the backroom at his favourite Vegas gay bar, Area 69. We were joined by some hot cage dancers lured by the generosity of his billfold, and the promise that they wouldn't be expected to make good if he won. Monsieur was really excited at first because he thought we were going to play strip poker. Which, given the milieu and company, wasn't completely farfetched. But if there was one thing Monsieur relished more than the potential of objectifying young men, it was the prospect of getting his hands on lots of unearned money without raising the suspicions of Interpol.

No way did I think he had a shot at winning. He didn't really know the game. But no one could read his poker face, or rather, poker faces. His heart of stone was matched by nerves of steel. Deceit was in his nature. Distraction turned out to be his secret weapon.

Even though I wasn't good at concealing my plays, I understood the cards. I stood behind him as an advisor. No one was more surprised when he cleaned up. He was so distracting that no one else at the table could maintain a poker face. He bedazzled the other players like Dracula hypnotizing his victims. Bit by bit, bon mot by bon mot, quirky mannerism by quirky mannerism, he whittled away at their attention spans. You could see them losing the plot. How many rings does he keep in his shoulder bag, and does he have to keep changing them? Does he have to freshen his lipstick again, and in another colour? Was he really Elvis Presley's secret lover? Why does he keep talking about dolphins and Communists?

"I used to get arrested for disorderly conduct, my dear," Monsieur gushed to our cabby. "Now I get offered free hotel rooms!"

He was right. Our suite at New York–New York was comped. In fact, Monsieur and I had been living in comped hotel rooms in Vegas for several months. They do that for the big spenders so long as they don't break the bank. Monsieur's prowess at poker was almost unassailable but he was a disaster at the roulette and craps tables, and anything else that involved throwing dice. He was lucky if one of them landed anywhere near the table, let alone on it. I told him it was like watching a jellyfish play basketball. He was pleased by my adherence to his current obsession with aquatic symbolism. I'd learned to play along with Monsieur's compulsions, waiting for them to play out. Once Monsieur settled on something, it stuck to his brain and circled incessantly, until something else caught his fancy and it fell with a thud, and was quickly forgotten.

Monsieur didn't mind losing because he could easily make up for any losses at the poker tournaments.

"You must come see our room when you're off your shift," Monsieur lilted, flickering his lashes seductively as the taxi turned onto a side street near the casino.

"That's okay, I'm good," our driver said wearily, his shoulders sagging.

Monsieur had that effect on people in small, enclosed spaces. His cyclotronic brain could suck your life force dry. You needed a strong cup of coffee to recuperate. Or a robust cocaine habit.

"Sir, you can't do that," said the driver, stopping at a red light. Monsieur had rolled down his window and was about to toss out his used nacho bag.

"Fine," huffed Monsieur. "I was just doing my civic duty. But no, let's put all the street cleaners out of business. Let's steal the bread off their tables. Let's force their families to line up at soup kitchens. I'm only thinking of the children. Early exposure to humanitarianism never ends well. And I'm surprised by you, driver darling. Whatever happened to blue collar comradery?"

Monsieur turned to me. His lips practically glowed in the dark, radioactive with synthetic cheese particles. "Here, you take it."

"I don't want it," I replied.

It was a toss-up which was the bigger purse, the one on Monsieur's face or the vintage pink Birkin Bag he flung his refuse into.

"I'm sure that Hermès didn't have this in mind or they would have called it the Trash Bag," he said, sulking.

Our driver eyed me in the rear-view mirror. "Are you guys for real?" he asked as the cab rolled up in front of our destination.

I could have asked the same question about Elysium.

Occupying the lion's share of a strip mall on Sin City's outskirts, Elysium boasted a kitschy babel of styles that bordered on blasphemy — if you were an architectural purist. The casino's 1950s take on Spanish Mission Revival conjured comforting memories of inquisitions, *autos-da-fé*, and gifting Indigenous peoples with smallpox blankets. Frontier fort flourishes reinforced the theme. There was a fake bell tower — or gun tower, it was kind of hard to tell — and a cupola imitating the dome at St. Peter's Basilica. At some point someone had added dark wood trim for a ye olde English Tudor touch. The original structure was overshadowed by a blocky, concrete hotel extension. Exuding Cold War warmth and charm, the monolith of Soviet Brutalism probably went up in the early 1970s.

To Monsieur, it was heaven on earth. Purity was his *bête noire*; cultural appropriation, his white knight.

"Contamination makes the world go around, my dear," he'd soapboxed that time in a *mehndi* parlour. I'd tried to talk him out of getting his hands hennaed like a bride at an Indian wedding, but my protests only made him want to do it even more. "When you throw something new into the mix, you get evolution. And fashion," he added, holding up his freshly tatted talons. "Cultural appropriation is biodiversity."

One person's cultural appropriation is another's cultural asphyxiation. From where I sat, Elysium looked like the end of civilization, and not in a good way.

We pulled up to the entrance. I tipped the driver and got out. He happily signed the non-disclosure agreement when he saw how big the tip was. I kept a few copies folded in my pocket. My companion was a walking-talking lawsuit on legs, which he seemed to have forgotten how to use. He remained seated in the cab, staring forward.

"Sir? Are you all right?" asked the driver.

"He's waiting for you to get out and open his door for him. Or for me to," I said, lighting myself a defiant cigarette and refusing to budge.

"This is a taxi service, not a limo, sir. And I have calls coming in. So would you please step out of the cab."

Monsieur ignored him and took out his compact. He checked to make sure that his beauty mark hadn't fallen off and then added a little more rouge to his cheeks. When he was done, he put the compact away and rolled down his window.

"Well?" he said. "I'm waiting."

"Oh, for Christ's sake," I muttered, butting out my fag. This entourage kick he was on was getting out of hand.

I walked around to his side of the cab and opened the door for him. Monsieur thought that a group of senior citizens taking snapshots outside their shuttle bus were paparazzi. He swept himself out of the taxi like a Hollywood It Girl and struck a red carpet pose. His delusion was contagious. They thought he must be someone famous and we were momentarily blinded by flashes.

Monsieur looked around and furrowed his brow. "Where's the velvet rope, my dear?" he stage-whispered.

"There isn't one. It's not that kind of place."

"Oh well, once we're inside I'm sure they'll whisk me to safety in a VIP section. I'm positively famished for bottle service."

"I don't think it's that kind of place either," I said.

"I suppose one night of humouring your morbid taste for

slumming it won't kill me," he said, flinging his Birkin Bag at me to carry.

"Don't count on it," I mumbled out of earshot.

The doorway to Elysium was designed to look like the Pearly Gates, sort of. It was made of wrought brass filigree intended to emulate gold, secured to a plexiglass backing. Instead of a cross on top, there was a dollar sign radiating rays of light. Two large cherub statues flanked either side. They wore gun holsters and played jazz trumpets. Their wings were spread as if poised for flight. I half hoped one of them would come to life, pounce on Monsieur, and whisk him away. It was bad enough that he was making me walk ahead of him like a bodyguard but the taser was pushing it. He had a taser custom-made to look like an old-fashioned Colt pistol, covered in rhinestones. He insisted I wave it around for show.

I blamed Liberace.

"HE WAS QUITE possibly the greatest American who ever lived," Monsieur commented a while ago when we were standing in the middle of the Liberace Museum. "It's a shame they're planning on closing it."

Monsieur was wary of change, unless it was cascading from a slot machine. With a new millennium fast approaching, he'd decided it was important that we tour fading remnants of the twentieth century before they degenerated into oblivion. That was one reason we were in Las Vegas. Another, more important reason hovered in the air around us. Unspoken and undetectable, it seeped through our skin, invaded our airways, and coursed through our veins, like nuclear fallout but worse. Monsieur's aversion to change was transparent too but couldn't have been more obvious to me. Both of us were entering the twilight of our prime. He feared the inevitable degradation of time.

Maybe he thought we could hide from time in the City of Second Chances. Maybe he thought that since everything else in Vegas was already an imitation of life, time was an illusion too. Although your local corner store physicist or Botox clinician would likely tell you it's illusory wherever you are. Maybe our cells conspire with the clock to deceive us too, copy after copy after copy until the original template is too faded to replicate. Maybe, at the end of the day, we're all imitations of life. Maybe I needed a cocktail.

"Of course, we're imitations," Monsieur said wearily. "You and I should know, my dear. We're experts at aping existence. That's how we've been paying the bills since day one. I haven't got a clue where this sudden descent into dime store philosophizing has come from. So please, darling, dial it down. Otherwise slink off to a Buddhist temple and light a joss stick. Or a hot dog stand — I'm not fussy. If life is a parade of false impressions, this place is a cavalcade, and I am trying to take it in."

Monsieur pulled a silver flask from his purse and handed it to me.

"And of course you need a cocktail," he continued. "I wish you'd stop second-guessing your addictions. They've been the only stable thing in your life since we met. And really, darling, if you can't trust your addictions, what can you trust?"

I took a sobering swig and looked around. Liberace had the museum built before he died, a shrine in his own honour. Once the highest-paid celebrity on the planet, and one of the most famous, the flamboyant showman filled it with symbols of his success like a braggadocious Pharoah desperate for his legacy to live on in eternity. The only thing missing was a sarcophagus. And the bones of dead slaves. Instead of hieroglyphics, spotlights led the way.

Monsieur stood transfixed in front of a vintage 1930s Roadster that looked like a crime syndicate's getaway car, covered with rhinestones. There was a similarly encrusted Baldwin grand piano beside it. Nearby, a pair of cowboy boots featured the star-spangled banner in sequins. Slack-jawed, wide-eyed, and filled with awe like a kid seeing all the presents under the tree first thing Christmas morning, Monsieur surveyed Liberace's boondoggle of gewgaws: outrageous jewellery and costumes, extravagant stage pieces, phantasmagorical furniture with a Versailles-meets-acid-flash-back vibe. I think it may have been the closest thing to a religious experience Monsieur ever had. It's not so much that he lacked the depth required for spiritual reflection. He lacked the attention span. Incapable of transcendence, he embraced the transitory. Hence his worship of pop culture moments.

"He was so gangster, my dear," Monsieur lectured. "He practically invented bling. That's why everyone calls Liberace the Godfather of Rap."

By everyone, he meant he did. Most people under fifty didn't know who Liberace was.

"More like Fairy Godmother," I said, taking another swig from the flask.

"Be careful, my dear, your internalized homophobia is showing," Monsieur sniped, giving me side eye.

"And so is your transference," I shot back.

Monsieur started to snicker. So did I. Things quickly escalated to giggle fits, then belly laughs.

"That fucking couples counsellor," I said, gasping for breath.

"Imagine forking out two hundred dollars an hour to be told that our problem is codependence," Monsieur managed to blurt out. He whipped out a lace handkerchief from his sleeve and dabbed his tears of mirth.

I'd convinced Monsieur to see a therapist with me once. We both regretted it the minute we sat down in his office.

"Oh my dear, I might have been able to live with the annoying pan flute and chimes on that incessant New Age sound machine of his, and even the cloying scent of sandalwood incense mixed with yoga sweat," said Monsieur. "But when he started talking about mindfulness all I could think is that maybe someone who wears sandals with white sports socks shouldn't be preaching self-awareness."

"In January," I reminded him.

"I still wake up with night sweats," said Monsieur. He shuddered. Fashion faux pas gave him PTSD.

The therapist got it all twisted around. Codependency was our solution, not our problem. Without it, we were nothing. Just two half-lives with broken centres. Loneliness glued us together. No, not loneliness: longing. I kept confusing the two, which our analyst said was a red flag.

I wonder what the shrink would've thought about the internalized homophobia all around us. We were standing in the middle of a monument to it. Talk about red flags. Hiding in plain sight, Liberace had decked himself out in campy outfits that were one sashay shy of drag. He fucked men. He minced all the way to the bank. But he went to his grave denying he was gay. He played the room, and the room bought it. Just like when Monsieur played poker.

But his museum was a house of cards. The massive memorials to Egypt's elite were built of stone. Liberace's testimonial to himself was tacked together with wood and stucco, as ersatz and impermanent as the unworldly possessions languishing inside. The shrines of the kings of Kemet were rooted deep. Liberace's skimmed the shallows. Scratch the surface and you wouldn't find anything except more surface. Monsieur was such a big fan that I didn't say anything. Besides, there was never any point in telling him that he was out of his depth. He'd just dig in his heels.

Monsieur was right, though, that there was talk of tearing it down. The piano player's fame was fading fast. Visitors were dwindling. Legends lasted thousands of years thousands of years ago. Posterity didn't mean what it used to. Now we consumed updated versions of the past at an astonishing rate, gnawing at them voraciously. Never sated, we kept hungering for fresh versions of it, or old ones with a saucy new twist. Liberace thought cosmetic surgery would be his one-way ticket to an afterlife that, if it didn't last thousands of years, would at least linger for a few news cycles. But it was someone else's face he wanted to cut open.

We stopped in front of a wall of framed photographs. They were mostly pictures of the performer and one of the parade of young male companions he preyed on then discarded. This one had lasted longer than most. Earlier photos showed them all cuddly and romantic but then they got weird. The young man's face morphed into a replica of Liberace's that was simultaneously youthful and ghoulish. The pictures revealed an adjustment in their relationship from romantic to master and servant. His companion became his chaperone, his driver, his bodyguard, and his merchandise manager, before Liberace kicked him to the curb for a younger model.

"What an excellent idea," Monsieur said.

He was staring at a photograph of Liberace standing on stage in a white ermine cape with an enormous train. His companion stood behind him in a matching white chauffeur uniform, holding open the door to the gangster-y car we'd looked at earlier. Their love had become a Saint Valentine's Day Massacre.

"No fucking way!" I said when Monsieur asked me how I felt about getting plastic surgery to look like him.

"It seems like a small request considering everything I've done for you all these years," he sulked.

He kept needling me until I couldn't take it anymore. Three little old ladies sitting on a bench watching a video of Liberace talking about his dogs looked up with alarm as I stormed past them and out the museum's door. I didn't slam it. I jammed it open, hoping that the surgical desert sun would spread its ultraviolet rays deep and wide, smash to smithereens the sepulchre's self-referential hall of mirrors, and cleanse the cancer eating away at Monsieur Delacroix's plastic soul. But nope, the door shut, loudly and abruptly, as though seized by a hand reaching out from the grave. Or maybe it was the museum's docent.

Things had been rocky between us since then. I'd spent most of my life following in Monsieur's footsteps, never questioning why. Blinded by self-deception, I'd fooled myself that we were equals when all this time he'd been playing his upper hand, distracting me with dears and darlings as we merged into one. Now I couldn't tell which of us was the mirror, and which the reflection. I was fed up with our chicanery, stunts. and shenanigans. It was time for a little mitosis. In the meantime, I half-heartedly humoured Monsieur's delusions of grandeur. But my servility was getting surly.

ELYSIUM WAS PACKED. We made our way passed the sweatpants and stovepipe jeans, through a cacophony of clanking slot machines and piped-in pop music, trying to keep clear of the walkers and wheelchairs. Every few minutes you could hear the roar of jet engines overhead. The casino was near the airport.

Elysium catered to local workers dreaming of a life beyond minimum wage, tourists on a budget hoping for a miracle, and cash-strapped retirees who'd dipped into their laundry coins, crossing their fingers for a windfall that would lead them to a light at the end of the tunnel. Vegas had a huge seniors population, and they weren't fooling around. Some of those old dolls were on a mission so you'd best get out of their way when you see them zooming at you in their scooters. God save you if they found you sitting in the seat in front of their lucky slot. It's legal to carry guns in Nevada nightspots, and testy gamblers make for itchy trigger fingers.

We found the show lounge and were ushered to our seats. Wagon wheel tables, chrome and Naugahyde chairs, red gingham tablecloths, and Chianti bottle candle holders — Monsieur was in heaven. He loved anything retro. But only if it was authentic. He didn't approve of irony, ironically.

"Oh, my dear, it looks just like that Appalachian boozer — the one in Virginia. Remember?" Monsieur effused.

"You mean the Damascus Dinner Theater," I reminded him.

A few years ago, we'd feasted on their festive if off-key production of *Oklahoma*. It was just after our last scam before we went mainstream with gay porn and poker. Monsieur and I made one of our biggest hauls ever when we spent several months driving up and down the Blue Ridge Mountains defrauding snake churches. Monsieur had a knack for handling serpents; no one could talk in tongues the way he did, and he oozed charisma, but he wouldn't listen to me when I suggested that most evangelical preachers didn't wear makeup, at least not so much. I needn't have worried. No one noticed his smoky eye or cheekbone contours once his forked tongue got going. The evangelicals were putty in his hands and we tithed our way to a pretty penny.

"Here you go, hon," said a pleasant server as she plunked down my two-dollar vat of merlot.

"And here's the house specialty you ordered, sir," she added sweetly, setting an enormous conch shell in front of Monsieur.

"It's called a Bikini Atoll," he informed me excitedly, pointing at a picture of it on the laminated drinks menu. "You'll be bombed like you've never been bombed before. That's the description. Isn't it fabulous?"

His tiki mug was filled to the brim and garnished with fruit chunks on swizzle sticks. The large cocktail umbrella grabbed my attention. I'd seen vintage pin-up girls on cocktail umbrellas before but not like this one. A stunning brunette struck a cheesecake pose, wearing a two-piece bathing suit covered in cotton balls shaped like a mushroom cloud, and a matching headpiece.

"That's the original Miss Atomic Blast," said our server when she saw me staring at it. She was hovering over Monsieur waiting for a tip. I reached in my pocket to pay it.

"Who?" I asked, slipping her a ten.

"Miss Atomic Blast," she said, lubricated by my conscientious gratuity. "She was the first one. She was a dancer at the Desert Inn Casino. It used to be where our hotel extension is now, but they tore it down in the '70s. There was a bar at the top called Sky Lounge where you could go to watch the nuclear tests. They used to do them all the time in the '50s, above ground and everything. You'd order your drink, put on your sunglasses, and bombs away. Anyhow, the chamber of commerce started a Miss Atomic Blast competition as a marketing gimmick, and she was the first one. It went on for a few years until people started getting radiation sickness. That kind of put a damper on things. Then they started testing underground. And, well, no more Miss Atomic Blast. There's a whole bunch of memorabilia about it in the gift shop if you're interested."

We had a few minutes before *Honky Tonk Angels* started, so I took her suggestion and skedaddled to see some souvenirs. There were Miss Atomic Blast postcards, Miss Atomic Blast fridge magnets, Miss Atomic Blast coasters, Miss Atomic Blast mousepads, and more. An educational display on one of the walls caught my eye, specifically a news clipping from 1952.

"World's First Atomic Pin-Up Girl Radiates Loveliness Instead of Radioactive Particles" said the title under a photograph of Miss Atomic Blast standing beside the mayor of Las Vegas, holding a key to the city. According to the newspaper, she was a good Baptist girl who dreamed of being a housewife and mother.

"I am proud to represent our American military. It took U.S. know-how to make the atomic bomb that ended the war, know-how that makes us the stewards of world peace and keeps us safe from Communists," she said in the interview. "My prayers go out to all the Christians who make America great."

Apparently, the rest of us could go to hell. I bought a postcard for Monsieur to send to himself and rushed back to the show lounge.

Monsieur and I weren't spring chickens anymore, but in this place, by comparison, we were practically fetal. The room had filled up with couples who were likely courting around the time Patsy Cline serenaded the airwaves with "Crazy" and "Walking After Midnight," before the legendary vocalist died in a plane crash in 1963.

The house lights went down and the show started. I fell to pieces. These women were real, not drag queens. What a rip-off. Now I knew why our cabby had been giving us strange looks. He thought we were complete knobs. A puppet show introduced the evening's gimmick, a doorway that would turn whoever passed through it into the entertainer of their dreams. When someone did, there were really bad thunder and lightning effects.

I guzzled merlot to make it better. My reservations were short-lived. The singers trotted out about a dozen of country music's greatest gals and they were magnificent. They were backed up by Cline's original band, the Jordanaires. Their voices were as powerful as a long-haul flatbed, and as bittersweet as an empty stretch of highway at dawn. My soul filled up with southern comfort. I hankered for chew tabacky. It was all I could do not to say, "Yup."

TWO DAYS LATER, Monsieur and I sat on a rock across from the Hoover Dam, waiting for a truck to fall. In Vegas, when you're on a roll, you don't stop. After Elysium, we went to some other saloons off the beaten track, but my interest in seeing the real Las Vegas eventually waned. So, I persuaded Monsieur to cross the desert with me. Lake Mead was a forty-five-minute drive. We brought a picnic hamper and a couple of bottles of Cristal.

After finding out about Miss Atomic Blast, I did some reading up about nuclear testing in Nevada. About the myriad cancers of thousands of downwinders. About the trillions of litres of radioactive water bubbling beneath the desert floor. And about the trucks crossing the Hoover Dam. Every day, several trucks carrying nuclear waste traversed the narrow road on top of the dam. If one fell, all hell would break lose. I wanted a front-row seat when it did.

We arrived just in time for daybreak. I cracked open one of the bottles and poured us each a glass. We clinked rims while we watched the sun rise. I took Monsieur's hand. I'd finally accepted that we were stuck with each other. We were in a holding pattern that only oblivion could end.

I acknowledge the sacred land of the Lkwungen People, also known as the Songhees and Esquimalt First Nations, upon which this book was written. The southern tip of Vancouver Island, the Gulf Islands, and the San Juan Islands are the traditional territories of the Lkwungen peoples. Lkwungen means "Place to smoke herring," and Lkwungen'athun refers to the language of the land.

— Guy Babineau

We acknowledge the sacred land on which Cormorant Books operates. It has been a site of human activity for 15,000 years. This land is the territory of the Huron-Wendat and Petun First Nations, the Seneca, and most recently, the Mississaugas of the Credit River. The territory was the subject of the Dish With One Spoon Wampum Belt Covenant, an agreement between the Iroquois Confederacy and Confederacy of the Ojibway and allied nations to peaceably share and steward the resources around the Great Lakes. Today, the meeting place of Toronto is still home to many Indigenous people from across Turtle Island. We are grateful to have the opportunity to work in the community, on this territory.

We are also mindful of broken covenants and the need to strive to make right with all our relations.